The Baby Package

Sarah J. Brooks

Sarah J. Brooks

ISBN-13: 978-1719195881

ISBN-10: 1719195889

Copyright © 2018 Sarah J. Brooks

Author's note: This is a work of fiction. Some of the names and geographical locations in this book are products of the author's imagination, and do not necessarily correspond with reality.

The Baby Package

Sarah J. Brooks

For my readers

Table of contents

Chapter 1
Chapter 2
Chapter 3
Chapter 4
Chapter 5
Chapter 6
Chapter 7
Chapter 8
Chapter 9
Chapter 10
Chapter 11
Chapter 12
Chapter 13
Chapter 14
Chapter 15
Chapter 16
Chapter 17
Chapter 18
Chapter 19
Chapter 20
Chapter 21
Epilogue

Chapter 1

Julia

"Are we going to Provoc?" I asked as we all piled into the cab.

"Oh, my God I love Provocateur," Teddy said in his usual flamboyant draw.

"Yeah, it's the only place to be seen right now," Sarah added. "I've got to find a hot stockbroker to give me some tips."

"Why do they need to be hot?" I teased.

"Technically they don't, but if I'm going to pretend to be interested in the guy so I can get free financial advice, I'd prefer if they were hot."

"You know you make enough money to actually pay for stock advice. You could date whoever you want," I said.

I was finishing my makeup while we rode in the cab. Teddy was perpetually relegated to the front seat while Sarah, Kendra and I sat in the back. He hated that we always made him sit up there but as our only male friend who came out with us, he sucked it up and sat up there.

Going out dancing at the clubs in New York was one of my favorite things to do. This evening it was particularly exciting because I'd just landed a huge client for our hotel chain and Teddy, who was also my supervisor at work, offered to pay the alcohol tab for the evening. There was no way we were going to turn that down; drinking in New York was expensive business.

"I'm not paying someone to give me advice when these guys will give it for free. Plus, when have you known me to ever actually date someone? I'm not looking for that sort of commitment," Sarah added.

"Right, who would want to have a guy for more than one night?" Kendra chimed in.

"I'm not opposed to more than one night. I just don't like these clingy guys who want to come over all the time and start getting mushy. Short term is all I have time for."

Sarah was perpetually single. She managed the marketing at King Hotels and was damn good at her job. The key was her ability to make anyone feel like they were wanted in both personal and professional environments. Sarah had the ability to walk into a meeting full of CEO's and have the whole lot of them eating out of her hands in a matter of minutes. I envied her ability to connect in that way.

"Let's remember this celebration is for Julia," Teddy added. "Thank you for making me look so good to my bosses," he laughed with his distinctive high-pitched cackle that made all of us smile too. Teddy was the first boss I had out of college and I was so lucky to have him. He was funny, supportive, and refreshing compared to what I'd heard about the hotel sales industry while I was in school.

"I'm just in it for the money," I teased.

"You'll get a huge commission check, girl. I'm telling you, this one is going to rattle your cage when it hits your account."

"I can't wait. I've decided I'm going to go ahead with the baby thing."

"What? No!" Sarah blasted from the other side of the vehicle. "You are way too young. Come on Julia, you're only twenty-five. This is something people my age do, not people your age."

Sarah was forty years old and totally right. Women her age in New York were deciding to have babies on their own, but I didn't want to wait until I was forty to have a baby. I'd always dreamed of a big family and nowadays blending families just wasn't as big of a deal as it was in the past. If I had a baby now, I still expected that somewhere down the road I could have more children once I met the man of my dreams. But the cruel reality was that might be way down the road and I just didn't want to wait.

"You know how I feel about it," Kendra said under her breath.

Kendra didn't like the idea at all. She and I were similar in age, she was only two years older than me but she didn't have a problem waiting to start her family. I'd always planned to have my family young and in this day and age, I just didn't need to wait for a husband in order to get started. Kendra and I had come to an agreement that I was going to do this and she was going to be supportive, even though she didn't fully agree with my plan.

"I'm all for it," Teddy said. "You know we offer maternity leave, and you can even work from home if you decide to."

"I think I'll just take a couple of weeks and then work from home. But hell, I haven't gotten pregnant yet so who knows. I did make an appointment with that fertility clinic near the office. It had a six-month waiting list and my appointment should be coming up soon."

"Did you pick a Daddy yet?" Sarah laughed. "Tall, dark, and handsome with an Ivy League degree?"

"Yeah, something like that. Anyways I don't want to make this all about me," I said as we pulled up to the club. I'd actually spent an exhaustive amount of time reviewing sperm donor profiles. I'd spent so much time looking at profiles and changing my mind about what I wanted that when I finally came across the perfect profile I still wasn't sure that was what I really wanted to settle on.

Picking a man based on his identifiable features and education wasn't exactly a romantic way to have a child. I'd chosen the hair color, eye color, and height as if this person was some doll I was ordering to fit predefined criteria. In real life, finding a mate was so much more involved yet in some aspect it was easier because you knew you loved the person. When you were in love I imagined that the specific looks of your partner wouldn't be an issue.

"Girl, tonight is all about you and if you're going to be having a baby soon then you should be partying like a rock star tonight!" Teddy said as we all climbed out of the cab.

Teddy knew the bouncer and we quickly made our way past the long line and into the club. He liked partying more than anyone I knew at King Hotels. It always surprised me that he managed to make it to work on time even after staying up until three or four in the morning on some nights. I definitely couldn't party that hard or that often. Once a week was about all I could handle and only on Saturdays so I could still sleep in and recover all day on Sundays.

My red sequined mini dress had been sitting in my closet for months just waiting for this night on the town. The fall weather was warm enough to handle the hurried rush into the club and not freeze my butt off.

We followed Teddy to a reserved couch he had near the main dance floor. He was never the sort who wanted to sit off in the VIP area or in a back corner. If we were coming to Provoc then we were going to be seen. It was fun to be friends with someone who was so outgoing because I certainly wasn't that way. I could fake my way through a sales meeting or even a night on the town, but the truth was that I always preferred an evening on my couch watching movies.

Ordering bottle service was a requirement for most clubs

if you wanted your own assigned area and this club was no different. Teddy had pre-ordered mixers, red bull, bottles of water, and Grey Goose for our group and the waitress brought it over to us as soon as we sat down. There was something so exhilarating about being with Teddy when he was splurging like this; it wasn't at all what our night was like when we paid for our own drinks and Kendra and Sarah knew it.

"Thank you, Teddy, for making this night amazing," I toasted as soon as we had all put together our drinks.

"Cheers," everyone said and tapped our glasses together.

"Let's make a pass around the club," Sarah ordered as she pulled me up from the couch. "I need to get my sights on a few options."

"Okay."

Being Sarah's sidekick was normal for me. I didn't have trouble with finding decent men to talk to for the evening but my issue was making any sort of connection that would last longer than just one night. The men in New York were more finicky than the women. Not many of them wanted a real relationship and instead were typically looking to get laid as quickly as possible and then drop the girl. I'd seen it so many times that I totally understood Sarah's outlook on casual dating, I just wasn't sure I could manage that much longer. I really did want to find someone who I could have more with and was willing to wait it out and find them somewhere down the road.

"Him?" Sarah asked as she pointed to a very young looking guy standing with a group of women.

"The one holding court with the bevy of twenty-somethings?"

"Yeah, I think he looks like a stockbroker. What do you think?"

"Maybe, but that's a large group of ladies to fight off. Are you really up for that?" I laughed.

"No problem," she pulled me with her toward the group. "Let's do a server-distraction," she laughed.

I had no chance to make a run for it. No chance to stop the madness before it began. This was going down whether I agreed with it or not. Sarah slipped me a hundred dollar bill and pushed me right into the middle of the group before I could protest at all.

"Hey, we'd like a bottle of Grey Goose. Keep the change," I said and handed the sexy looking guy in a suit the hundred dollars that Sarah had given me. This move worked for Sarah a lot and she had only recently started making me do the initial contact. I'd agreed the first time and then been roped into doing it ever since. I walked away right after handing him the money and joined Sarah a few feet away.

Just as planned, the guy quickly caught up to me and handed me back the money. "I'm not a server here," he said with an annoying look on his face.

"Oh, my gosh, Julia he seriously doesn't even look like

the servers. Wow, I'm so sorry," Sarah said and I slipped her the hundred dollars as I got ready to walk away and leave her to her man hunting.

"It's okay, I'm sure she didn't mean any harm."

"Now that I've gotten you away from the girls, how do you feel about buying a real woman a drink?" I heard Sarah say as I gave her a glance and headed back toward our table.

When I rejoined the table there was a group of guys talking Kendra up and Teddy just rolled his eyes at the commotion. Kendra was a goddess, that was the best way I could describe how she looked in her tight black mini dress. Her ebony skin glowed and her long black hair was curled and looking especially lovely that night.

Often I'd found that men just couldn't resist hitting on her when we were out. It usually felt like she was the primary target of affection and I was a secondary target. Not that I didn't look amazing in my red dress, but she just had that sexual vibe that radiated off of her. My vibe said something a bit different, or at least that was what I chalked it up to when the men picked her over me.

"Our server disappeared, I need some cranberry juice," Teddy said. "Want to walk with me to the bar?"

"Yep," I laughed as I looked at the three men talking to Kendra.

If I had wanted any of them I easily could have joined the conversation, but I wasn't feeling the vibe from them. I was looking for a fun guy to bring home for the night, but just for the night. With my newly found commitment to becoming a mother, I definitely didn't want to get involved in more than a short fling.

"No gay guys here at all tonight."

"Teddy, I bet there are more than you think. You've got to get out there and socialize. Sitting with the three of us might be clouding your gaydar."

"I know, but it's not that easy to pick up dudes here. This is a sausage fest for hetero women."

"Maybe you shouldn't be walking around with me then," I laughed. "You look straight as a board."

We both knew that was a complete lie. Teddy had on a decorative purple button up shirt and some fantastic Versace shoes; he was dressed to impress. As we waited for our turn at the bar I glanced up at a tall guy standing to my right. He was a remarkable-looking man, beautiful really. He towered over me, even with my Jimmy Choos on. I was staring at him as he looked over and caught me right in the act. He looked familiar although I wasn't exactly sure until he started to talk.

"It's busy tonight," he said with a boyish grin.

I knew right away who he was. Mike Cooper, a friend of one of my older brothers and some sort of doctor, although I wasn't sure what type of medicine he had gone into. For a minute I thought he might have recognized me.

"Yeah, it's always wild here."

"Do you come here often?" he asked and then laughed at his own line. "Wow, that was as generic as they come."

"Actually, I don't come here very often."

Teddy moved up ahead of me in line and I saw Mike look at him and then at me. He seemed to realize we weren't together rather quickly and continued his pursuit of me. Or perhaps he just didn't care if I was with Teddy or not and was going to flirt with me anyways.

"That's an amazing dress. Would you mind if I bought you a drink? I'm Mike, by the way."

"Hi, Mike. I'm Julia," I said in anticipation that he might actually realize who I was once I told him my name.

Mike and my brother Rob had been fairly close friends growing up. Rob was seven years older than me and I was very much a child when Mike had been to our home. The last time I remembered seeing him was when he came home for Christmas break during my Junior year in high school. I'd tried to find reasons to be in the same room as him and Rob and my other brothers but I was always relegated to leaving the room. I was pretty sure Mike Cooper didn't even know I existed. And as I waited for him to recognize me, it was clear he did not.

"Well that's a beautiful name for a beautiful girl," Mike said as he shook my hand lightly. "How about I get you a drink and you come sit with me at my table for a little bit?"

"Still pretty generic," I teased him.

"It is, but the problem is that I would really like to talk with you and we certainly can't keep standing here in this mess of people."

"I'm heading back to the couch," Teddy busted right between the two of us. "Yeah, I'll catch up to you later." He winked at me and then looked at Mike. "Good catch."

"Well, you have his approval so I guess I have no other choice but to say yes," I shrugged and walked up to the bar beside Mike. I was about to tell him what I wanted to drink when he leaned into the bartender and placed the order himself.

I had no idea what he had told the man but we left the bar without our drinks. Mike slipped his hand down to hold mine and I followed him to the far back corner of the club where he had a private table.

Holding hands in a club like this wasn't exactly the same as holding hand normally. It was a necessity to ensure you didn't lose the person you were following. But, his hand was strong and firm while also being extremely soft. He didn't act like the surgeons I'd met in clubs before; they typically had an attitude about them that was fairly distinctive. I wracked my brain trying to remember what type of doctor Mike had become, but for the life of me, I couldn't remember what my brother had said. In all fairness, it had been several years since we had talked about Mike. When I first moved to New York Rob had brought up that his friend also lived there.

"Our drinks are on their way," Mike said and held his hand out for me to slide into the small booth.

Mike sat down right beside me instead of across from me. At this point, it didn't seem romantic; more a little pushy. If he really didn't recognize who I was, then he was basically just sitting with a stranger and trying to get laid.

Guys in New York weren't all jerks. I'd met plenty of decent guys, the problem was finding any decent guys who I also found attractive and had a connection with. In the twenty-first century women no longer had to settle for a man who was only half of what she was looking for and I just didn't feel like dating around with men I knew weren't a good match.

A few guys here and there seemed promising, but the spark fizzled quickly and I jumped back into concentrating on my career. So far, there was a definite spark with Mike, but nothing too outrageous and a lot of my emotions about him were probably just a girlhood crush that I still carried over.

"Oh my God, Julia, you need to come with me," Kendra said as she approached the table and stood over the two of us.

"Kendra, this is Mike," I said.

"Hi, Mike, I promise you can have her back in a minute, I need her." She was insistent and reached for my hand to pull me out of the booth. Mike had no choice but to move out of the way.

He was polite and smiled at the interruption but he was clearly annoyed. Kendra wasn't the type of grab me away from situations though so I was a little curious to see what was going on and why this was such an emergency.

"Ten minutes?" Mike asked Kendra and me with a playful raised eyebrow. "After that, I'm stealing her back."

"Yes, ten minutes is good," Kendra said and yanked me off into the crowd behind her.

"What was that all about? He's super cute, you can't really be this worried about me sitting with that guy?"

"No, nothing about him. It's about Sarah, she um..." Kendra stopped dead in her tracks.

I looked around trying to figure out what was going on. There was a crowd of people around us and when I looked at the couch where we had all been sitting I saw what the emergency was.

"She's not!" I yelled and my hand flew up to cover my eyes.

"Yeah, I'm sure the cops have already been called, or maybe they will let her finish?" Kendra shrugged.

Sarah had taken her new boy toy to the couch we had reserved. She was riding him, screwing the hell out of the guy, right there in the middle of the club. At first, I wasn't sure I actually believed my own eyes. Sarah was extremely sexually free, and she'd been known to have a voyeuristic side, but this was extreme even for her.

"Where's Teddy?" I asked.

"There," Kendra pointed to Teddy standing about ten feet away talking to a man wearing purple shoes. They actually looked like an adorable couple with their matching styles.

"Should I stop her?" I asked, hoping the answer was no.

"Yeah, because I sure as heck am not going over there. She's going to get arrested. Why does she do this stuff?"

"I don't know," I replied and reluctantly made my way over toward the couch. I was almost there when three police officers came down the steps and moved in on Sarah and her new friend.

There was no big commotion. No yelling or any sort of scene at all. One of the officers just stood next to the couch and both Sarah and her man looked up at him. For a minute I wasn't sure they were even going to stop having sex, but they did and as Sarah stood up and slid her dress back down, a few people clapped around the two of them.

Both Sarah and her guy were being handcuffed when I hurried over to see what I could do to help. I wasn't a rule breaker like she was, I was terrified to even be by the police officers, but she looked calm as could be.

"Do you want me to call someone?" I asked.

"Yes. Teddy has the number for my attorney. Which precinct am I going to?" she asked the officer.

"Just around the corner," he replied.

"Okay," Sarah shrugged. "Just have him meet me there."

The officers walked her away before I could clarify where she was going so I really hoped Teddy knew what was going on and how to help her. Teddy was in the middle of full-on flirting mode when I interrupted him. He hadn't even realized what was going on at all.

"Sarah was just arrested for having sex right there on the couch! She said you have her attorney's number. Can you call him and have him meet her? The police officers said they were taking her just around the corner."

"Wait, was she having sex with the police officer?" Teddy laughed.

"No, this is serious."

"Yes, I can handle it, just a second," he turned back to his friend and basically ignored me.

I didn't know what to do. Teddy was likely to totally ignore what was going on and not call her attorney until tomorrow if he and this guy hit it off. I waited impatiently off to the side as Teddy and his guy friend talked for what seemed like forever.

It was nearly twenty minutes before Teddy finally exchanged numbers with the guy and came over to me. By that time I was close to screaming at him I was so frustrated, but the one problem with being friends with your boss was that you couldn't scream at them even when they were being a jerk.

"Teddy, come on. Just call her attorney already," I said as Kendra found her way over to us. "Where were you?"

"I got caught up."

"What is going on with the two of you? Our friend just got taken to jail; you really don't have anything better to do than flirt with people? She needs our help," I said in a panic.

Teddy laughed and Kendra just shrugged her shoulders. I was at my wits end with these two and about to just go over to the jail myself if one of them didn't start helping our friend.

"She got arrested three weeks ago when we were out together," Teddy said when he stopped laughing. "This happens to her more than you would think. Is this the first time you've been with her when it happened?"

"What? How have I never heard about it?"

"Maybe she didn't want you to know what a pervert she is," Kendra laughed.

"So what's going to happen? Does she have to stay in jail for a long time?"

"No," Teddy patted me on the back. "They will book her and she will pay a fine. Her lawyer will go down and either they will drop the charges or she will get a day in court. Then her lawyer negotiates a fine or community service and it's all over with. It's really not a big deal. Calm down."

"Really?" I asked a little bewildered by what I was hearing.

"Yeah, she will be just fine. I'll text her attorney. I've got his number. Go back to having fun. Where is that hot guy that was hitting on you at the bar?"

My heart stopped when I realized how long I'd been away from Mike. He probably thought I had totally ditched him. How embarrassing it would be to even go back over there at this point.

"We will figure it out," Kendra said reassuringly as Teddy walked away texting on his phone. "Don't worry. I'm sure he will still be over there."

The two of us walked back to the table where we had left Mike. Instead of Mike, there was an equally handsome blonde haired guy sitting there with a woman. They were eating strawberries and drinking champagne, probably what Mike had ordered for me.

"Well, I ruined that."

"He's still around. Let's go find him," Kendra said.

"No, actually, I think I'm just going to go home. I'm exhausted and I don't want to date right now anyway. I'm ready to just get pregnant and be a mom. How about I meet you back at home?"

"Sure, I'll text you if I find someone to play with this evening and I'm not coming home. But are you sure? This was supposed to be your night to celebrate."

"I know, but it really is just fine. I like being at home," I laughed.

Kendra was looking at me when her eyes darted over my shoulder. I felt someone walk up behind me and knew it just had to be Mike. Kendra smiled so big that there was no other possible option. Kendra winked and then turned to walk away.

Slowly I turned around.

"I don't think I've ever been ditched before the first drink," he smiled down at me.

Chapter 2

Mike

She didn't respond to my playful quip and instead just stared up at me like I'd actually caught her in the middle of something. Up until that look, I had honestly thought she just got caught up with her friends or something. Now I was beginning to wonder if she had intended on ditching me.

"Yeah, I guess I'm not great at ditching people," she mischievously touched my bicep and leaned in close to me. I leaned down so she could say something in my ear. "My friend was caught having sex on one of the couches. Sorry. I got distracted taking care of that."

"Best excuse ever," I said. "But I did give our drinks to my friend. Should we get some more or go dance?"

I really couldn't shake the feeling that I knew Julia from somewhere. She was being much too nice to me to be a girl I had slept with and forgotten, so there had to be some other explanation as to why she looked so darn familiar.

Her long brown hair was curled slightly and pinned back to show off her neck, a neck that I desperately wanted to kiss. Sometimes when I met a woman there was a good amount of chemistry between us but with Julia, it was dripping off of us. Her sequined red dress hugged every curve like a professional race car driver.

She smiled at me while contemplating which of my offers she wanted to take me up on. I was happy to go buy some more champagne and strawberries if that was what she wanted, a good conversation with her was certainly on the menu. Or if she wanted to take me for a spin on the dance floor I was up for that as well, it would give me the opportunity to feel her body against mine.

"Dancing first, then drinking," she finally decided.

Sometimes I don't know what comes over me when I'm around a beautiful woman, but I grabbed her and lifted her off the ground a few inches as I carried her out to the dance floor. She was light as a feather and her lips were oh so close to mine. It would have been the perfect opportunity to kiss her if I hadn't just met her an hour before and been looking for her in the club most of the time since I'd first talked to her. No, I had to restrain those primal emotions, at least for the time being.

"Wow, okay then," she laughed and threw her head back. "That's a bold move."

"You deserve a bold move."

I didn't know much about this girl but there was something drawing me to her like I hadn't been drawn to a woman in a very long time. In college, maybe, there had been Lisa, but even that was short lived when our professional drives got in the way. This girl excited me and not just the physical excitement that was bulging in my pants. We started to dance to the house music.

The dance floor was much too loud to be able to communicate effectively. It gave us the opportunity to use the physical charisma between us as a barometer for our communication. The music thumped and I did my best not to let Julia feel just how excited she was making me with her sexy hips and flirty dance moves.

I didn't get to be one of the most eligible bachelors in New York City by being bad with the ladies. I knew how to be kind, sweet and attentive. Often though it felt like a game I was playing, and it was becoming an old game. Women knew who I was, usually. They had seen an article or watched a story on television. Julia didn't look at me like those women did though. Her gaze delved much deeper than I was used to; it made me slightly uncomfortable, she made me feel off my game.

As we dance I kept a few inches between the two of us until Julia took control and slid her delicious ass right up against my body. There was no way to hide my excitement and I prepared myself for her to move away quickly. But instead of moving away from my hard member, Julia pressed her ass against me even harder. She looked back at me with a mischievous smile and I was done. At that moment I knew I was going to be bringing Julia home with me.

I couldn't behave another minute longer and grabbed her

hips to hold her there against me. My normal suave etiquette was barely holding on as my desire for this girl throbbed harder and harder. Even as I gripped her and held her against me, Julia continued to dance seductively, enticing me to continue with our little game.

"You're killing me," I mouthed when she turned around and pressed her body against me.

I felt her soft breasts pressed into my body and let my hands move down the open back of her dress. When I reached to curve of her ass I was nearly able to stop myself, but I couldn't. One of my hands slid into the top of her dress and I cupped her perfectly formed ass in my hands. This girl was delicious.

It didn't matter that the club was playing upbeat music, Julia and I were dancing to our own music. She slid her hands around and pulled the back of my shirt out of my pants so she could let her fingers glide up and down my back.

Chemistry was the only way I could describe what was going on between the two of us; sexual chemistry. Our bodies were made for each other. Honestly, I'd met women that I'd wanted to manhandle like I was with Julia on the dance floor, I just hadn't met a woman who actually reciprocated the level of lust I had.

We danced for nearly an hour in the hot sticky dance club. Neither of us was phased by the environment as we kept our eyes on each other. She would smile sweetly up at me but then her smile turned into desire and I'd feel her hands exploring under my shirt. I half expected that she was going to grab onto my erection right there in the middle of the club, but she never went quite that far.

"Can I steal her for a minute," Julia's friend yelled as she came up and joined us on the dance floor.

I didn't believe it was going to be for a minute, but I nodded my head in agreement. This time I followed the two women off the dance floor and kept my eye on them. Julia's friend said something in her ear and then pointed to a good looking guy standing nearby. The two women hugged and then Julie came back over to me. It was the perfect opportunity for us to take a break and I motioned for us to go back over to the table I had reserved in the corner.

Julia reached down and held onto my hand as I guided us back toward the table. Her delicate fingers fit perfectly into my hand and I squeezed them playfully when we approached the table and I saw Taylor sitting there with a woman.

"He's my friend, let's join them," I said loud enough for her to hear me.

Coming to the clubs was fun because the women were always ready to have a good time, well most of them at least. But it did make it really hard to have a conversation with someone like Julia.

"Wow, I think I saw him in a magazine," Julia said.

"Maybe," I couldn't help but laugh since the magazine she had seen Taylor in was the same one I was in, but I wasn't about to admit that to her.

Women were lovely, I enjoyed them in all aspects of my life and truly cherished the female form. There was a limit to my understanding though and when women became pushy or rude to each other in an effort to talk to me, it really bothered me. I noticed a group of women watching Julia and me as we sat down at the table. I gave them a quick glance and then slipped my arm around Julia's shoulders as I introduced her to Taylor.

"Taylor, this is Julia," I yelled so he could hear me.

"Hi Julia, this is Star," he said as he introduced his blonde bombshell that had been sharing the champagne I'd left for the two of them.

"It's nice to meet you," Taylor said and reached over to shake hands with Julia.

We had barely finished the introduction when the group of four young women made their way over to our table. Surely they didn't plan on interrupting our dates I thought, but then I realized they definitely planned to do that.

"Oh, my gosh guys. I'm so sorry for interrupting, but can we get pictures with you two?" one of the women said as she looked at Julia and Star for approval.

"Sorry ladies, not right now," I said.

"Please, we promise not to take too long."

"No, sorry," I repeated and then turned toward Julia.

Instead of looking agitated by the interruption, Julia was actually smiling and nodded that I should go take the pictures. She practically pushed me out of the booth while she laughed at the absurdity of the whole thing. Following Julia's lead, Star also motioned for Taylor to go ahead and take the photos although she didn't look nearly as amused by the whole thing.

"Do you girls want me to take the picture?" Julia asked as she popped out of the booth and grabbed one of the girl's phones.

"Yes, thank you," a few of the girls replied.

This group of young women was probably barely old enough to be in the club. They certainly weren't my type of woman and their pushiness was a huge turn-off. By this point, I was just taking the pictures to get them on their way.

Taylor joined me and the two of us stood between two women and smiled into the camera. But after Julia took one photo, one woman asked for a picture alone with Taylor, then another woman asked for a picture alone with just me. This went on for at least ten minutes before we were finally able to get them to move on.

I felt terrible by the time I sat back down with Julia. This wasn't at all the kind of guy I was. "I'm so sorry, I apologize for the interruption," I said as I poured us both a glass of champagne.

"Not at all," she said with that same playful grin. "That was really entertaining. I bet those girls will be talking about the two of you for weeks now."

"Normally I would say no to anything like that if I was on a date with a woman. Please know that it's not normal for me."

"It's a good thing we aren't on a date then," Julia laughed. "And I don't mind. There will probably be a group of guys coming around to take pictures with me really soon too," she dramatically rolled her eyes and I couldn't stop laughing.

"Oh yeah?"

"Yep, I know, it's hard to compete with the likes of me," she continued. "I'll try and keep you in the loop though."

"Yes, please do! How about I get us some more champagne and food?" I asked and everyone nodded.

I pulled Julia's hand up to my lips and gave her a quick kiss before making my way to the bar to get what we needed. Julia was again throwing me off my game. Her lighthearted way of handling that situation was so ideal that I couldn't have dreamed of a better response. She saw those women and was welcoming and inviting to them and even helped with the photo, it was pretty damn amazing.

So far Julia was checking off so many boxes of what I wanted in a woman and we hardly knew each other. I really had to get to know her and suddenly my mind was shifting from bringing her home to actually talking and getting to know what she liked and didn't like. If you would have asked me just a few hours before if I was interested in any sort of dating, I would have vehemently denied it.

"Wow bro, I like her," Taylor said as he joined me at the bar.

"I know, she looks familiar to me though. Is she famous or something?"

"Not that I know of, but she handled those girls like a pro. It wouldn't surprise me if she was in television or involved in publicity somehow. Either way, nice catch."

"Thanks. I just can't shake this feeling that I know her though. It's really weird."

"What's her name?" He asked.

"Julia is all I have so far."

"Well, let me know if you figure it out. I'm going to get my date onto the dance floor and then head home in a bit. It was nice catching up with you. Let's talk this week, let me know if you ever figure out who she is."

"Deal." Taylor and I gave each other a quick hug and then he went back to the table to get his date. The two of them were on their way to the dance floor as I came back with some more champagne.

"I thought at these tables you were supposed to get someone to do that for you?" Julia asked.

"I know, haven't seen her all night though."

"Well, that seems unusual," Julia said and grabbed my hand when I sat down with her.

"They will bring some snacks over soon. I hope you're hungry."

"Starving, famished. I could eat a small child," she joked.

"Hopefully it doesn't come to that."

It was by far the weirdest first kiss ever but I couldn't resist. As I looked at her cute little smile I leaned in and let my lips touch hers. At first, she pulled away a little, I think it was out of surprise that I had just kissed her though and she soon leaned into the kiss. Her hands wrapped around my neck and her fingers worked up into the back of my hair.

Julia parted her mouth and turned to the side as she let me thrust my tongue inside of her. The delicious taste of her mouth electrified me and it seemed to have a similar reaction to her as I felt one of her legs cross over the other and slide between mine. She wanted me, her body was telling me that she wanted me and I just couldn't ignore it.

"Wow, that was nice," Julia said when we finally pulled apart.

"Yes, it was."

I poured a couple of glasses of champagne and handed one of them to her. Her red lipstick wasn't even smeared after our kissing session. My eyes stayed fixated on her lips while they wrapped around the edge of the glass and then she slowly lifted the glass and the alcohol slid into her mouth.

"What?" She asked playfully as I stared at her.

"I feel like I know you," I finally said.

"Oh, you do?" She asked and then coyly looked away. "That's a pretty good line."

"It does seem a little cheesy, sorry."

"I know what you mean. I feel like I know you too. Maybe we really do know each other?" She winked and then went back to drinking her champagne.

"Do we?"

Just as I asked the question the waitress came to the table and put down the food I'd ordered. I'd ordered way too much of it. In fact, I felt like a maniac as soon as the food arrived and there were six different platters for us. I had thought Taylor and his new friend were going to join us but now it just looked like I planned on force-feeding Julia a ton of appetizers.

"I'm starving," she said and drank another glass of champagne while we both went head first into the various foods.

"You are so beautiful; I just want you to know that before I start stuffing my face with food."

"You're pretty good looking yourself there, Mike," she replied before putting a stuffed jalapeño into her mouth in one bite.

Her eyes got large right away and then started to water. She was looking at me as if I could help her and all I could do was pour her some more champagne. I wasn't even sure that champagne could help cool her tongue after eating that hot piece of cheese-filled pepper.

"You didn't know that was a jalapeño?"

"No," she said with the food still in her mouth. Her cheeks were filled with the food and she continued to chew it though. "It's okay," she said more to herself than to me. "I'm okay."

"Just spit it out, it's fine, here," I said and handed her a napkin. "They aren't everyone's cup of tea."

"No, no, it's fine," she insisted and continued to chew. "I like it. I just wasn't prepared for it to be a pepper," she laughed a little even though she didn't look like she was having fun at all.

Her dewy white skin had turned the same shade as her red dress. She finished off one glass of champagne and then another one before she managed to finish chewing and swallowing the pepper. The whole time she still had half of a smile and looked cute as could be.

"I feel horrible. I'm sorry I didn't tell you that was a jalapeño. I bet they look a lot like fried stuffed mushrooms."

"Yeah they do," she laughed.

"I'm so sorry," I pulled her in for a hug and held onto her

for a minute. "You looked like you might die from that thing. Was it horribly hot?"

"No, I'm okay. It just caught me off guard."

The room and the people around us disappeared as she stayed wrapped up in my arms for a minute. I wasn't exactly a protector or anything like that, at least that had never been the persona I identified with when I was around women, but being around Julia made me feel different than normal. I'd actually just let her eat that pepper and I should have said something, it had happened so fast though. For a moment I expected she would get annoyed or agitated with me, any other woman would have. I expected her to lash out at me, but she didn't. I was trying to manufacture a reason not to like this girl and it had totally backfired on me.

Julia didn't seem annoyed at all; as she lifted her head up she was smiling and laughed at the whole thing. This was the sort of laid-back personality I'd been hoping to find in a woman, it was how my buddies and I always reacted when something like this happened to us. The women I usually met didn't seem to think things like this were very funny. The last girl I'd been on a date with actually called me a jerk before we had even finished our appetizer.

"Probably good that this isn't a first date," Julia laughed. "I don't think I would have liked having snot dripping down my nose on a first date," she gingerly wiped her nose with a napkin.

"You still look really good, even with snot," I laughed.

"How would you feel about doing a real first date some time?"

"I think we could manage that. So does that mean this doesn't count as a date? Because I'd really love to bring you home for a night of fun. Of course, if it was a first date I wouldn't do such a thing," she said playfully.

"This is definitely not a first date," I replied, eager to please her.

Who was this girl? How was it that I felt so connected to her and yet knew nothing about her at all? She had a great sense of humor and a body with curves that I couldn't stop looking at.

The music drifted off and it was just the two of us sitting there again as if everyone else had disappeared while we continued talking and having an amazing time. We talked about a lot of things, but nothing really personal. Our opinions on the new Broadway show, what we were looking forward to this fall around town, and even the subway and its constant inability to allow a phone signal while you were traveling through the city. I didn't have the heart to tell her I hardly ever rode the subway anymore but it did seem odd that in this day and age they couldn't figure out a way to get cell service or Wi-Fi down there.

The conversation between the two of us flowed easily from one topic to the next while we sipped our champagne and ate our bar food. It was the best first date I'd had in a really long time, especially considering it wasn't a date at all.

Perhaps that was why we were getting along so easily; there was no forced intimacy like what happened on first dates normally. There were no expectations of what would come next in our night and I felt more at ease than I typically was, it was as if I already know Julia, but I didn't know her at all.
+

We both switched to water as it got to the early morning hours and the night started to wind down. It was nearly three o'clock in the morning when I finally settled the tab and walked Julia out to my hired car. I wanted to bring her home. Normally after a night even half as good as this one I would have brought the girl back to my house. Not tonight though, I wanted to see her again. I wasn't about to ruin this whole thing.

"If you give Joe your address I'll drop you off," I said when we climbed into the back of the big SUV.

I handed her a pad of paper and she wrote her address down and passed the slip of paper to my driver Joe. Although she had teased about bringing me home with her, I really was just fine with dropping her off. The connection we had was intriguing to me and I planned on asking her out again.

"Thank you, Joe," she said before turning back toward me. "Thank you for the ride home."

"You're welcome. I'm happy to do it. I really wouldn't feel right just putting you in a cab. You should give me your number too, so I can call you and arrange our real first date."

"No, I think I'll give you that later," Julia said as she slid onto my lap and hiked her dress up and over her thighs. Instantly I was aroused and ready to slide inside of her. Knowing that there was only a small bit of fabric between my body and hers was exciting, but I wasn't trying to have sex with her that night. The plan was simple, get her number, drop her off, and give her a kickass goodnight kiss.

"I had an amazing time tonight," I said between kisses.

Her lips pressed erotically against mine and she pulled in a deep breath while we played with one another. I tried not to concentrate on the feeling of her hips slightly moving on top of me. I wasn't going to be able to hold out for much longer. There was only so much a man could do.

As we pulled up to her apartment Joe came around and opened the door so I could walk Julia up to her apartment. Julia climbed out of the car first and whispered something in Joe's ear before heading to the front door to get it unlocked.

"What did she say?" I laughed as Joe shut the door.

"That I wouldn't be needed anymore tonight." Joe gave me a knowing smile.

Apparently, I was sleeping over.

Chapter 3

Julia

Mike was going to be mine. I should have said something to him about who I was, but I just couldn't ruin our night. It didn't matter. I'd fantasized about him for so long and now I was going to have him. We probably wouldn't see or talk to each other again, but at least I would have one fun night to remember. I wasn't even sure if he was still talking to my brother Rob at all.

"I had a great evening," Mike said as we got off the elevator on my floor and walked toward my apartment.

"Yes, it was really fun. More than I was expecting."

"Oh, so you weren't expecting me to be fun?" He laughed and raised an eyebrow at me.

"I think you have far exceeded what I thought you were like," I knew I'd said too much when he looked at me with a slightly cocked head. How would I of had expectations for a man I'd just met. Dang. I had let it out of the bag; he was going to see through this whole thing. I leaned in to kiss him in an effort to distract him from any thoughts regarding what I'd just said.

He grabbed my hips and pulled me toward him as he found a way to wedge us both in between the doorway. If he had figured out that we really did know each other, he wasn't saying anything about it just yet. He looked down at me and smiled a little before taking my lips as if he'd had them a million times before.

I was glad to be pressed up against the doorway since I felt my knees getting shaky and I likely wouldn't have been standing without the support behind me. I liked kissing Mike. It was better than I'd fantasized about and yet I still felt like I was in a bit of a daze as I looked up at him when he pulled away a little.

"Come in," I managed to whisper.

"Okay," he replied without an argument at all. His hazel eyes glistened with desire as the light from the hallway flickered above us.

"We can have a night cap," I suggested in an effort to hide my desire to take him straight to bed. Knowing that Mike was a decent guy took away the normal trepidation I had about bringing a man to my house. I knew him well enough to know he wasn't going to hurt me or doing anything crazy; he was a good guy, he was the perfect fling for me.

Who was this person that I'd become though? I wasn't the sort of girl who lied to guys and took them home. Normally, on the rare occasion that I wanted to take a guy home, or go home with him, I didn't lie to get my way. Something had come over me and I just knew he wouldn't want to sleep with me if he knew who I really was. He'd balk at the fact that he knew my brother or that he knew me when I was younger and none of that should matter. We clearly had a connection and that was real; the rest of it didn't matter.

"Sure, let's have a night cap," Mike agreed.

I turned around and fumbled with my keys as I tried to get into my apartment. Normally, even with some alcohol in my system, I didn't have a problem getting into my door. But on this night there was an extremely handsome man with a throbbing body part pressed up against me. He hands slid around and under my skirt hemline as he kissed my neck. None of this was helping me as I tried to concentrate on sliding the key into the hole. His fingers moved up my thighs and then all the way to my stomach as he took in the touch of my bare skin. My lacy black panties were exposed as my ass pressed up against him.

"Hey now, I need to concentrate," I teased.

"I'll help," he offered and took the key from me.

He didn't help at all. Instead, Mike held onto the key while he continued to kiss my neck and drive me wild. I could hardly stand still as my body longed to have him. I pressed my hips back against him and leaned my neck into his kisses. The touch of his fingers on my bare skin made me want him more and more. I couldn't take this anticipation much longer. I was dripping with excitement.

"You're not even trying to open the door," I said softly.

"Oh, sorry," he laughed.

With one quick movement he had the key in the door and

swung the door open. He wrapped me up in his arms and flipped me around to face him as the door shut behind us. The quick movement made me giggle at first, until I saw the serious nature of his desire.

I dropped my bag and he dropped the keys as our hands thrust onto one another and started to remove our clothes. My fingers shook with excitement while pulling his shirt off and then sliding up and down his amazingly defined chest. How was it possible that a human could look so perfect? Guys like Mike weren't usually the ones I went for. I didn't trust a guy who looked that good; surely they were just sleeping around and having their way with every hot girl that came around. I was more comfortable with Mike than I would have been if I truly had just met him that evening. But Mike didn't know that was why I was comfortable with him. Perhaps he thought I was just full of self confidence? Or maybe he believed I was the sort of girl who just brought men home right away?

As much as I tried not to over analyze what was going on, my insecurities were ruling me and I had to stop them. This was my problem. Not just with Mike, but with everyone... I over thought things. I thought about decisions so much that sometimes I didn't make a decision at all...which was still a decision. It was one of my major flaws, or at least I thought it was.

"Bedroom... this way," I managed to say with the tiny bit of confidence I had left.

"Okay," he smiled and pulled me into him.

As we stood in the entryway, Mike let his hands tease my outer thighs before pulling my dress up and over my head. I cringed with self loathing and not wanting him to see me in the full light of the hallway. We needed to get to the bedroom; the dark of the bedroom offered me the opportunity to at least pretend I had confidence.

"This way," I pulled on him as I moved away a little.

"Wow, that ass," he groaned and slid his hands over my ass and pulled me back toward him. "You're amazingly beautiful."

"Thanks," I laughed.

"Seriously Julia, this ass. I can't get enough of it."

His eyes were fixated on my behind and he slid his fingers over the edge of my lacy panties. He was definitely an ass man; there was no doubt he was telling the truth as he gawked at my behind. The way he was looking at my butt gave me a little burst of confidence. He really liked it; the roundness that I always felt self conscious about seemed to be fueling his desires.

"Let's go to the bedroom," I urged and pulled forward.

Mike let me pull in front of him but he stayed there staring at me as I walked a few steps. His eyes utterly fixated on my ass. I paused and wiggled it a little for him. Hell, if he liked my ass then I could work with that.

"Damn, I could look at you forever," he said and flipped

on the lights in the living room as he followed me to the bedroom, flipping the lights on in there too.

"No need for those I laughed."

"Oh, yes. I want to see every inch of you while I make love to you."

"No," I groaned.

"Julie, there's something you should know about me," Mike started to say. "I love the female form. I appreciate curves and you are stunning. I'd really love to see you."

"Um, okay," I said without an ounce of confidence that I was going to enjoy this.

Having the lights off was my way of letting go and forgetting about all the body flaws that bothered me. My curvy frame wasn't too fluffy, but in New York it was hard not to compare myself to every model walking down the street.

"Look at me," Mike said as his gaze fully enveloped me and I did as he asked. "You are beautiful and I'm so glad I met you tonight. If you would like to wait, I have no problem heading home and calling you tomorrow for a first date."

"No," I said instinctively before the pessimist inside me was able to re-think what he was saying. "I want you now."

I grabbed him and started to kiss him before I lost my nerve. It was erotic to have the lights on and to have heard what he just said to me. There was a part of me that felt like this was a line he said to a lot of women, but was it totally horrible of me to think that instead of just taking him at his word? Yeah it was! But I couldn't help myself.

I made a conscious decision to believe him though. Sure, he could have said that same thing to many different women, but it didn't matter. In fact, it didn't even matter that we would probably never go on a real date. So why did I even care if he was making things up to make me feel more comfortable?

My thought process shifted to just enjoying our evening and not worrying about anything else. It was one night. One night of passion and love making.

I grabbed his pants button and undid it while we kissed. In the process I felt the massive member that had been pressing up against me earlier. This was going to be one hell of a night.

For a few minutes we stood there in the doorway of my room playing and kissing with each other. My fingers wrapped around his hard body as his hands softly moved up and down my back before settling on the clasps of my bra and unhooking it. Mike groaned a little as he guided my black bra onto the ground and his hands moved back up to cup my breasts. He played with them gently at first. Slowly caressing me as we kissed and started to move toward the bed.

I kept my eyes closed in an effort to forget about the lights being on and Mike being able to see every curve of my body. His hands were warm and helped me feel at ease, even comfortable there in his arms.

I tugged on his hardness and pulled his underwear off. He was standing totally naked, erect and excited for me. In that moment it was clear that nothing else matter because he was there with me and I was there with him. I had to stop ruminating about why or how we had ended up there together and just enjoy the night.

"Your hands feel so good," he groaned.

Then I did something that I hadn't done in years. I slid down to my knees and took him into my mouth. Giving oral to a man was such an intimate thing that I really didn't do it unless I had been dating the guy for a long time. It was a sexual act that was even more intimate to me than actually making love. But I wanted to feel his body inside my mouth. I needed it.

My lips wrapped tightly around him and I took his body in. He groaned with each sucking motion and I thrived off of his noises. The louder he was the more I wanted to continue doing what I was doing. I move deep around him and took in each inch that I could savoring the slight bit of power that I felt in that moment. For such an intimate act, oral sex was also a powerful sign of the confidence I was feeling that evening. I moved harder and faster while pressing my hands against his thighs. His cock dripped with excitement from my touch and I knew if I continued he would certainly explode any minute.

"Julia," Mike groaned as his hips moved softly against my

mouth.

I didn't answer him. I was busy. Busy trying to drive him crazy. Busy taking his body into my mouth and powerfully building up his desire until he couldn't take it any longer and pulled away.

"What?" I laughed as his arms wrapped around me and pulled me up toward him.

"Oh, you're going to get it," he teased and tossed me onto the bed.

"Oh, no," I said playfully.

Mike started to kiss up my legs and stopped to look at me. His smile was childlike and his excitement clearly visible as he looked at my panties. He didn't pause for long before I felt his teeth take hold of the fabric and pull the panties all the way down my leg in one swift movement. He didn't even wait for me to lift my ass to make things easier.

The desire in his eyes was like a drug that had taken over him. He let the panties fall out of his mouth and then quickly pressed my legs apart and looked down at my naked body. At first I wanted to close my legs and hide from the embarrassment I was feeling, but I looked at Mike and realized he was in awe of me. His desire was in full.

"So sexy," he groaned before using his fingers to spread me open. "I can't wait to taste you."

His words flashed through me and I felt my body react instantly to them. I was already wet with desire, but I got even wetter. Then his tongue gently touched me and I moaned a primal sound that it caught me a little off guard.

Mike was gentle, slow, as he moved his tongue up and down my body. He played with every inch of me in a seductive dance to build up my desire. His tongue magically found the little spots that felt like they hadn't been touched in years. First moving up to the top of my clit and then pulling me into his mouth with a long sucking motion that felt so powerful.

I moaned louder and he pulled harder on my body. He'd let me out of his grip for a moment or two while he licked and played with me and then pulled me into him again and again. The buildup was powerful, so powerful that I found myself holding onto the sheets as I thrusted my hips up toward him wanting more and more.

If he wasn't careful, I was going to cum in his mouth. The powerful lick of his tongue and enticing sound of his own groans was turning me on more than I thought possible. The primal need to release started to build up in me and I grabbed his head and tried to pull him away.

"I'm going to cum," I warned him. "The condoms are in that drawer."

"Cum for me," he said without moving toward the drawer at all.

"No, no, no, I want you inside of me," I said.

"Later baby, I want you to cum," he practically ordered

before returning to play with my body.

I didn't have the energy to fight with him. His tongue felt so damn good and I did really want to release. He moved with a new vigor and intensity as I moaned out in pleasure. I couldn't take much more of this, that was for sure.

When he slowly slid two fingers inside of me that was the last straw and I thrust against him with pure desire. He grabbed my clit with his mouth and formed a delicious suction around me as I wiggled and moved against him. The harder I moved though, the more he held onto me. His fingers curled inside and stroked me as the power of the moment built up more and more.

Shit, I was going to cum, I felt myself letting go. I didn't have control in that moment. I was totally and utterly succumbing to his powerful touch. My pelvis thrust into his grip and I let go with a loud scream of pleasure. "Yes, oh my God," I yelled and felt my whole body tense up with the feeling of total pleasure.

"Go baby," Mike groaned as he released my clit but sustained the stroking of my g-spot as I continued to cum hard.

I opened my eyes slightly to see him watching as my body gave in to the pleasure he was serving me. I was too wrapped up in the moment to even think about the shyness I normally had. Instead, I gave him a show as my body shook and shivered in front of him. I drenched his fingers with my release and couldn't stop as he continued to play with me.

Then he started to do something that I was totally unfamiliar with. Instead of stroking inside of me, Mike used one of his hands to press down on my pubic bone as he started moving his curled fingers up and down inside of me. He moved slowly at first and the unusual sensation caught me off guard. It felt good and new to me. As I felt a weirdly new feeling building up, I couldn't help but relax and let my body give in to this new sensation.

Soon I was in a totally foreign state as Mike moved his fingers faster and faster. He continued to hold me in place and the buildup got more and more intense.

"Oh, my God, that feels so good," I muttered.

"Try to relax."

"Okay," I agreed and took in a deep breath and tried to relax.

The second I relaxed my pelvic muscles the building sensation took over and I felt like I was going to cum, but a weird way that I had never felt before. Mike moved his fingers quickly and then suddenly pulled them out of me and started rubbing my clit back and forth as I gave into his movements and felt a gush of fluid rush out of me.

At first I thought I had just peed the bed. I opened my eyes in terror as he continued to rub my clit vigorously.

"Relax, you're squirting," he said and leaned down to kiss me.

"I am?" I said in total shock.

"You did. That was fucking hot as hell."

Mike kissed down my body and then continued to lick me totally soaked body. His pleasure in licking up my juices was evident by the moans he was making. This experience was so new and utterly unknown to me that I had my eyes opened and was trying to see how wet I had just gotten the sheets.

To my total dismay there was a huge wet spot down by my legs. I couldn't believe what had just happened. It was cool though, exciting even.

"Wow," I muttered looking at the mess I'd made. "Should I go get a towel?"

Mike was still licking me as he looked up and smiled a little at my concern over the wet spot.

"You're not going anywhere. Don't worry about it."

"I'll just go grab it real quickly," I offered and tried wiggling away from him.

"No way," he ordered and just pulled me over to the other side of the bed while he reached into the drawer and grabbed a condom.

"Oh no," I teased as he ripped it open and started to roll the piece of rubber over his hard body.

"Oh, yes," he smiled down at me.

He was kneeling over me as he finished putting the condom on and looking down at my body like he still couldn't get enough. The funny thing was, I couldn't get enough either. I wanted more, like a drug that I'd tasted and couldn't stop. I looked longingly up at him as he lowered himself onto me and kissed my neck softly while he pressed his body slowly into mine. The feeling of him entering me filled me up and I held onto him and adjusted to this new feeling.

Mike moved slowly at first and then his thrusts grew in intensity. Harder and longer each stroke continued. We moved together in a rhythmic motion of perfection with my body meeting his speed and intensity.

I saw the look on his face when Mike lost total control and turned into the primal beast that I was more familiar with in a man. He thrust harder and harder toward his goal of release and I clawed into his back with the feeling of total completeness that was building up in me. I'd already cum so much that it was a little shocking to me that I felt so close to giving in again. Was it even possible for me to cum again?

With a few more strokes I knew that I was indeed going to release and closed my eyes to feel the pleasure that was building up. In our very short time together I was already feeling more sexually satisfied than I'd felt in months, maybe even years.

"Yes," I said and urged him on.

My voice seemed to give him power and he pushed harder toward his release. I thrust my hips harder and felt my body brushing up against his as my center rumbled and I tightened with pleasure.

As if we had planned the perfectly timed orgasm, I started to release just as Mike gave a few final thrusts of pleasure and let out a deep moan of pleasure. It was utterly perfection.

"What an amazing night," Mike whispered when he slipped next to me and wrapped his arms around me.

"It was pretty perfect," I agreed as the exhaustion of our evening weighed heavily on my eyelids.

"Let's get some sleep," he whispered as he held onto me.

I was comfortable in his arms. Weirdly comfortable and totally willing to fall asleep with him there in my bed. The morning would be an awkward good bye and then we would both move on with our lives. I was okay with that too. I was planning on moving on with my life and having a baby.

Guys like Mike weren't actually out there, or at least I hadn't found them. He was an anomaly that I felt like wasn't possible for me in real life. This thing between us wasn't real, it was a fabrication of our feelings of comfort for each other.

It wasn't a bad thing. I was okay with it. The reality was that I really did want to have one last night of fun before having a baby and becoming a single mother and this night had been more perfect than I could have imagined. Mike was a gentleman and really damn good in the sack. I could move on with my plans now without feeling like I was missing out or that I was giving up something.

The power of the sleepiness I felt overwhelmed me more quickly than I was prepared for. I was only snuggled in Mike's arms for a few moments when I felt him wrap the blanket around us and the warmth was so inviting.

By morning, this fairytale feeling would be over and the flush of alcohol would be gone from both of our systems. We would go about our normal lives and this moment would just be a pleasant memory.

"Goodnight, Julia," Mike whispered and rubbed my arm as I snuggled up to his chest.

"Goodnight, Mike."

"I have to work early in the morning. Do you want me to wake you up before I leave?" he asked as the reality of the morning started to bleed into our evening of romance.

"No need," I said and closed my eyes. "It's okay."

"Okay, I'll call you for our date though," he offered.

"Goodnight." I wasn't convinced that I'd ever hear from him again. "Sweet dreams."

"The sweetest of dreams to you too," he kissed my forehead and started to stroke my hair as I felt myself drifting off to sleep.

There was a tiny bit of uneasiness about the idea of him being gone when I woke up. It wasn't going to feel great and I knew it, but it was what it was and I couldn't change that. This was a one night fling for both of us. He was trying to ease the feelings about it all by promising a date but what guy wouldn't make that promise? Not many would admit that they were just trying to have a night of fun.

None of it mattered in the end though because I was going to be a mom soon. I was going to bring a beautiful life into this world and dedicate myself to being the best mother possible.

Chapter 4

Mike

She looked sweet and utterly adorable sleeping so soundly next to me. I climbed out of bed and was about to grab my clothes and head out but stopped. I didn't want to leave without saying goodbye.

After getting dressed I went to the kitchen and fumbled around a little to make a couple cups of coffee for us. Even though I'd already given her a fair warning that I had to leave early for work, I wanted to talk to her one last time before I left.

"Good morning Julia," I whispered when I sat down on her side of the bed.

She moved a little but barely opened her eyes. It was only six am and we certainly hadn't had a full night of sleep. I was use to getting only a few hours though and was ready to head into the office. Sunday was my paperwork day. I didn't work every Sunday, but this week I'd gotten way behind because my partner Bruce had been missing in action which meant I was taking on his patients.

We named our practice RMA, or reproductive medicine associates. Bruce and I had been in business for the last five years together and up until recently things had been rather uneventful. Never in all my life had I thought I'd end up being the responsible one in a business partnership. But here I was always hounding Bruce and trying to get him to show up for work more. He spent more time philandering with the ladies than he did in the office, that was for sure.

We had arranged to meet up on Sunday to touch base on all his patients I'd seen, and I also needed to talk to him about why he had been gone so much. With just the two of us running our practice, it was pretty damn difficult when he disappeared for whole days at a time.

"Julia, here's some coffee. I'm going to get going," I said again as I let my hand rest on her cheek. "I've got a work thing today."

"You made coffee?" she said softly.

"I can't guarantee it's very good."

"That was sweet of you."

She pulled herself up and sat against the large white headboard. Her dark brown hair cascaded around her bare breasts and I did my best not to stare at her form. My cock, on the other hand, was paying very close attention.

"I'll call you, okay?"

"You know Mike, it's totally alright if this was just a one-night thing. You don't have to call. I get it. We had fun and I'm perfectly fine with that."

"I'll call you," I replied to her skepticism.

"Okay," she leaned in and pressed her lips softly against mine. "But if you don't..."

"Wow, I've never had a girl so sure I wasn't going to call," I laughed. "I'm not sure if I should be offended or not."

"Oh, you should definitely be offended," Julia laughed.

"Listen here young lady. I had a great time getting to know you and I'd like to take you on a real date. I'm going to call you up and we are going to schedule it. Deal?"

"Deal," she said with a little smirk on her face. "Now get going so I can go back to sleep."

I kissed her one last time and downed my coffee before heading out. Julia ended up following me to the front door and locked it behind me as soon as I left. The skepticism of this girl made me laugh out loud as I walked into the elevator to head downstairs. Maybe she didn't want me to call. I'd never had a woman try so damn hard to make sure what we had stayed a one night stand.

Our Sunday morning meet up didn't go as planned. Bruce wasn't there so I spent most of the morning finishing my notes on patients and clearing out some old files. It wasn't until noon that Bruce decided to show up, strolling in with a huge smile on his face and not a care in the world.

"Nice of you to show up."

"We said noon. It's noon. I don't know why you're so agitated," Bruce fell into the big leather couch in my office and put his feet up on the coffee table.

"Dude, I said eight o'clock and you said noon. Then we decided on nine."

"That's not how I remember it."

"Okay, well you're here now. So let's go through a few of the cases I saw for you. I have a couple questions," I said and pulled out the charts that needed updates.

"These three women don't have numbers listed by their sperm donors. You know that's a huge error. How are we supposed to know if we have the right numbers now? Did you keep notes somewhere? We need to update these."

"There are no numbers for these three," Bruce said and smiled down at the charts. "I am the donor."

Bruce Simon was a perpetual playboy bachelor. Up until that moment I'd always assumed that he was just a sloppy bookkeeper. I'd seen other files of his that needed notes and numbers added, but never went back to check if it was done. We were partners, after all, I wasn't his keeper. It wasn't my job to babysit him. But this was huge. This was not at all what I'd expected to hear and I was pretty damned shocked to say the least.

"Bruce, please tell me you aren't saying what I think you are saying."

"I'm saying that I'm the sperm donor for these three women. I thought I was pretty clear about that," he laughed.

"This is serious. You can't be doing that. There has to be some sort of legal thing saying this is not allowed. What the heck?"

"I have a lawyer. He drew up some papers. It's iron clad."

"But you're their doctor. Come on, man!"

"Mike, I was going to be their doctor no matter what sperm swam up and grabbed a hold of their egg. I don't think that should matter. Plus, it's not like I'm tricking these women. They come in here begging for me to do this. I'm just being of service to them."

"Bruce!"

"Mike!" he yelled back at me.

"No, you can't do this. The medical licensing board would be all over this. Stop doing it! If you want to father people's babies at least send those women to me to be their doctor. Or just stop doing it all together. God, we are going to be sued," I put my head into my hands in utter disbelief.

"It's fine. I will start telling them no. To be honest, I can't believe no one has asked you."

"Perhaps I'm just better at setting boundaries with my clients?"

"Or maybe I'm just the better looking one of the two of us," he started to look at himself in the mirror off to the side of the couch.

Bruce was blonde with blue eyes and an olive complexion, I knew from working in this industry that those assets were very popular among women looking to have a baby. Not to mention his willingness to participate had made him an easy option for women. I had never even considered participating something like that and I'd never been asked either.

"I don't care what the reasons are, Bruce. It's not ethical if you're going to be their doctor. Can we at least agree on that? And I would like to talk to our attorney to mitigate any other potential issues that could arise from this."

"I already talked to Bob, he helped me with the contract that the women sign."

"I'm still going to talk to him and you still need to stop being the doctor for these women. Understood?"

"Yep."

"Now, let's talk about these other files and I'll get you up to speed on what was accomplished."

"Sure thing," Bruce said and continued to look just as relaxed as the moment he came into my office.

Nothing seemed to bother him at all. I used to be like him. I used to be carefree and unconcerned about boring business stuff. Somewhere in the process of building up our successful practice I became worried about the longevity of things. I became semi-responsible.

We spent nearly two hours getting everything back on track and rearranging some patients, so I could see the people he had this intimate relationship with. I gave him some of my patients and he gave me some of his so everything ended up working out.

"By the way, I'm going to need you to cover a couple patients tomorrow morning too. I've got a thing tonight," Bruce added as we wrapped things up and were heading out of the office to the parking lot.

"Dude, I'm getting burnt out here. Why can't you come in on time or just reschedule your patients?"

My blood pressure was boiling at this point. We had already hired an office manager and had several other support staff in our office, all these people were there to help reduce the strain on the two of us. But the way Bruce was operating lately, I was going to have to start looking for a new partner soon.

"I've got a hot date tonight and I hate leaving early in the morning. It's a little rude, don't you think?"

"Wow."

"What?" he asked as if he was totally oblivious to the real world that one of us had to live in. "How's your dating life going?"

"My dating life is going well. I actually left a hot new girl this morning so I could be here. It wasn't rude at all. It was me being responsible."

"Impressive."

"It's your job, Bruce. Get in here by eight and see your patients or reschedule them. I can't keep picking up your slack." I didn't wait for him to respond and climbed into my vehicle and slammed the door.

Done, I was done with this crap. Not only was Bruce putting our whole practice at risk with his shady side deals, he wasn't even covering his end of the work that needed done. Charging clinic rates for women that he fathered children with couldn't be within the ethical boundaries of the practice. But I called our attorney Bob to see what he had to say.

"Bob, it's Mike Cooper. Did you tell Bruce he was cleared to father children with his patients?"

"Good morning to you, too," he scoffed.

"Come on, I trust your legal counsel and Bruce is saying he got your okay. Why wasn't I told about any of this?"

"Here's the deal. If a friend of yours asked you to take care of her during her pregnancy you would do it, right?"

"Yes, I'd probably do it. But that's not crossing an ethical boundary."

"What if a friend of yours asked you to father a child?"

"I don't know if I would do that. I really want to be a father, but it would be hard to know there were children out there that I wasn't involved with raising."

"Okay, so your issue with that is that you wouldn't get to raise the child, not any sort of ethic issue with the woman asking you or with the sperm being provided?" Bob asked as if this was all leading to some final answer that I just wasn't seeing.

"Yes. That's right."

"Read the contract. It's clear that I'm simply stating Bruce, as a friend of these women, is providing them his sperm. There is an agreed upon fee and the contract is over once he's delivered the specimen. It has nothing to do with who they choose as a doctor. Although, I did suggest to Bruce that he not be their doctor and refer them to someone else. I actually suggested someone outside of your practice."

"Thank you. That's what I was saying."

The rest of my Sunday was rather uneventful and I had to try my best not to pick up the phone and call Julia. Her trepidation over me really asking her out was bugging me the more I thought about it. Perhaps she really didn't want me to ask her out and this was her way of pushing her agenda?

Was that possible?

Sure, up until that morning I wouldn't have thought my own partner was lying to me and going behind my back and it turns out he was. So it was possible I'd misread the signs between Julia and I. I'd just sit on her number for a day or so before calling her and see if I felt the same about her after a little time.

Weekends in general weren't for relaxing. Most of my errands had to be done on the weekends and by Sunday night I was usually totally exhausted. This particular Sunday was no different and when I finally crawled into bed around ten o'clock, I couldn't wait to get some sleep.

Chapter 5

Julia

"How was your weekend? I didn't even hear you come home last night," I said when I saw Kendra sitting at our kitchen table Monday morning.

"I didn't come home until this morning."

She had a cheeky grin that I'd seen before from her. Kendra had a way with the guys, she was much better at picking them than I was. I envied her. If I had as much luck as she did, I probably would be more willing to wait to have a baby in hopes of finding the man of my dreams.

It was totally plausible that my own lack of confidence was why I struggled with meeting decent men. I could admit it. When a woman was confident she carried herself differently. When a woman didn't care if men liked her or not, there was something totally different about how she walked and even the aura around her. I wasn't one of those women. Even though I felt like I had a normal amount of confidence and I could fake it for an evening or so, I was always rethinking what was going on in my mind. There was constant self doubt in my head during interactions with men. And my night with Mike was no different.

"So that guy turned out to be decent?" I asked.

"Yes, we had an amazing weekend together. You know when you just click with someone and everything seems perfect? That's what it was like."

"Nice! That's really great, Kendra," I was so happy for her. The last few months both of us had been so jaded about the guys in New York, maybe our luck was changing. Although Kendra had also managed to meet a great guy just last month, who she had promptly dumped after she found out he was only in town for a month of work. "The guy I brought home, Mike. He was spectacular. But I don't think we will see each other again."

"Why not?"

"He's really hot and was extremely nice, but to tell you the truth I just don't think I'm his type at all. He probably dates models and women like that. And well, there's something else..."

"So just to be clear," she said as she interrupted me, "he's not the one saying any of this? You're deciding for him that you aren't the right one for him?"

"Yes," I laughed. "Plus, my appointment is today with the fertility place. I thought it was next week but it's today. I'm moving forward with it. Not exactly the sort of thing a guy is going to want if we were to date. He's not the love of my life and I'm not going to sit around and wait for that person to appear. I've made up my mind."

"Julia, why don't you wait just a little bit? You are still young; you have plenty of time to start having babies. Just wait a year. Or maybe two. Hell, you are still so young. I can't believe you are even considering this."

I totally understood where Kendra and my friends were coming from. I was still young and I knew if I really wanted to wait I could do that. The thing was though, I'd already decided that I was ready to be a mother and I didn't want to wait. It was unconventional, I knew, but I was ready to get pregnant and have a baby. I was going to be one of those cool young moms with a great career and the perfect life. I just couldn't wait.

With all the second guessing I did in my personal life, this was something that I was sure of. I knew deep down that I was ready and to be honest there wasn't much that I still had to think about. It was very unlikely anyone could have talked me out of this plan, not even my best friend.

"I know, I know. But I'm okay with being a single mom. Really, I'm excited about it. I don't need anyone else around. Actually, I'm more excited about being able to do this all on my own than anything else. I'll get to pick the name, I'll get to pick my new apartment and decorate the baby's room. I make a great living and I'm on track to move up the ladder in a couple of years. Now is the perfect time for this."

"Julia, this is a little crazy, you have to admit it."

"No I don't. Women are having babies by themselves all the time. Just because I didn't pick some dude up and accidently get pregnant doesn't make it weird. I'm financially responsible and since we've been roommates for so long I have been able to save up a lot of money. I'm ready."

"Fine, I'm not going to argue any more. I'm sure the process takes time, right? You'll have the ability to change your mind somewhere down the road."

"Yes, although I don't think I'll change my mind at all. This is an expensive process and I wouldn't be moving forward if I hadn't already made up my mind. But today I'm just meeting with Doctor Simon and discussing my options. I have picked out a few possible sperm donors from the registry and I still need to narrow that down before I could move forward."

"Sperm donor, eww! That sounds gross."

"It's not that gross."

I tried to defend it but Kendra was right on this one, it did sound a little gross to be talking about sperm at all. I didn't even want to imagine what it was like for the men to be hiding away in sterile doctors' offices spewing their seed into a cup. But I liked this plan much better than having to be tied to some random dude for the rest of my life.

If I happened to get pregnant from a guy I dated for a night or two, well, that seemed like a recipe for disaster to me. There could be custody battles and child support hearings and all sorts of messiness. Nope, my way was much easier. I just paid for some sperm and hired a doctor to squirt it into me, then BAM! It was baby making time.

"Well do you want me to go with you? I'm not totally on board but I'll go with you if you need support."

"Kendra! That's so nice of you!" I wrapped my arms around her and held on tight. This was the sort of friend she was. She clearly didn't like my plan, but she still offered to be there for me. "You are amazing! But I think I should do this alone. I want to be focused and plus it's good for me to practice my independence."

"Good! I really didn't want to go to that place," she laughed. "But you let me know if you ever need some backup, I promise I will go with you. And I'm sure I'll come around to this whole idea if you end up going through with it. I'll be here for you."

"Thanks again, Kendra. You're a really good friend."

"I know. I know. I'm the best. The baby can call me Auntie Kendra." We both laughed at the idea, but it was likely what would end up happening. Since I didn't have any sisters Kendra was as close as I was going to get to that sort of relationship.

"That's a plan," I said with a hug before finally heading out of our apartment and to my doctor's appointment.

My heart was pounding out of my chest as I maneuvered my way through the city to the clinic office on 56th street. After much rumination I'd settled on Doctor Bruce Simon. His online reviews were stellar and many of his patients had noted going back to him over and over again.

The first appointment was supposed to be more like a blind date, or at least that was what I had gathered from everything I'd read up on this process. I was going to interview him and his practice to see if we were a good fit and he was basically going to be making sure I was a good fit as well, but honestly I couldn't imagine any doctor not working with a woman that was willing to pay them.

My fingers were freezing as I pressed the button for the elevator up to his office. It was a beautiful fall day and the weather was in the mid 70's so I shouldn't have felt as cold as I was feeling. But as I looked at my hands I saw I'd been clenching my fists the entire trip to the office and still had fingernail marks on my hands from the tight grip.

I took in a few deep breaths as the elevator door closed and I did my best to try and calm down. Getting pregnant with the help of artificial insemination wasn't all that hard, but there were a ton of steps to jump through. Doctors had liability issues if they helped a woman who wasn't healthy get pregnant, even if it was something as little as squirting some sperm inside of her. The rules, or what I understood up to this point, were daunting. Especially if you consider I could have decided to lie under some random dude and get pregnant without so much as a check of my pulse before I did that.

As the elevator doors opened I took a few steps and stood in front of the fancy glass doors to Doctor Simon's office. My vision was blurry as I stared at the sign on the door. I couldn't even read the names on there but I saw the large RMA letters and knew I was in the right spot.

I pressed open the door and took another deep breath in an attempt to calm down. It wasn't helping much though, I still felt like I could hear my heart beating in my ears and my breathing was so heavy that I was sure everyone in the waiting room could hear me.

"Good afternoon and welcome to Reproductive Medicine Associates. How can I help you?" the young blonde at the desk said with an annoyingly chipper smile.

"Um, hello. My name is Julia Rivas. I have an appointment with Doctor Simon."

"Miss Rivas, here you are," she said with her fake smile. "I have some paperwork for you to fill out. The doctor is running a little behind, but it shouldn't be too long."

"Thank you." I grabbed her clipboard with my shaky hands and found a spot in the corner of the room.

The waiting room was filled with happy couples and only a few single women. I didn't necessarily feel out of place, but I didn't feel comfortable either. Handling new situations on my own was just one of the things I needed to adjust to if I was going to be a mother though. So I took another deep breath, wiped the sweat from the palm of my hand, grabbed the pen, and started filling out my life story on the clipboard stuffed with papers.

It was nearly a half hour before I'd completed my large packet of paperwork. The questions went on and on as if they were never going to end. When was your first period? How long have you been considering having a child? What steps have you gone through to try for a child? Some of the questions seemed absolutely ridiculous to me while others were clearly more geared toward couples who were having fertility issues. But as I walked back up to the young blonde at the desk, I finally felt my breath calm. This was what I wanted and filling out thirty minutes of paperwork wasn't going to sway me from my dream. In fact, I was even more certain of my plans now that I'd managed to navigate that road block.

It was a road block, I was sure of it. They put this enormous packet of information together to deter young women who just wanted to gather information and weren't really interested in moving forward. Of course, some of them would stay and stick through the paperwork for the appointments. But I suspected more than a few women had dropped that clipboard and made their way out of the office. If the months of waiting for an appointment was enough of a deterrent, the paperwork might have been.

There were a steady stream of names being called to go back to their appointments, but my name wasn't called at all. There were a few women in the waiting room that had been there longer than I had, but soon even they had been called back to a room. I waited patiently. Certainly this was just another road block put up to keep women out of the process who weren't totally dedicated, or at least that was my theory.

Then a woman, who had just come in five minutes earlier, was called to go back to the patient area. I couldn't take it any longer and jumped out of my seat, about to lose my cool before I realized this was not going to help me get accepted into this office. I had to keep my cool. Certainly a woman who could easily fly off the handle about a late appointment wasn't going to be considered a good mother.

"Excuse me, do you know how much longer it will be? I've been waiting for quite some time."

"Oh, yes, I'm sorry. I was just about to have you come up. Doctor Simon is still running late. If you'd be okay with seeing his partner I could squeeze you in, or we could reschedule you for a later date."

I'd already taken the day off from work and waited most of the morning. As much as I really wanted to meet Doctor Simon, since he was the one I'd picked, at this point I just wanted to get through this appointment and onto the next step in the process.

"How much longer will the doctor be?"

"I'm sorry, I don't know. He could be just a few minutes or he might not make it in at all today."

"Oh."

"His partner is very good and I know they share notes when they have to cover for each other. It's possible you'd even end up with his partner delivering your baby since they rotate their on-call nights. It might be a good thing to meet him now."

"Okay," I said with all the fake acceptance I could muster. "I'll see him."

"Great, it should be less than an hour and I'll have you back there."

I clenched my fists tight and pressed my lips even tighter as I made my way back to my little corner of the waiting room. Another hour! This place was ridiculous. My stomach grumbled with hunger as I waited out my time and watched as other women went ahead of me.

By the time my name was finally called I was in a thoroughly bad mood. Even her upbeat banter was lost on me as the nurse took my vitals and went over my pile of paperwork with me. When she finally stepped out of the room I was livid about the whole situation. This doctor's office wasn't behaving like one of the top-rated fertility centers in the city. They certainly didn't appear to be the rising star that so many women were talking about.

Granted I might have been confused by the dozens and dozens of offices I'd looked at. Each of them had blurred together and I couldn't have been sure about everything I'd read, but I was positive the women who had come to see Doctor Simon loved him and to be honest I wasn't even sure who his partner was.

When I heard the doctor outside my room I hurried to

get my agitation in check. Deep breaths, smiling, and I prepared for him to enter the room.

"Where's the chart?" I heard him said to the nurse.

"Just go in, I'll get it to you in a second. I'm finishing something up," the nurse replied.

As the door opened I took a deep breath again but then stopped breathing all together when I saw who was standing in the doorway.

"Julia?" Mike asked with an awkward look on his face.

"Hey, Mike. Wow, you're a fertility doctor? I didn't see this one coming," I laughed nervously.

He was totally silent as he sat down on the rolling stool across from me. I was sitting in a rather uncomfortable metal chair and laughed nervously about the whole situation. How did I not know that this was the sort of doctor he was? It was rather humorous, especially after the morning I'd had already.

"Wow. I have a really busy day today. I thought we sort of handled this whole thing that morning when I left," Mike said curtly as he crossed his arms.

"What?"

"I didn't take you as the sort of girl who would do something like this."

"What are you talking about?"

"I'm flattered, Julia, really. But I have a busy day. I'll call you, okay," he said and stood up to leave the room.

"I have no idea what you're talking about. I didn't come here to stalk you. Is that what you think is happening here? Wow, you are really full of yourself." I felt the blood nearly boiling inside me at the insinuation that I'd purposely ended up in that room waiting for him. I had no idea he worked there. I certainly wouldn't have showed up pretending that I wanted to get pregnant and hoping that would get me another date.

"So, you just happened to make an appointment with me but didn't know it was me? Come on now," Mike said as he stood in the doorway.

The nurse appeared behind him. "Here you go, doctor. Sorry it took so long to get her chart. She was another one of Doctor Simon's patients that needed to be seen today," she said and handed Mike what I assumed was my medical chart.

He held onto it and looked back at me with only the slightest bit of remorse. In fact, I wasn't even sure it was remorse at all. As he stood there about to open the chart that held all the secrets to my medical, sexual, and fertility history, I slapped the chart out of his hand.

"I don't know who you think you are but I've been waiting for months to see Doctor Simon. I waiting for hours in the waiting room and just finally agreed to be seen by his partner. I had no idea it was you and the fact that you'd even think I was someone like that means you obviously didn't get to know me at all the other night. What sort of crazy narcissist thinks a woman who wants to have a baby would stalk her one night stand and show up at his office? That's utterly insane."

"Wait a second. You don't need to be so upset, Julia. I was just confused."

"Right. And the first conclusion you jumped to was that I was a crazy stalker? Great. Perfect. Could this day get any better?" I stood up and gathered my purse. There was no way I was staying. No way I was going to continue to talk about the biggest life decision I have ever made with a man who was so stuck on himself he thought I'd come there for him. Nope, I'd just wait for Doctor Simon and set up a new appointment with him.

"I'm sorry, Julia. Please sit back down. I will see when Bruce is going to get in and you can see him."

"Sir, Doctor Simon hasn't been answering his phone at all," the nurse said quietly. "I've been trying him all morning."

"It doesn't matter," I yelled and pressed past Mike. "Schedule me with him and call me with the time."

"Julia," Mike called after me.

"You know what?" I turned back to him in a furry of anger. "I actually thought you were a good guy. I had heard Rob talk about you for years. I had a crush on you since the moment you went off to college. But I definitely didn't think you'd turn out to be such a jerk."

Then I realized that I'd just given away my own little secret. I just connected Mike to my brother Rob. His face was pale with acknowledgment as everything started to click for him. I could tell by his expression that he still hadn't realized who I was until that very moment.

I turned to leave. This was done. Whatever had been between us was done. Clearly I wasn't going to run off and live happily ever after with Mike. I'd known it when he left that morning after our night together, but I knew it even more as I stood there in front of him watching his face contort at the realization he'd slept with one of his friend's sisters.

I was halfway down the hall before Mike even made an effort to respond. "Julia Rivas," he yelled after me. "Rob's little sister. I..."

I didn't wait to hear what else he had to say. I pressed through the waiting room door and stormed out the glass front doors to the office.

Nervously I waited at the elevator, hoping desperately that Mike didn't come running out there after me. I was mortified by the whole thing. Not only by the fact that he never realized who I was, but by the fact that now he knew I was trying to have a baby and that he actually thought I'd stalked him and snuck into his office like that. Mike definitely wasn't thinking as highly of me as I had been thinking of him.

Even after realizing that I hadn't stalked him, the whole thing was just horribly embarrassing. I was sure I wouldn't be coming back to see Doctor Simon either and now was going to have to find a new doctor and wait months and months to get into them.

As the elevator doors closed tears poured down my face. Nothing was turning out the way it was supposed to. My entire life had gone from feeling perfect to feeling like I would never be happy again. How quickly life could turn around.

Chapter 6

Mike

"What was that all about?" Sheryl asked.

She bent over and picked up the chart that Julia had thrown onto the ground. I just stood there in utter disbelief over all the information that was jetting through my mind. I still wasn't really sure I understood what was going on.

"I thought she was a crazy stalker like that one girl, remember that red head who showed up after I didn't call her?"

"Oh, yeah. That was crazy! So this girl was a stalker? That doesn't make sense though, she was scheduled with Doctor Simon and not you."

"I know that now Sheryl!" I snapped. "It would have been much more useful information to have before I opened the door to the room."

"Sorry. How was I supposed to know she was one of your girlfriends?"

"Don't act like I have this long line of women I date. Come on, I'm not like that," I tried to defend myself.

"Maybe not DMV size long, but it's definitely Starbuck

size," she laughed and I couldn't help but smile. "So you did know her? She was pretty upset. Let me guess, you didn't call her back either?"

Not calling women back wasn't something I did. Even if I wasn't going to see them again I'd usually call and make some sort of excuse. I'd tell them how busy work was, or make some other excuse for why it just wasn't a good time right now. At least since the stalking incident I'd made more of an effort to let girls down over the phone so they wouldn't show up at my work. But none of that had anything to do with Julia.

"Apparently it was just a wild coincidence," I said. "She was really scheduled with Bruce?"

"Yeah, looks like she had her appointment booked several months ago."

"But she had to have known it was me who worked here. She knew me. I was friends with her brother."

"So, you think she stalked you and set up an appointment three months ago with Bruce, knowing he was a basket case who wouldn't show up for work today and that way she could wait in the waiting room for three hours and then get scheduled with you?"

Sheryl was smiling at me. No, of course I didn't think she had done all that. And if I had had a moment or two to think about things before going into the room I would have noticed Julia's last name and I was sure I would have realized who she was. It was just a comedy of errors.

"She is also my high school friend's little sister. I met her at a club over the weekend and went home with her," I ran my hand through my hair as I contemplated the fact that I hadn't realized it was her. "I thought she looked familiar but I just couldn't place where I knew her from."

"Oh, shit. You are a jerk," Sheryl laughed.

"Thanks for the vote of confidence."

"No, really. I mean, I thought you were sort of a jerk for the way you acted when you saw her in the room. But wow, you really slept with your friend's sister and didn't even realize it was her? That's pretty epic."

"Yeah."

"And this poor woman was planning on having Doctor Simon help her with artificial insemination. So now she is probably utter embarrassed that the man she slept with, who didn't know who she was when he should have, also now knows about her fertility. Wow, if I could find her and give her a hug I would. And yep, you're a jerk."

"Shit, yeah. So, she was really coming in here to start the process?"

"Yeah, she was doing her initial consultation."

"She's like twenty-five and beautiful, funny too. Why on earth would she want a baby with some sperm donor?"

"I don't know. Maybe because she's tired of meeting jerky guys who don't call her back and have no idea they actually know her?"

"Ouch."

"You deserved that and you know it. Now we have a shit ton of work to do, so as much as I'd love to continue on with this conversation about your shortcomings, we really need to get through this day."

"I'm going to kill Bruce next time I see him," I said as Sheryl handed me the next patients chart. "He better be dead already or there's no reason for this shit. I just talked to him about showing up and being more accountable."

"Maybe he's really dead?" Sheryl shrugged as we went back to work.

We both knew Bruce wasn't dead. He was just shacked up with some woman and had his phone off. He liked to pretend like he was totally dedicated and turn his phone off so the girl would feel comfortable with him. In reality, he had his phone off so all the women texting and calling him wouldn't disturb his date with the new woman. And of course, so his business partner, me, wouldn't be able to reach him when he abandoned me with all his patients for the day.

The rest of the day was a blur. Patient after patient came into the rooms. I focused on them as much as possible and took copious notes to ensure I could look back over them later when my mind was clear.

It was impossible to get Julia off of my mind though. I'd planned on calling her and setting up a date. I was going to make things happen between the two of us despite the way she'd pushed me away when I left that morning. Her distance was starting to make more sense too. If she knew who I was the whole time and I hadn't realized who she was, well that probably didn't sit well with her by the morning. Plus, she was planning on having a baby! That's a pretty big deal.

As the last patient left the building, I collapsed onto the couch in my office. The stack of patient charts was piled at least a foot thick on my desk and just then my phone rang with a call from Bruce.

"It's him, isn't it?" Sheryl laughed.

"He just called the main desk," Miranda added as we all hung out in my office.

"Oh, I'm going to kill him," I said just before answering the call.

"Don't kill me," Bruce said as if he knew exactly what I was thinking. "I'm sorry. I ended up breaking up with a girl and it went badly. The police were involved and I had a horrible day. I'm going to be there tomorrow. I promise this sort of thing isn't going to happen again. Our conversation the other day is still true. I'm going to make an effort."

"Bruce, I don't even know. To be honest, I don't believe a thing you're saying right now."

"I understand."

"You're not even going to argue with me?" I asked a little concerned that my friend who normally argued about everything wasn't even making the effort.

"No, I really did have a horrible day. The woman tried to jump off my balcony after I broke it off. It was awful. I barely pulled her back and had to call the police. They took her to the psychiatric hospital."

"Shit, I'm sorry, man," I said as I realized this story was likely true and not something he was making up.

"Yeah, I'll be there tomorrow and tell you about it. I need to crash. Emotionally exhausted," he said before hanging up.

"So what sort of crazy excuse did he have this time," Sheryl laughed.

"I'm not sure it was actually an excuse. He didn't seem like himself at all."

"Well, I'll be the judge of that tomorrow. You have a good time with all those notes tonight," she said with a sympathetic smile.

"That's what he gets paid the big bucks for," Miranda added as the two women waved good-bye and headed out for the night.

"Don't worry about me. I'll still be here in the morning when you come back," I hollered after them.

"We aren't worried," Sheryl laughed.

I heard her lock the front door after it shut. I often had to stay for an hour or two after patients left. It was a normal part of keeping up with my paperwork. But since I'd seen so many patients that day I hadn't had time to put any notes into the computer or the patient's charts officially. Instead, I had taken notes on paper during their sessions. Now I had to go through each chart and nicely write my notes for the day and then make a pile of patients that I'd have to talk with Bruce about.

Our notes in the medical charts were a legal part of the patient's case. If it was a patient of Bruce's I liked to make sure I was reviewing the case thoroughly before adding to the chart. The last thing I needed was to say I gave a patient one medication when I really gave something else. Or to miss something important about their case.

Luckily this day was filled with consultations and routine checkups. We liked to keep certain days of the week for certain types of appointments as much as possible. If it had been a Friday, I would have been much more upset with Bruce since Fridays are our complicated cases that really require the assigned doctor to review them.

I moved to my desk and groaned at the amount of work I had to do that evening. It was entirely possible that I'd be there well into the night. But before I got too far into my paperwork, I dialed Julia to see if I could apologize to her.

"This is Julia, leave a message after the beep," her sweet voice said right away after the first ring.

"Hey, Julia. I'm really sorry about what happened today. And about not realizing it was you. I did feel like we had a connection and I honestly felt like I knew you from somewhere but I just couldn't place you. In my defense, you're much prettier now than I remember you before. Crap, sorry. I didn't mean that to sound bad. Sorry, just give me a call back. I'd like to apologize."

I hung up and then let my head fall into my hands with exasperation. That was by far the worse apology voicemail in the history of men. Why hadn't I thought things through a little more before calling her?

In every other aspect of my life I was fine with taking notes and precautions to ensure I said or did the right thing. With my patient charts I was meticulous. But yet I dialed her up without even thinking through what I wanted to say, without writing down any notes. And I basically said she was ugly back when I was in high school. She had to hate me!

Reluctantly, I pushed my phone away and got started on my paperwork. It was highly unlikely that Julia was going to call me back anytime soon. In fact, I wasn't sure she'd ever actually call me back.

***

Three days later and I still hadn't heard back from Julia. It was driving me nuts. She had to know that I wasn't intentionally a total jerk. Even if she didn't want to see me again, even if she didn't want to use my office for her pregnancy, I still couldn't live with the idea that she thought

I was a monstrous jerk of a man. Finally I decided to call Rob and check in with him, maybe feel him out to see if Julia had told him about what happened.

"Hey, what's up?" Rob answered.

"Not much, just checking in. Want to grab a drink soon?" I said.

"When have I ever not wanted to get a drink?"

"Very true. How about tonight?"

"You know me so well."

It was true, I did know Rob well. If we tried to schedule something a little further out he would cancel on me. My best bet was always the same day invitation. I was the same way. Most of the time I didn't make plans for my weekend and just grabbed whoever was available to head out, or I'd have a woman I could call for a date.

"So meet you at nine down at Henry's?" I asked.

"Shit, no I can't do it tonight. I forgot I was doing this thing with Marissa."

"Oh, Marissa?"

"Yeah, just this stock broker I'm dating. Nothing serious."

"Yeah, we can catch up another time," I said as nonchalantly as I could manage. "Maybe you could invite your sister too. Isn't she in New York now?"

"Julia's been here for a few years Mike, I told you about

her job at the Hotel. Remember, she's a sales consultant for big wigs at King Hotels?"

The second he mentioned what Julia did, I remembered the conversation we had over a year before. It was a brief talk in the middle of a noisy bar just before we went and picked up some girls. It was one of the only times we had hung out in the last year and to be honest, talking about his sister wasn't really hitting my radar that night.

"Oh, yeah. Sorry, I forgot. King Hotels, that's pretty cool. What else is up with her lately?"

"Man, I don't know. I can't keep up with her life. You know how she is."

Actually, I didn't really know how she was at all. I'd been trying to reach her for days without any luck. But I wasn't about to unload that juicy piece of information on Rob. I wasn't sure he would think me sleeping with his sister was a great idea.

"Oh, I know how it is. Okay, well, call me sometime and we can grab drinks. It was nice catching up with you."

"You too," Rob said and we both hung up.

One of the best things about having a friend like Rob was that we had been friends for so long that a quick conversation was enough for the both of us. There was no need to fill each other in on why we had been too busy to call earlier. No need to pretend or keep secrets from each other, except for the part about me doing his sister. I was going to continue to keep that secret.

With only a small amount of effort I called around and was put through to a Mr. Schneider who was the head of the sales team at King Hotels. A few white lies and five minutes later I had the address of the hotel where Julia worked.

I grabbed my coat and hailed a cab with only an intention of scoping out the building and seeing what was in that neighborhood. Nothing more than that. I would just get the lay of the land so perhaps sometime down the road I could do lunch in that neighborhood and run into Julia.

It was freezing out. Not at all normal for a September afternoon. I had my coat buttoned up as high as it would go and still had to tuck myself into the collar in an effort to stay warm as I climbed out of the cab in front of the hotel.

As I stood in the freezing wind in front of the large glass building, I decided to head inside. The lobby of the hotel was modern and decorated with glass sculptures and odd pieces of art. There were several leather seats organized in a square off in the corner of the lobby, so I grabbed a seat and pretended to look at my phone for a minute.

Casually I looked around every few moments and tried to get the lay of the land. Unfortunately, even after thirty minutes I hadn't been able to ascertain whether or not the marketing and sales team offices were on the main floor or somewhere else in the building.

Then I saw Julia. My pulse quickened as I looked down at my phone and tried to peak at the offices where she had just walked out of. My technique of looking at my phone and then looking up was working fine until I made eye contact with Julia as she walked toward me.

The jig was up. She clearly had seen me looking at her. Now all I had to do was decide what sort of story I was going to tell her about why I was there. Maybe I had a meeting there? No, I didn't even know what offices were in that neighborhood. There was no way I could pull that story off. Perhaps I could just say I was supposed to meet a friend there in the lobby.

"Mike, what are you doing here?" Julia asked as she took a seat across from me.

There was an open seat right next to me, so it was a telling sign that she had chosen the seat as far away from me as possible. She leaned forward with her elbows resting on her knees and a stern expression of disapproval on her face.

"I'm stalking you," I said with a shrug of my shoulders and a smile. Hoping that a little humor might lighten the mood.

"I know you're trying to be funny, but really, what are you doing here?"

"I'm here to tell you I'm sorry. I've said it a few horrible ways on your cell phone, but I needed to make sure you really heard me. I didn't mean to act like that."

"Okay, thank you," Julia said and got up to walk away.

"That's it?" I ran after her. "You're just going to forgive

me and then walk away?"

"What else do you want Mike? Do you want to embarrass me here at work like you did at your office? No, thank you. I accept your apology, so now you can go about your life and not worry about my hurt feelings any longer."

She turned to walk away and I instinctively reached out for her hand and grabbed it. Electricity flooded my body at the touch of her soft skin. A visceral reaction pulsed into me and I was throbbing with excitement within seconds.

"Can I take you to dinner? You have to be getting done soon. We could go someplace close and I promise to be a gentleman."

"Now you want to take me to dinner? That's not necessary."

Her eyes locked onto mine and she softly shook her head back and forth as I kept my gaze locked on her beautiful brown eyes. I wasn't ready to let go of her. With her hand in mine I knew I wanted to spend more time with Julia and if the only way she would agree was for us to do it right then and there, I was game.

"Mike, I'm not sure if you understand why I was in your office. But that doesn't exactly make this a possibility," she motioned down to my hand which was still wrapped around hers. "Let's just call it good. You apologized, I accepted. We can both move on."

"So you're saying no to a free meal?"

"I'm saying no."

"Julia, is everything okay?" A man asked as he stopped next to us. He eyed my hand on Julia's and I quickly let go of her.

"Everything is okay, Teddy," she reassured him.

"Hi, I'm Teddy Schneider, the supervisor here. Is there something I can help you with?" He asked me as if I was going to book a dozen hotel rooms or something like that.

"No, I think Julia has it covered. She just offered to come to dinner with me so we could discuss me booking a conference here later next year."

"Fabulous idea, yes. Please go and discuss it. Julie is my top sales woman. She will help you with anything you need."

As Teddy Schneider walked away I tried to pull another playful smile out to see if it would help reduce the tension, but Julia's stern face never cracked at all. She stormed back toward the hallway of offices and I followed her to the one that had her name on it.

I was about to put up a new argument when I realized she was grabbing her coat and purse. My smile took over my face as she pushed past me and walked quickly toward the front of the lobby. Her three-inch heels clicking away on the tile floor of the large room while I took large strides to catch up to her.

"Thank you, Julia," I whispered while holding the front door open for her.

"You're going to have to book a convention with me now."

"Ok," I replied without a moment of hesitation.

I happened to be on a convention committed for fertility doctors. I certainly could throw King Hotels name around at the next meeting and try to book with them. I had a new bounce in my step as I followed Julia across the street to where we were going to eat. I was happy that Julia had agreed to come on the impromptu date.

"We are going to eat a meal here and that's it," Julia said pointing at the Italian restaurant we were standing in front of.

"Perfect."

"Nothing else, Mike."

"Okay, that's perfect."

I held the door open for her and she gently brushed up against me as we made our way into the tiny local Italian restaurant. Giovanni's was nicer on the inside than it looked from the street. I never would have considered taking a woman there on a date if I'd only looked at the rusted sign outside the building. Once inside, the floors were a brilliant stained wood and the sitting area roomier than many high end eateries in New York. Each table was dressed with a white tablecloth and artificial candles. It was actually really romantic and I could see Julia hesitating as we stood near the main dining area and waited to be seated.

"I've never been here before. I thought it was going to be different," she snuffed just before a server made his way to us.

"Hello and welcome to Giovanni's. Do you have a reservation?"

"No, I'm sorry, we don't," Julia said. "We can come back…"

"I'm sorry, it's my fault. This is sort of a last-minute date," I interrupted before Julia could tell the man we were leaving. "Is there any possible way we could get a table? I'd be very grateful," I said and handed the man a hundred-dollar bill as I shook his hand. I figured it was worth a try to get a table. Sure enough the man started looking at his seating chart and whipped a name off the list and made room for us.

"Your name?" He asked looking at me.

"Doctor Cooper," I said pulling out the doctor card to push even further.

"Thank you. Yes, it looks like I do have a cancelation tonight and can squeeze you in. Please, come this way," the man said as we followed him to a back corner of the restaurant. "I'll be your waiter; my name is Jessie. I'll give you a minute and then come back with some menus."

"Thank you," I said and held Julia's chair out for her. "This is a nice romantic spot," I said as she sat down.

"You know I didn't want a romantic spot. I thought this

place was a dump."

"We can make the best of it," I said and sat down across from her. "Now, will you let me apologize?"

"Go for it."

"First, about how I acted at the office. I'm so sorry. That was disrespectful and rude of me. My only defense is that my co-worker, Doctor Simon, abandoned me and I was doing double duty. One time in the past a woman I'd dated snuck into the office and when I saw you I jumped to conclusions. I'm very sorry and I sincerely want to apologize."

Julia looked away from me and tears welled up in her eyes. She went from being hard and distant to sweet and vulnerable in a blink of an eye. I reached out and grabbed her hand in an effort to comfort her.

"It's okay," she managed to say through tears.

"I had a great time with you the other night. I honestly thought we connected and was looking forward to taking you on a real date."

"I'm not really looking to date," she said as she continued to look away and only glanced back at me for a moment. "Obviously, from me being at your office, you know I'm looking to start a different phase of my life."

"Yes, I concluded that after I realized what was really going on."

"Mike, I'm sorry I didn't say something about knowing

you," she said and turned her tear filled eyes toward me. "I thought it was fun when we were at the club. It was exciting that you saw me as this beautiful woman instead of a little girl. I should have said something."

"No, that's fine. I really did feel like we had met before or I knew you. It's my jerky self who is to blame for that too. I should have asked you more questions and gotten to know you more. I'm sure it would have come out. But the truth is I was just enamored by you and well, attraction seemed to be in the lead of my brain that night."

I squeezed her hand and she smiled back. It was the first smile I'd gotten and I finally thought we would be okay. I handed her a napkin to wipe her eyes with as our waiter approached the table and handed us our menus.

"Can I get you guys something to drink?" he asked.

"I could really use a drink," Julia said before I could get a word in. "Bring us a bottle of red wine. Something good."

"Yes, what the lady said," I echoed.

"Our special is pasta primavera tonight. I'll get your wine and be back shortly," the young man said eagerly. "Our best red wine is three hundred dollars," he whispered in my ear. "Is that what you want?"

"Yes, that sounds perfect," I replied.

"Three hundred dollars, wow," Julia laughed a little. "You really do want me to forgive you."

"If buying wine is all I have to do, I'm all over that," I

held onto her hand still and didn't want to let go. The soft touch of her skin was calming to me and I really could have sat there all night long holding onto her. If she didn't want to pull away from me then I wasn't about to give up the chance to hold onto her.

"So I guess I should tell you why I was at the office," Julia said dramatically and pulled her hand away from me. "I am ready to have a baby, but I'm still in the beginning stages of the process and was basically wanting to interview Doctor Simon to see if he would be a good doctor to work with."

"Can I ask you why?"

"Because I've heard women are really happy working with him and often come back to him over and over again for their babies."

"No, why do you want to have a baby this way? I don't mean any disrespect at all. Of course I know that women choose to have children this way all the time. But you're a beautiful, smart, funny, young woman; it seems like you wouldn't have any trouble finding a man who wanted to have a baby with you." I smiled at the thought.

Truthfully I couldn't think of a man who would turn Julia down if she asked them to father a child with her. She was a beautiful woman who clearly had her head on straight and a thriving life. She was the cream of the crop in New York and having a baby through artificial insemination didn't seem to suit her at all.

"Don't you think women who choose artificial

insemination have it easier though?" She asked. "They don't have some weird guy they have to deal with. No legal issues. No relationship issues. It's easier this way."

"Some of that is true, but sometimes..." I started to say and then stopped myself from going any further. "Let's change the subject, should we," I said nervously. "This seems a little heavy of a topic for our first date."

"Oh, so you're still going with the dating story here?" She laughed out loud.

"Um, yeah, we are at a romantic restaurant and I just ordered wine. This is definitely a date."

"I thought this was supposed to just be an apology," she laughed.

"Yes, it's an apology and a first date. We don't need to put so many labels on things though do we?"

"Hey, how did you find out where I worked anyways? I never told you that did I?"

Julia looked fantastic as her face softened and she leaned forward on the table. Her big brown eyes glistened from the tears that were still in them, but her smile lit up her face and I could tell things were better between the two of us.

"I called your brother," I shrugged.

"Oh no! You didn't tell him I was at your office did you?" she exclaimed.

"Of course not. There's doctor patient privilege there," I

said. "I just called to catch up with him and then snuck in some questions about you and how you were doing here in New York."

"I've been here a few years. You really hadn't talked about me before?"

"Not really," I said making a face and shrugging. "We are sort of self centered and we usually talk about me or Rob and what we are doing. I don't think we ever talk about other people much."

"Yeah, that sounds like you two," Julia laughed. "I haven't told any of my brothers my plans yet. I just don't think they will understand why I'm doing it."

"Why you're having a baby on your own?" I asked.

"Yeah, I know it's unconventional. But I've made up my mind and I'm moving forward with it. I just need to pick a baby daddy," she laughed.

"And you're using a sperm bank?"

"Yes, why? You have a weird expression on your face. Is there something I should know?"

"No, no, I mean they clear their donors of diseases and some even do gene testing and I know they are very safe. It's just..." I was going to keep talking but saw the concern on Julia's face. "Don't worry about it. I'm sure you'll find a donor that is exactly what you're looking for."

The waiter interrupted us and poured our wine before taking our food orders and disappearing again. I'm sure he could sense the intensity of our conversation and he quickly made himself scarce.

Julia and I were both leaning forward toward one another with our hands on the white linen table cloth. There was only a few inches separating the two of us, but it felt like a huge divide that I wasn't sure Julia wanted me to cross for her.

"Mike, if anything, I really consider you a friend. This is your area of expertise and I would like your opinion. Is there a certain sperm bank I shouldn't use? Or something more specific I should be asking them? Don't let me make a huge mistake with this if there's something you know that would help me."

"Okay, I've been doing this a few years now and I have to say that many times mothers start worrying about not being able to have a real father they can introduce to their children. Even if that is just through pictures and stories, like a letter he writes to the child or some other information about who the father is. Many times women who find a friend to father their child seem to be much happier with the process in the long run."

"So they don't like not knowing who the man is?"

"Not all of them. I'm certain many of the women I've worked with were very happy with the anonymous donor process. You're right. They don't have legal issues or anyone else involved in the process. There are definite benefits to that process."

She looked confused as she sipped her wine, the sweet red nectar softly touching her lips before sliding into her mouth. I got hard just watching how her lips took the glass in and let the wine enter her. For a moment I imagined those delicious lips wrapped around my body and I had to look away. God she was amazingly beautiful.

"So people ask their friends to do it? How does that work? I have a few gay guy friends that I've thought about asking."

"Yeah, something like that. People work out all sorts of arrangements that work for them. I even know a man who donates to women and then doesn't have any involvement. But the women know who he is, they know they can get medical information if it is ever needed, he even puts a clause in the contract that he will meet the child when they are older if that is something the woman and child want. I don't know, I think there isn't a right or wrong way. But definitely something you should think about before making your decision."

"Thanks Mike, I appreciate your help. It's weird, but I appreciate it."

"Of course, you can feel free to ask me anything about this stuff. I might not know the right answers but I'd be happy to help."

As our dinner arrived we sat quietly eating and drinking our wine. Where the heck were we supposed to take the conversation after we'd talked about sperm donors? Not exactly a normal first date at all.

"How do you like working in this field?" Julia finally asked.

"I love it. My patients are going through an exciting and scary time of their life. It's an honor to be there to help them through it."

"Seems like a good field to be in. Everyone is always happy and having babies."

"Not everyone, unfortunately. Many couples come in and are trying desperately to have a baby and nothing we do seems to work. It can be heartbreaking at times."

"Oh yeah," she said softly.

"So how do you like your job? You look like a boss lady there at the hotel. Are you doing well there? Do you love it? How do you like that boss of yours? He seems like quite the guy."

"So many questions for a first date, geesh. Slow down, dude," she laughed.

Our dinner continued for over two hours with a combination of awkward first date questions and intermittent fertility questions. As much as I saw Julia as a sexually attractive woman and I wanted to take her to bed, I did feel her pushing me away into a friend zone the longer we talked. By the time dinner was over I'd been shoved right into the depths of friend zone.

"Thank you for dinner and the talk, Mike. You're going to

be a great resource as I go through this. You're a good friend," Julia ended with a kiss on the cheek as I walked her to a cab out front.

"Anytime. I'm more than happy to help and I promise next time you're in the office to see Doctor Simon, you'll love him. He's got better bedside manner than I do," I laughed.

"Thanks again, I'll talk to you soon. I'm sure I'll have tons of questions throughout this process. Good night," she said and waved to me as her cab drove away.

Chapter 7

Julia

"How was your date with Mister Hottie McHotster?" Teddy asked the next morning when I showed up to work.

"Date?"

"Don't play coy with me. That's the guy from the club the other night. I'd remember those dreamy eyes anywhere. So you've got him chasing you. Girl, you are the boss!"

"Teddy, it's not like that. He's an old friend. It's a long story but we are just friends."

"No, I'm not buying that at all. Any man who looks at you like that isn't thinking about a friendship with you. What did you do, Julia? Did you friend zone that hot man? Tell me it isn't true?"

"You know this isn't appropriate work talk. What happened to you working on your boundaries of supervision?" I laughed as I handed him the Starbucks coffee I'd grabbed him on my way into work.

"I can do better. How about you get your sales up or I'm firing your ass," he joked.

"That's better."

"Seriously, Julia. What's up? Give me the deets. You know I live vicariously through your heterosexual love life. My life is so full of head cases lately I can't find a decent guy to save my life."

"You and me both," I giggled and sipped my coffee. "But seriously, Mike is a friend of my brother's and things just got super weird. It turns out he's a fertility doctor and when my doctor didn't show up for the appointment, Mike stepped in. Wow, what a mess that was and so embarrassing."

"Serious? That's cool though. It would be nice to have someone you know helping in that process, right?"

Teddy didn't understand much about women and love, but I certainly wasn't about to have the man I slept with become my fertility doctor. No way, no how. That wasn't about to happen. Not to mention all the drama that would surely surround this process if I was constantly trying not to flirt with my doctor. Nope, I was going back to Doctor Simon as soon as I could and I'd deal with him for the rest of the process.

One thing that Mike said had me thinking a lot though. Maybe I should consider a sperm donation from someone I actually knew? I could see his point about how I might want actual medical information in the future and my child would certainly be curious about who their father was and what he looked like. It would be nice to show them a picture and maybe even tell them about their father.

"I'm going back to my original doctor as soon as he gets

in, but there was something else that I was thinking about," I paused to try and find the right words. "How would you feel about being my sperm donor, Teddy?"

"No."

"What? Wow, that was really fast."

"I thought about it actually. When another friend of mine asked me. The thing is, I do want to be a father some day and I think I'd want to be really involved in my child's life. I don't think I could handle having a baby and not being involved. I'm sorry."

"Please, Teddy, don't be sorry. I totally understand. I just thought it was worth asking."

"I could ask around to some of my friends and see if any of the guys might be interested for you, if you'd like?"

"Yeah, maybe that would work. I'd be open to talking to them if someone was interested. It does seem like a pretty big deal and I wouldn't want to force it on anyone. I might still go with the plan for an anonymous donor, but I'm going to look a little closer at the possibility of using someone I know."

"What about Ed from accounting? He's had the hots for you since you started. I'm sure he'd volunteer his soldiers for the cause," Teddy laughed. "But I bet he'd want to give them to you the old fashion way."

"Eww no, Teddy! I'm not looking for someone who wants to have sex. That's exactly the reason I asked you," I laughed.

"Yeah, yeah, I know you just wanted your child to have my sense of style," he did a spin to show off his outrageous suit of the day.

"My son or daughter would be lucky to have your style. I mean, they'd probably get beaten up a lot in school, but…"

"Ha, ha, ha. Very funny. Why don't you ask the hottie who was here to take you on the date? Maybe he'd do it?"

I froze at the suggestion. Would he consider doing such a thing? We had moved past the first night and one night stand thing. I really did think we could be friends now, but would he be interested in donating his DNA to my cause? I didn't think he would. Mike seemed like the sort of guy who wouldn't consider being a sperm donor, but then again he was the one who had suggested I ask someone I know.

"I don't think he'd be into it. Plus, I still think he's really hot. Probably wouldn't be the best plan."

"That's exactly why you should ask him. Your kids would be so friggin adorable! Plus, he's obviously smart and you know him so that would help down the road if you wanted to get back in touch."

"No, I mean, I don't even know how I'd ask him. I probably should have asked while we were at Giovanni's yesterday, but now it would just be weird."

I couldn't help thinking that Mike would be a good option though. He was drop dead gorgeous, he obviously knew how the process worked, and he did seem a little into himself, so he wouldn't want to be involved in the child's life. My heart pounded at the thought of Mike being the father to my child. I liked the idea. I liked that fact that I know him and I thought he was a relatively good guy. He just might be exactly what I was looking for.

But thinking about asking Mike made me so nervous. Out interactions had already been way out of the realm of what I was use to having with someone. We'd had a one night stand, a horrible office visit, and then a romantic dinner. The polar opposite emotions during all of those encounters made me nervous to even consider another such encounter with Mike.

"I'd just call him up and ask him. If this is his business he's probably considered if he'd ever offer to do it. Just ask. It can't hurt," Teddy said as if I'd be asking Mike for a piece of chocolate and not his DNA to give life to a baby.

"I don't know..."

"Or ask him on a date. Maybe not something as romantic as Giovanni's if you're not trying to have a relationship though," he rolled his eyes at my choice of restaurants.

"Okay, yeah, maybe bowling or something that friends would do?"

"Sure."

"Um, yeah, I think that might work. I'll think about it and call him later this week," I lied. There was no way I was getting the courage up to call Mike and ask him. I already knew I wasn't going to be able to do it.

"What's his name again?" Teddy asked as he grabbed my phone off my desk.

"It's Mike Cooper, why? I don't have any pictures of him on there. You can look at his Facebook page..."

"Okay, you're calling him," Teddy said as he thrust the phone back into my face.

I could see the call being dialed and then connecting. I froze out of utter and total fear. I couldn't just talk to him like that. I needed to prepare what I was going to say. There had to be some time between when I wrote down my notes and when I actually called, if I actually called. No, I couldn't do this.

"Hello?" I heard him say as Teddy held the phone near my face. "Hello, Julia? Are you there?"

"Um, hi," I managed to bumble.

"How are you? It's nice to hear from you," he replied and then waited in awkward silence as I didn't answer him.

All the blood had drained out of my head and I felt like I would pass out at any moment. Why the heck was I so damned nervous just to talk to him? I hadn't felt this way before? I'd already slept with the man! He'd been inside me! Yet I could barely manage to think as I considered asking him to father my baby.

"We should go bowling," I blurted out in a much louder

voice than I had intended.

"What's up with your phone?" Mike laughed. "I couldn't hear you before and now it sounds like you're yelling."

"Um, I don't know. Probably just because I'm inside. Well, I get if you're busy and stuff. I don't want to intrude, I was..."

"I'd love to go bowling with you, Julia," he said softly. "How about Friday night?

"Yep, come pick me up at seven," I said and then hung up the phone.

"Julia, that was rude." Teddy laughed and put the phone back on my desk.

"He probably thinks I'm some sort of maniac! Oh, my God, I can't breathe. I'm really going to do this. I'm really going to ask him to be the father. Am I doing it? Oh I don't know."

"Yes, you are. He seems like a good guy and if you're going to have a baby it should be with a good guy. But, maybe you could just have the baby the old fashion way with him? You like him, right?"

"No, no, I don't want that. We just got together for fun. It's not serious and I'm certainly not going to offer a relationship and ask for a baby, that's crazy. We are friends, I'll sell it like that. We are friends and I just want his sperm and I don't want his money or anything like that. Just his sperm so I can have a cute baby."

Teddy shook his head in agreement and we both sat back down sipping our coffee in silence. If Mike would agree to be my sperm donor that was going to be the best possible outcome. The more I thought about this plan the more I liked it.

The problem was going to be getting up my nerve to ask him. But once I got the nerve to ask him everything would work out, I just knew it.

"So how are you going to deal with your sexual attraction to him and his to you?" Teddy asked as I'd finally calmed down.

"What? No, there's no sexual attraction. We are friends now, it's decided."

"Yeah, I don't buy that for a second. But you keep telling yourself that lie," he snickered at me.

***

Friday night seemed to take forever to arrive. I was a ruminating mess throughout the week contemplating how I was going to ask Mike. The idea that I would actually be able to say what I wanted to say without it sounding crazy was all I could think of. Surely I wouldn't be able to find the right words and I'd mess the whole thing up, I was sure of it.

When Mike buzzed from the lobby of the apartment complex I looked at Kendra as if I was a deer caught in headlights.

"Answer it," she said and pushed me toward the intercom.

"Hello."

"Hey, it's Mike. Buzz me up and I'll come to your door and get you."

Did I want him to come to my door? That was more like an official date sort of thing and I wanted this to just be friends. I should just go down and see him in the lobby.

Buzz.

Kendra pressed the button to let Mike into the building. "What are you doing?" I yelled in a panic.

"Letting him up. Stop being so weird about this."

"I'm not being weird. This is just me," I shrugged.

"Yeah, well stop over thinking everything and just go have fun. If the topic comes up then ask him. If there's a love connection then maybe you should go for that instead of worrying about this whole baby thing. Maybe he's the one?"

"He's not the one," I rolled my eyes at Kendra. "I've already established he's not the one. Do you remember me telling you how he acted at his clinic? No, we are going to be friends."

"Okay, Julia."

She was patronizing me, I saw it in how she pressed her lips together and gave me a slight look from the corner of her eyes. It didn't matter if she believed me or not. Mike was going to be my friend and nothing more. I'd already done all the work to decide on this baby and Mike was helpful in giving me the idea of using someone I know. Certainly hearing that from him made me think about it much more than I had before. But we were just friends.

I opened the door right away when he knocked and pushed myself out into the hallway before Kendra could talk with Mike. The last thing I needed was for her to start in with her questioning and innuendo about what she knew. Nope, she wasn't getting near him.

"Hey," I said as I held onto the door so Kendra couldn't come out. "Should we get going?"

"I could come in and say hi to your roommate, if you want me to?"

"No, no, we better get going. Kendra hasn't been feeling well," I grabbed Mike's hand and pulled him down the hallway as I heard Kendra open the door behind us.

"Have fun you two love birds," she yelled just as we got to the elevator.

I shook my head back and forth as Mike smiled at the outburst. I couldn't even bring myself to respond to her though and instead just stepped onto the elevator in silence.

Mike looked so handsome in his dark washed jeans and funky t-shirt. His effortless look probably took him two minutes to put together while I had agonized over which jeans and t-shirt I should wear for over an hour. Then I tortured myself over how to wear my hair and how much makeup to put on. It was a whole afternoon process for me and I still wasn't sure I'd made the right choices. Finally, I settled on my loose-fitting boyfriend cut jeans with my favorite Kansas City Royals t-shirt. My hair was pulled back in a simple ponytail and I'd only put on some mascara and blush for makeup.

This wasn't a date, this was my chance to get to know Mike and see if he really would be a good option for my donor. If things felt right I was going to ask him that night... Well, if I managed to get myself together enough and muster the courage. But it definitely wasn't a date.

"Thanks for asking me out on this date," Mike said as I froze solid in place. "I was worried you wouldn't want to get together anymore after all that happened. I'm glad you called."

"What are friends for?" I said in a bit of a panic.

"Yep," he replied while pressing the button for the ground floor.

"It will be fun to get to know each other some more. Plus, I haven't been bowling in ages. I'm really excited."

"Me too."

It was awkward between us as we sat in the Uber and made our way to the bowling alley. Mike looked like he wanted to say something to me but every time he was about to talk he got quiet and then turned to look out the window.

When I tried to make an effort at small talk, it didn't turn out that well either.

"The weathers been much warmer lately, that's cool," I said randomly.

"Yeah, better than how cold and windy it was earlier this week."

"Yep," I replied lamely.

Ugh, the tension going on between the two of us was insane. I had to think of something to loosen us up or there was absolutely no way I was going to be able to ask Mike to give me his sperm.

As we pulled up to the bowling alley Mike held the car door open for me and out of nowhere I slapped him on the butt as I walked past him. Something took over me, some demon flirting part of my brain that I wasn't even aware existed.

"Game on," he laughed and slapped my ass back on our way into the building. "I'm going to kick your butt."

"I doubt it. I'm pretty damn good at throwing balls around."

"Nope, I'm not buying it. Prove it," he laughed.

We gathered our overly stinky used shoes and went to our assigned lane to start the evening of bowling fun. The light hearted feel of the night was finally there and I was optimistic we could work this out and I might just have the sperm I needed to get pregnant.

Mike was a funny guy. Throughout the evening he threw out one liners and jokes that had me laughing harder than I remembered in a really long time.

"Knock them out, those pins deserve it after the way they've been acting tonight," he rooted me on as I went up for my last frame of our first game.

Sure enough my ball went straight into the gutter. I clearly remembered being much better at bowling than I actually was. I'd barely managed to bowl 100 while Mike was closer to 300 in his score.

"Dang, I think you're going to win," I joked.

"Let me show you how to do this," he said as he grabbed the ball and came around behind me.

His arms wrapped around my body and I felt his breath on the back of my neck. Every inch of my body tingled with excitement. His touch was invigorating, it drew out so much lust in me that I had a hard time remembering to breathe.

I swallowed hard as he put the ball in my hand and wrapped his around mine. He wiggled his hips a little behind me before pulling my arm back and checking my swing.

"It's okay, you don't have to show me," I said trying to cut the sexual tension, but it didn't help.

"So you start with the ball here," Mike said as he ignored

my comment and put the ball in front of me. "See that second arrow on the ground? Let's aim for that one."

"Um, Okay," I nervously muttered. "But I'm sure it's just going to go into the gutter."

"Nope, let's think positively. You're going to pull your arm back and then when you release I want you to twist it like this," he rolled the ball a little in my hand to show me the twisting motion.

"So pull it back and twist while I release it?"

"Try to wait until just before you let go of the ball and keep your eye on that spot on the floor so you know where you're aiming," Mike said and took a step back.

"What are you doing? You're not going to help?"

"I think you should give it a go. It's my final frame, I'm counting on this strike," he smiled back at me.

I closed my eyes and took a few steps back to start my walk up to the lane. I could feel him looking at me and tried not to think too much about it as I envisioned the ball flying out of my hand the way I had seen him throwing it so far that evening.

Slowly I held the ball in front of me and took my steps up to the lane while pulling it back and twisting the ball as it released from my fingers. I kept my eyes on the spot of the ground, just like Mike said and then watched in amazement as the ball barreled down the lane. At first it looked like the ball was going to go straight into the gutter but then something started to happen. The slight spin I gave it made the ball curve toward the center pin and then bam!

"I got a strike!" I yelled and jumped into Mike's arms.

"That's my girl," he said supportively as he hugged me.

Our hug turned from friendship to much more though as we held onto one another. I felt so comfortable in his arms, so welcomed, it was nice. The problem was that I was bad at relationships and I didn't want to ruin this friendship by making it into some short term relationship when I could have so much more with Mike. He could be my baby's father. This friendship could be exactly what I was looking for and the perfect solution to me wanting a baby and needing to find a sperm donor.

As we pulled apart from our hug I finally felt the nerve to ask Mike what I'd been contemplating all night long. In a sudden burst of courage I pulled his hand and brought him back to the chairs so I could ask him.

"Mike, will you be my sperm donor?" I asked as I held onto his hand and looked into his eyes hopefully.

He blinked a few times and then pulled his hand away from me. Before the words came out of his mouth I already knew the answer was going to be no. It was written all over his face. "I can't," he said. "I'm sorry."

"No, no, it's fine. I liked your idea of asking someone I know and I thought about you and how we had become friends. It's totally okay," I said as I tried to hold tears back.

"Should we play one more game or head out? I'm feeling really tired, maybe we should go."

"Julia, I can explain."

"No, there's no need for all that. I totally get it. Let's just go," I said and hurried over to the counter as I pulled my rental shoes off.

"I had a great time with you tonight, Julia. I was caught off guard by your request though. I thought we had something going here. I'm sorry."

"Of course, don't worry. We are still friends. I'd love to go bowling with you again very soon. I'm going to just go with the anonymous donor. I think that's the best option for me." I really was just saying anything I could so Mike didn't talk anymore.

We grabbed an Uber and drove in silence back to my place. When we got there, I jumped out and said, "Thanks for a fun night. I'll talk to you soon," as I hurried toward my building.

"Julia," Mike started to say. "We can talk about it more if you'd like."

"No, no, I totally get it. No worries. Have a great night," I said and hurried into the building.

Chapter 8

Mike

All she wanted was my sperm.

I had genuinely thought she wanted to go on a date with me. We had the chemistry and there was that something extra between the two of us that I just couldn't explain. A level of comfort that I really enjoyed when I was around Julia, but it wasn't at all what I thought it was.

How had I been so wrong about everything?

Julia had me locked into the friend zone harder than I could ever remember being. It was probably for the best. A relationship likely wouldn't have worked out anyways, but damn I sure would have like to give it a try.

"You look out of it today," Sheryl said as I showed up for work Monday morning. "Is everything okay?"

"Yeah, a rough weekend."

"Aren't all of your weekends rough?" she joked.

"Please tell me Bruce is actually here."

"Yes, he's in his office."

"Thank God, I couldn't manage another Monday like we had last week. I swear I didn't eat or drink a thing for twelve hours trying to jam all those patients in. How does today look?"

"Half as busy as last week," Sheryl laughed. "Dr. Simon will be taking care of his own patients."

"Ha, ha, you're so funny," I snarled back at her as I walked down the hall to Bruce's office.

We had worked out our issues over the last week and things were normal between us again, but I honestly was still waiting for the next time that Bruce didn't show up again. I didn't trust his promptness would stay. Building our business to the size that it was had taken a lot of hard work. I just didn't understand why Bruce wasn't taking part in it anymore. For so many years he had wanted the same thing I did, but now he always seemed distracted by his love life.

"Morning," I said as I let myself into his office.

"Good morning. I'm here and ready to work again," he said barely looking up from his paperwork.

"I appreciate your newfound dedication, Bruce."

"Yes, I am dedicated again. This is my stack of patients for the day; I'm just making sure I'm up to date on what's going on with each of them."

"Cool. Alright, I guess I'll leave you alone to work then," I said and made my way back out of his office.

Something definitely seemed off with Bruce. Maybe that whole incident with the woman at his house had thrown him off? Or maybe there was something else going on with him, I wasn't really sure but I was very happy to have him in the office to see his own patients that day.

The day was relatively uneventful until about three o'clock in the afternoon when I saw Julia in the waiting room. She was there for her appointment with Bruce and I did my best to stay out of sight. I certainly didn't want her to be uncomfortable about coming to our office. Just to make sure I was out of the way I grabbed Bruce after I heard the nurse call Julia's name. I pulled him into my office to talk really quick before she came down the hallway.

"Hey, this girl Julia Rivas is a friend of mine. I'm going to take a little break while you see her. I don't want it to be uncomfortable if she sees me here."

"If she's your friend, why would it be uncomfortable?" Bruce asked.

"Well, she asked if I would be her sperm donor and I told her no. I just don't want it to be weird now."

"Oh, okay," Bruce said as he left my office. "I'll offer her mine if she wants. I'm happy to do it."

"No, I didn't mean..." I started to say and then heard Julia walking down the hall with the nurse and quickly shut my door.

For a moment I stood at the door contemplating coming out and running into Julia. It wasn't the cool thing to do, but at least I could talk to her and try to explain why I had said no to her offer so quickly.

I was flattered that she had asked me. And if it had been

some other female friend of mine I might have said yes. But something told me that it was wrong to do that for Julia. Maybe I was afraid that it would have put me in this endless friend zone when I really wanted to have more with this girl? Maybe I was just a jerk who didn't want to help a friend out? Either way I definitely wasn't comfortable with Bruce being involved.

What had I done? I didn't want her to have Bruce father her child. There was no way that was a good idea. She should use an anonymous donor, that was best, or so I thought. There was no way she would want Bruce to do it. He wouldn't offer it to her and I knew she wouldn't bring it up to her new doctor on their first visit. Or at least I really hoped they wouldn't have that conversation.

I continually opened my door to see if Bruce was done seeing Julia. Five minutes went past and then five more. How long was he going to stay in there? This was getting ridiculous. I'd never known Bruce to spend so much time in one room. Then again I didn't normally pay attention to how much time he was in a room, but I was sure it wasn't nearly as long as he was in there with Julia.

The anticipation was killing me. I finally came out of my office and was pacing in the hallway when Sheryl found me.

"You have a patient in room two that's been waiting for a little bit," she said and handed me the chart. "You should probably head in there if you want to stay on schedule today."

"Yes, I'm sorry. Just a second, I need to talk to Doctor Simon really quick."

"He's doing an initial consult with that woman you know. I think he takes a little bit with those. You probably have time to see your patient. I'll tell him to wait for you when he comes out."

Reluctantly I hurried in to see my patient. It was a quick check up to monitor the gestational progress of her early pregnancy. I took ten minutes with her and focused on her issues as much as possible while trying not to worry too much about what Julia and Bruce were talking about.

Sure enough as I came out of my room Bruce was standing there waiting for me. He had a cocky smile on his face like he knew he was about to say something I wasn't going to like. My stomach sank before he was able to say a word.

"So, she's interested in having me do it. Are we okay with this now? Did you go over the contract with the lawyer? I'm cool with it if you are."

"No. No I'm not cool with it," I said in a panic. "You can't father Julia's baby. Bruce, you are not going to be giving her your sperm. No, absolutely not. Your swimmers are not going anywhere near her."

"So the legal stuff is not in order?" he said playfully.

"No, I think that is fine. The lawyer didn't have too many concerns but I haven't finished checking all of that out. I mean you can't father Julia's baby. You are not putting your fluids inside of her. I won't allow it."

"Why?" he asked still smiling at me annoyingly. "And you won't allow it? I wasn't aware that this was a decision you were part of. Perhaps you should have come and sat in on the consultation," he laughed.

"You are not saying yes to her. Please tell me you didn't already agree to that?"

"I haven't agreed to it. I told her I needed to step out. There seems to be a little unfinished business between the two of you. She asked about you. I saw it in her eyes. She doesn't want me to father that baby. So is there some unfinished business?"

"Yeah there is," I said. "Where's your damn contract at?"

Bruce walked into his office and grabbed a contract which was scarily located right on top of his desk, as if he was ready to use it at any time. I took the contract from Bruce and went right to Julia's door and knocked.

My hands shook and I tried to calm myself down before entering the room. I didn't want to act like some crazy jealous boyfriend but I was not okay with Bruce fathering her child. Especially since she and I had been together. I'd already had my body inside of hers. I'd already felt her orgasms around me. No, if anyone was going to father this child it was going to be me.

"Come in," she said softly.

"I'll do it," I blurted out. "Sign this and I'll do it."

"Mike, what are you doing here? Wait, what is that? What do you mean you'll do it? The donation? You'll be my donor?"

"Well I'm not about to have Bruce father your child! That's insane," I said a little louder than I wanted to.

Julia's eyes watered and she started sobbing. She was crying so much that I instinctively wrapped my arms around her and held onto her. I wasn't quite sure why she was crying. Had I said something wrong or was she crying from happiness? I stood there with her in my arms for well over a minute. I alternated rubbing her back and taking in her scent while I waited for her to calm down and tell me why she was crying. I couldn't exactly guess at this point.

"Thank you, Mike," she finally muttered.

"You should read through the contract first. I should probably read it too," I laughed. "It is Bruce's. I mean Doctor Simon's."

"I don't need to read it. Just tell me what it says," she said as she wiped the tears from her eyes.

"Let me read it to you," I replied softly as we sat together in the chairs.

I read through the entire document as if it was some sort of story I was telling her. I used vocal inflections to make it sound less boring, but overall it was a very bland read. It was nice to give it a good look before signing it. Although I'd looked it over with the lawyer, I certainly didn't have any stake in the document before and was much more interested in it now.

"So I pay you and you give me the sperm. And I'm agreeing that I won't sue you for child support, right?" Julia asked when I was finally done.

"You should take it to a lawyer and have them look it over though. I really don't feel comfortable with you signing it right now."

"You're right. I want to make sure and do this the right way. Thank you so much Mike. I really appreciate you agreeing to this. You are my ideal candidate."

"Candidate, like a contestant on a game show or something?" I laughed.

"You know what I mean. Thank you so much. So what comes next?"

"Like the actual act?" I laughed.

"I mean if I have my lawyer look over this and everything is okay, then what?"

"Then come back in and we will figure it out with your doctor. I think Doctor Simon should continue your care so we can keep our friendship intact."

"Perfect. Thank you again, Mike," Julia said and gave me a kiss that took me off guard.

It was a quick peck, more friendly than anything else, but

my body still reacted firmly to her touch. How had I let things get so far off course? I'd gone from eating up her delicious naked body to standing there hugging my friend who I was now going to have a baby with. This wasn't at all how I thought things were going to turn out when I brought this lovely woman to bed.

"Okay, I better get back to my patients. I'll talk to you soon," I held the door open for her as she hurried out and down the hall.

"Thank you again, Mike. You're the best friend ever," she blew me a kiss and then made her way into the lobby.

Julia was smiling now and happier than I could have imagined. She really did want to have this baby. I couldn't believe I'd just agreed to be part of the whole thing, but I also liked the idea of getting to be around Julia more. It was an odd mix of emotions for me as I watched her practically dance out of my office.

"Ouch, best friend," Bruce said from behind me.

He put his hand on my shoulder as if consoling me through a hard break up. I wasn't sure I liked the idea of being called her friend so much, but it was better than not being her friend at all. This whole thing with Julia was a new frontier for me.

"Yeah, I'm not loving hearing that."

"So she's going to have your baby? Did you guys do it in there? Should I have housekeeping clean up the room before the next patient," he gave me an elbow nudge.

"No, we didn't do it. Didn't you hear? I'm her best friend now," I growled back at Bruce and stormed off to see my next patient.

I was busy reading the next patient's chart when Sheryl came up next to me. She stood there, silent, not saying anything but waiting for me to say something. I narrowed my eyes onto her gaze and shook my head.

"What?" she asked.

"You want to say something, just say it already."

Sheryl and I had worked together for a long time. She was my employee but also a friend since we worked so closely for so long. I could see it in her eyes. She had something to say about this whole situation and if I didn't just let her say it right away I'd have to look at the stare the rest of the day.

"Friends make the best couples," she shrugged, smiled and then walked away from me.

"Interesting," I mumbled before heading back to work.

It true though. The best couples I knew were friends first. Perhaps this was the start of something that would last for a very long time. Or it was possible I'd just gotten myself into a heaping mess that I'd regret forever, only time would tell.

Chapter 9

Julia

"Mike agreed!" I yelled at Kendra when I returned from my doctor's appointment. "I was totally going to go with the anonymous donor and then Doctor Simon started talking about how it was better to use someone you know. I told him I asked Mike and he said no, but Doctor Simon went and talked to him and Mike agreed! I'm so excited."

"Yeah, you seem a little excited," she laughed as I sat with her on the couch.

"You don't even understand. The big thing holding me back was deciding on the donor. Then when I started thinking about Mike I knew he was the right one. But when he said no I started to question everything all over again. Now I'm so excited! I'm going to be a mother. Can you believe that?"

"No, I actually can't."

"It's happening, girl, it is happening!"

"So did you guys do it in his office or something? How is this going to work since the two of you have already slept together?"

It was a good question and one I'd worried a little about on the way home. I hadn't clarified with Mike that I was totally fine with doing this through artificial insemination. I absolutely didn't want to make him uncomfortable or put him out anymore than I already was.

"We will do it the medical way. He's already doing so much for me I don't want to make it weird."

"Then wouldn't it be better for him if he got to have real sex instead of using a cup?" Kendra asked.

"No, no, he didn't even want to agree to this before. I really want to keep things as friends and try and not be weird about it. If we are sleeping together it would be more like a relationship and I don't think that's what he wants. I'll stick to the cup."

"Probably something you two should talk about and you need an attorney and some sort of legal agreement. I have a friend who could help you out, let me get you his number."

"Perfect, I've got a document about this already from Mike's office. I just need someone to look it over and make sure it is good and I'll be ready to go."

"Wow, Julia. I really can't believe this."

"I know, it's so exciting!" I yelled and hugged Kendra who wasn't hugging me back all that much. I could feel the tension in her body regarding this whole situation but I wasn't going to let it get me down.

Everything was working out better than I could have

imagined. I just couldn't wait to get things started and hurried off to my room to get my new ovulation kit out. It used an app on my phone to measure my temperature and last period in order to find the perfect ovulation day for insemination.

For the next few days I did all my due diligence. I followed a healthy diet, got good sleep, and took my prenatal vitamins. I met with the attorney and scheduled my insemination for Friday since that was my perfect fertility day and so I could spend the weekend resting after.

The week flew buy with so much to do in order to get ready for my big day. I had waited and planned for so long that it really seemed impossible that it was going to happen this Friday. I was trying to hold back my expectations a little bit since I knew it possible that I wouldn't get pregnant with the first try. That was okay with me though, now that I'd found Mike I had a great feeling about the overall process and if I had to give it a go for a few months I could manage that.

By the time I walked into the clinic for my appointment I felt like a girl getting ready to go on a date. I was so nervous. All my confidence from the week was gone and I had to make a purposeful effort to take deep breaths while I waited in the lobby.

"Miss. Rivas," Doctor Simon's nurse called me.

"Yes, that's me. Oh, okay," I babbled as I grabbed for my purse but only grabbed one handle so all the contents went tumbling onto the ground.

A nice pregnant woman was next to me and leaned over to help me. She ended up holding my purse for me while I threw all the items back in there. My hands were shaking I was so nervous.

"Is today the day?" she asked when I stood up.

"Yeah, I'm so nervous."

"Don't worry. It is easier than the other way," she laughed and then rubbed her belly.

"I guess it is," I said nervously as I walked back to the room with the nurse. "Um, is Mike around? I mean Doctor Cooper? I, think I need something from him."

"He's going to stop in and visit with you before Doctor Simon," she laughed. "I think he's been as nervous as you are all morning."

"Really?"

"Yes, go ahead and have a seat. I'll go get him."

I tapped my feet on the ground and flipped through a magazine without reading any of the pages. I couldn't even focus my vision I was so distracted by everything going through my mind. This was really it. This was going to happen.

Knock. Knock.

"Come in," I said and dropped the magazine on the floor.

"Are you okay?" Mike asked as he closed the door behind

him.

He had on the same light blue set of scrubs that I'd seen him wearing every time I had been in the office but on this day he looked different. His smile was brilliant white and the dimples on his cheeks seemed a little bigger than I remembered them before. He was so handsome standing there that my breath caught and I couldn't even respond to him.

Mike leaned over and grabbed the magazine from floor and set it on the table then grabbed the extra chair in the room and pulled it up right in front of me. His knees touched mine and he put his hands on my hands and squeezed them softly.

"Julia, are you doing okay?"

"Yes," I finally managed. "Oh, I have the document too. It's in here somewhere," I grabbed for my purse and spilled the contents on the ground again. I couldn't believe just how out of sorts I felt around him. "Sorry, I did this in the lobby too. I don't know what's wrong with me."

"I think you're nervous."

"Maybe, but I know I want to do this. Are you still going to do it? Please don't back out."

"I'm still game to do this. I brought my favorite ammunition back in my office."

"Oh," I said a little in shock. "You mean you are going to go do it right now? I um…"

"The fresher the better," he laughed.

"So here's the contract," I thrust the paper between the two of us. "I don't want you to think that we have to date or anything like that. I did accept your request for yearly updates on the child if you and I weren't in contact anymore. Um, what else?" I tried reading through the contract and remembering what else the lawyers had updated but I just couldn't think straight.

"It's fine, Julia. I read it over after the last update. I'll sign it right now," he said and pulled a pen out of his pocket and signed the document. "Here you go."

He handed me the pen and his fingers lingered over mine for just a second. The warmth of his hands calmed me down almost instantly. Why was he so calm about this whole thing? He was the one who had said no before and now he appeared to be perfectly fine with it all. And why was I so damn nervous all of a sudden? All week I'd been excited and ready for this day and now with Mike in the room I was losing my shit.

"We don't have to date or anything like that. I really meant it when I said we could be friends. As much involvement as you want is cool with me. I'm just so excited you agreed to do this. I feel so much more comfortable about this all."

"It's kind of exciting, isn't it?"

"Yeah it is," I said as his hands touched mine.

"Are you sure? I just want to ask one last time."

"Yes, I'm sure. I'm so excited to be a mother, Mike. I never wanted to be an older mother and I didn't want to get stuck with some loser guy. I love that this is working out and I absolutely can't wait to meet this baby."

"Well then, I better go get to work," he winked at me.

"Wait," I jumped up from the chair as he was just about to leave the room. "Can I give you a kiss for good luck or would that be too weird?"

"Right here," he smiled and pointed to his cheek. "I won't need luck though."

My lips pressed softly against him and he let one of his hands wrap behind my back as we stayed in that spot for a moment. This was the start of the rest of my life, I could feel it. It was unconventional and a little crazy, but it was my life and I was so damn excited for it.

"Okay, go get um, big guy," I said and gave him a pat on his butt as he left the office.

He flashed me a mischievous smile before disappearing down the hallway. Did I just flirt with my sperm donor? Well, he was also the man I'd slept with only a few weeks before and my brother's friend from high school so maybe that gave me a little more leeway in the flirting department. But it was probably sending the wrong message to him since I didn't actually want a relationship from him. Friendship would be nice, though. I had already fantasized about what it would be like to stay friends with him while my child grew up.

We wouldn't have to see each other often but a couple times a year we would get together. Mike would comment how much our son looked like me and I'd tell him about all the things our son did that reminded me of Mike. Or maybe we'd have a pretty little girl and I could dress her up for her visits with Mike. I still wasn't sure if we would call him their father or not, that seemed like a sticky situation. Also, what would happen if I met someone and decided to get married somewhere down the road? There were a lot of little details I'd have to work out along the way but I was really excited to get going on that path already.

The nurse knocked softly but didn't wait for me to answer before she entered the room. She had a gown in her hands and some paperwork for us to go through.

"This is the office paperwork that we need to have you sign. Take your time reading it and then sign and date each page. The doctor will be in after you push this button to turn the light on outside your room. Please disrobe from the waist down and wait for the doctor on the table."

"Okay," I said trying to take in everything she had just said.

She closed the door behind her and I glanced through all the paperwork. It seemed like pretty standard paperwork to me. Talked mostly about the procedure and the minimal risks that there were, infection seemed like the big one and I wasn't concerned about that. There was a form stating that this was a one-time procedure and I would have to pay additional fees for additional procedures, that seemed pretty normal.

I signed all the papers and got undressed before clicking the call button to show that I was ready. Quickly I hopped up onto the table and tried to look as put together as possible with my naked butt sticking out behind me and a blue paper drape across my lap.

Knock. Knock.

"Are you ready?" The nurse asked.

"Yep."

"Doctor Cooper wanted to know if you'd like to have him in here for the procedure," Doctor Simon asked.

"No," I said.

"Okay then, let's get this baby-making going."

The nurse had a small container in her hands and turned to work at the counter for a minute while the doctor and I talked. Doctor Simon was just as handsome as Mike, but in a different sort of way. He was a little older with blonde hair and blue eyes. He seemed a little rougher around the edges than Mike but still was a very nice man.

"Can you tell me about the process first?" I asked with my hands crossed in front of me.

"Sure, the nurse is putting the specimen into a device

that I'll use to insert near your cervix. It will only take a moment but then I'd like you to lay here for thirty minutes or so after. There's a lot of research that says lying down isn't really necessary, but I've just got a thing about it and would appreciate you giving it a try."

"Of course, no problem."

"Then I usually suggest patients take it easy for a few days. But you don't have to go too far out of what your normal activity level is. And that's it. I'll have you back into the office in two weeks, but you can also get an over the counter pregnancy test that sometimes works as early as ten days."

"Great, okay, let's do this," I said and eagerly lay back onto the table.

The paper under me crinkled as I adjusted myself as the doctor guided my feet into the stirrups. It seemed just like a normal doctor appointment, in fact, the whole process was much faster than a normal OBGYN appointment had ever been.

"Okay that's it," Doctor Bruce said about a minute after he started.

"That's it?"

"Yep, I'll have the nurse get you a few magazines and you just lie back and relax. We will come let you know when thirty minutes is up."

"Thank you."

"I know Doctor Cooper was interested in visiting with you. Would you mind if he stopped in sometime during the next half hour?"

"Sure," I said just as the nurse helped to pull the blue paper drape over my legs and situate them so they weren't in the stirrups anymore.

"We will see you in two weeks," he said as he shut the door.

"I've got a warm blanket I'll grab for you," the nurse said. "Here are some magazines too. I'll check on you in a few minutes."

"Great. Thank you."

She quickly came back with a blanket and covered me up so I didn't look quiet as weirdo lying there waiting for Mike to come into the room. I kept my knees pulled up a little but otherwise just tried to relax and let the baby-making process happen.

When Mike arrived he had that damn adorable smile on his face again and it was infectious. I couldn't help but smile back at him.

"How's the baby-cooking going?" he asked and pulled a chair up next to me.

"It's good," I said and rolled my eyes.

"So would now be a bad time to ask you on a date?"

"Ha, ha, very funny." There was a nervous silence

between the two of us. Obviously he was joking. Why on earth would he want to take me on a date now? I was clearly trying to get pregnant. "Don't you have patients who need to be seen? I'm going to be fine. Just going to let this soak in for a little bit and should be out of here soon."

"I've got a few minutes free."

"Is it weird?" I asked.

"What?"

"Cumming in a cup and then having it put inside me?"

"Well, I would have preferred the old fashion way, but the cup will do."

"Thanks again. I'm so excited. This is the most perfect way I could have imagined this happening. I'll never be able to thank you enough."

Mike's pager went off and he pulled it out to look at it for a minute before putting it back on the side of his pants. I'd never realized he even had that thing. He didn't pull it out at all the night at the club or even when we sat and ate at the Italian restaurant.

"Duty calls. I've got some twins on the way tonight or maybe tomorrow if they are stubborn."

"Of course, I understand. Go take care of your work. I'm just going to head home and spend the weekend vegetating on the couch."

"So that was a no on the date option then?"

"I'm going to be eating pizza and watching Netflix on the couch all weekend. You're welcome to come hang out if you'd like."

"Sure, that sounds fun. I'll text you after these babies make their debut."

"Okay."

"Congratulations, momma to be. I've got a good feeling about my swimmers," Mike gave me a hug as he talked. The sweet scent of his cologne and stubble of his days' worth of beard growth sent my body into a fit of tingles.

My face flushed at his touch and I even felt like I got wet with excitement. We had made a baby with just a hug and a kiss on the cheek, but that didn't mean Mike didn't turn me on like crazy.

"I'll see you, um yeah, tomorrow then," I stuttered.

"Yep, let me know if you want me to bring anything. I'm an excellent pickle and ice cream shopper if you want to get ahead of the cravings."

"Oh you are?"

"I assume I am. I love food, so pretty much any craving you have I'm ready to deliver the goods at a moment's notice."

"Thanks, Mike. I'll see you tomorrow."

"Take care of yourself, see you tomorrow," he said and shut the door behind him.

By the time I left the office I was giddy with excitement over the idea I might have a baby on the way soon. I counted down the days I'd have to wait before taking the test and made sure to plan the next two weekends at home to rest.

Of course I knew that resting wasn't likely to have an effect on my ability to get pregnant, but I just wanted to make sure that everything I was doing was helping me be in the best possible health to make this baby happen.

On the way home I even downloaded a local grocery story app which could deliver food just in case I didn't feel like going out this weekend at all. I'd already told Teddy I'd be taking it easy at work over the next week and I wouldn't be working any overtime during this pregnancy.

Teddy was supper supportive of me. Even Kendra had come around to being supportive throughout the week. She'd gone and drank up all our alcohol and caffeine as her way of saying she was on board with the lifestyle I was going to be leading the next few months.

By the time I crawled into bed that night I was on cloud nine thinking about all that was ahead for me. I was going to be a mother soon. I was going to get to raise a sweet baby of my own. This was a whole new life for me and I absolutely couldn't wait.

It was even more exciting as my friends had started to come around and be more supportive. Also, having Mike agree to be the donor was the icing on the cake. The only thing I was worried about was the intense sexual chemistry I felt when I was around Mike.

The last thing I wanted to do was ruin the friendship we had. He was a great guy and however much he wanted to be involved in the life of my new baby, I wanted him to be there. But I'd have to hold back my urges so that I didn't ruin the friendship. My baby deserved the best and having Mike around as a friend was the absolutely best thing I could think of. As I closed my eyes, all I could think about was the smell of Mike's cologne and the touch of his hands as we said goodbye. This thing might be harder than I'd expected it to be.

Chapter 10

Mike

I was already turning out to be a crappy friend. After 48-hours at the hospital, my patient had finally given birth, but I hadn't slept all weekend and needed to head home and crash. I apologized to Julia and she seemed okay with it all, but it was a huge disappointment to me. Before I fell asleep I texted her in an effort to save our date.

MIKE: How about next Saturday night?

JULIA: For Netflix and pizza?

MIKE: For whatever you'd like to do.

JULIA: Netflix and pizza again sounds great.

MIKE: Perfect!

She could have offered to sit and read books and I would have agreed. I was drawn to Julia now more than ever. The week dragged on as if I was waiting for something huge and not just a tame night at Julia's house. I kept distracted with work and Bruce helped me with a new project we had been contemplating for a long time.

We were looking at adding a new doctor to our practice. It was a huge deal for us and considering the turbulence

Bruce and I had had lately I wasn't so sure it was the right time, but the process could take months or even years as we search for just the right person to bring onboard, so we decided to get the word out. The resumes rolled in from physicians looking to move into their own practice.

"This is hard," Bruce grumbled as we sat and looked through files late Friday night after our work day had finished.

"I know, everyone seems way more qualified than we ever were when we started this place."

"I know! I'm afraid we'd bring one of these people on board and they would take over!"

I had the exact same thought as we looked through our early list of candidates. Bruce and I did a damn good job running this place, but we weren't perfect. It would be a balance trying to find someone to fit in with us without being too meek or too over powering.

"Maybe we should bring on two new staff doctors and no partners," I suggested. "Then they will both know they are not in charge and we are the bosses."

"Do we have enough patients to support that?"

"Hell, you and I don't need to be taking so many patients all the time. We could just be the handsome faces of the business and keep small patient loads. We could let the new docs be patient heavy."

"I'm liking the sound of this."

"Let's have your business guy run some numbers for us and then we can look at that. I also think we could take over the rest of this floor as soon as that tech firm goes bust."

"Ha, yeah, they always end up going bust, don't they?" Bruce and I both laughed.

Every firm that had shown up across the hallway was in and out of there within the year, sometimes only a few months. It was a combination of bad management and just young people who were too eager to get big. It was the exact reason I wanted to have a clear plan of our expansion before we made any big moves.

"I'm going over to Julia's house tomorrow," I said a little desperate for a man's take on what I was doing.

"Cool, how's she doing? Any word on the little one?"

"It's only been a week."

"Oh yeah, the days just blend together for me lately. I haven't been myself since I've had to start showing up for work every day."

"Yeah, I think you're going to like this new plan a lot."

"Damn right I am. I can't wait to be one of those jerky doctors who doesn't show up except for once a week."

"Again," I added.

"Yeah, yeah. So you're going to hang out with your baby momma, that's sweet. A little dangerous, but sweet."

"What do you mean dangerous?"

"You're going to screw her and then ruin that nice little contract that I gave you. Emotions always ruin things."

"For your information I've already screwed her, well before the whole baby thing though," I laughed. "But I know what you mean. I'll keep it friends. She would be a nice woman to have around as a friend. Plus, I've known her since she was like ten, so that might make the whole baby thing even sweeter."

"If you don't screw her."

"That's what I'm saying, Bruce. I'm keeping it friends."

"Okay," he said looking utterly unconvinced.

I wasn't even sure that I was convincing myself that I was going to be able to keep things as just a friendship with Julia. I knew it was the best plan though and I genuinely wanted to do what was best for her.

We wrapped up our resume explorations and called it a night. On the way out of the clinic I couldn't help but glance over at the tech firm across the hall with all their lights on. There was an office full of workers who clearly weren't heading home anytime soon; the burnout rate on those tech guys had to be pretty damn young.

***

I grabbed the pizza; a half meat and half veggie. I also picked up some ice cream and movie snacks before making my way to Julia's apartment. With a quick buzz of her intercom she let me in and I was up the elevator and knocking on her door shortly after.

Her apartment was small, with a bedroom for her and one for her roommate. The living room was in the middle with the kitchen attached to it. They had a soft grey sofa and big television in the room but not much else. It was cramped quarters and I couldn't help wondering if she was planning on staying in that same apartment after the baby came.

Maybe the roommate would be leaving? Maybe it was none of my business because I was just a donor in this situation and not supposed to be involved in Julia's life like that.

"I brought food!" I said as Julia opened the door. "I wasn't sure if your roommate would be around so I got plenty if she is."

"Nope, she's off with her new man."

"The guy from the club?"

"No," Julia laughed as if I was being ridiculous.

"So what's on for the night? Anything good? Movie or television series?"

"I'm flexible. I was really hoping to watch that new series based in the medieval times or whatever. You know the one with that sexy blonde lady and the dragons who are taking over."

"Yeah, perfect. I haven't watched that yet."

"I'm glad you're here, Mike. It's good to see you," Julia

grabbed the pizza from me and I followed her to the kitchen.

She was pregnant already, I just knew it. Her skin was glowing more than when I'd seen her last. She looked so happy. Like a woman who was in the process of making a baby.

"How are you feeling? You look great!"

"I feel normal. I think I'm just eating more because I'm nervous," she laughed.

"Well, you look great," I said again watching her bend over and grab a big bowl from the cabinet below. Damn her ass looked fine in those shorts.

"Thanks," she laughed as she caught me staring at her butt. "I think it's getting bigger alredy."

"Perfect. I love big butts."

She just laughed and finished putting some chips in the bowl she had grabbed. Together we filled our plates with pizza and snacks and then made our way over to the couch to get our night of television started.

Julia had on a pair of tight workout shorts and a big oversized sweatshirt. But she'd cut part of the top off the sweatshirt so it hung down on one shoulder and had shorter sleeves. Her hair was up in a messy ponytail and she didn't have a touch of makeup on, yet she looked absolutely stunning.

I sat on the couch while she fiddled with the remote and found the show we were going to start watching. It was one of those series that had several seasons and could easily keep us occupied for days and days. Exactly what I hoped for, days and days of hanging out with Julia.

She found a spot on the couch a little further from me than I had hoped, but then again if we were going to keep this situation as just friends then distance was good. It was hard for me to imagine being just Julia's friend though. The more I was around her the harder that thought became.

"So I should be able to take the test in a couple of days, right?" Julia asked and pulled her legs up next to her on the couch.

"Yep, but remember, the whole first trimester is about growth. It's also the time when people have miscarriages the easiest. Try not to get too excited until things are a little further along."

"Oh, okay," Julia said as the smile dropped from her face. "How often do women have miscarriages?"

"Didn't Bruce go over this with you?" I asked as I moved closer to her to comfort her a little.

"I'm not sure, I wasn't paying attention. I was so excited I might have missed it. So I could get all excited for the baby and then lose it? What happens with a miscarriage? I hear women talk about them all the time but I really don't know much about how it happens. Will I be in pain? How will I know it's happening?"

She was starting to panic and I felt horrible for even

bringing it up. Having her blood pressure up and worrying about the baby wasn't going to change anything that was happening inside of her. At least it wasn't going to make it better, in fact, I believed that stress could actually make things worse for a growing fetus.

"Julia," I said and held onto her hand. "You can't worry about it yet. I'm just saying to try and take a little bit of a muted approach in the first few weeks. You can still get excited. You should definitely get excited. In fact, I want you to call me right away when you take the test and tell me all about it."

"But be prepared if something bad happens?"

"Well, sort of. Just know that it could happen. Keep taking care of yourself and doing the best you can to keep your health in top order. That's all you can do. Nature sometimes messes things up and there is just nothing we can do to fix that."

"So I shouldn't buy that new condo I was thinking about just yet?"

"You can buy your condo. You can buy your crib. You can do any of those motherly things you want to do. Because if it doesn't work this time all you have to do is try next month and then the month after. You're young and healthy, I don't think the process will take you very long at all."

"I can't help but be excited," she said as she hopped up onto the side of the couch. "I don't think I'll be able to hold it back if I'm pregnant. I guess I'll just have to go with it."

"Yeah, I don't think you will," I smiled up at her.

She slid back down to her seat on the couch and flipped the show on. I stayed there next to her and decided not to move back to the other side of the couch. It was more comfortable being there close to her than in the corner anyways.

As we watched the show I found myself inching closer and closer to Julia. Soon she had her head tucked in next to my chest and we were cuddling watching Netflix for hours. Her hair smelled of coconut and I couldn't stop taking in her scent as we sat together.

When she let her hand fall onto my lap I froze though. The touch of her fingers on my thigh had my whole body aching for her. I knew we needed to stay friends, or at least that was what I'd been telling myself, but there was a calmness about me when I was with Julia.

I didn't move her hand. I tried not to focus on it. But I loved that she was touching me. My eyes continued to watch the show yet I wasn't paying attention to any of it. Instead, my full attention was on everything about Julia. Her scent, her movements, even how she breathed. When she moved her fingers slightly, I mentally urged her to keep moving up my thigh.

Oh, how I would have loved if she'd just grabbed a hold of me and started stroking me right there. Sex was on my mind, there was no doubt about it. For all my talk about being friends I did want more with Julia, it didn't matter that she wanted to have a baby. But I knew that should matter to me. I should care that this was the life she wanted and me trying to have sex with her was going to confuse her, I really should have cared.

"I swear if that guy gets any more kills under his belt he's going to end up the King," Julia said as she lifted up her head and looked at me.

"I know, right?" I laughed, not knowing at all what she was talking about.

In the process of looking up at me, Julia had moved her hand off my leg and back onto her own leg. The disappointment was real. I reluctantly went back to watching the show and paying attention to what was going on, at least for a little while.

Soon I found myself drifting off though. It was well past midnight but Julia was still watching the show and I didn't want to leave. I repositioned myself a little lower on the couch and found a spot for my head on the pillows behind me. Moments later I was drifting off to sleep.

When I started to wake up I wasn't exactly sure if I was waking up or still in the middle of a dream. Julia's hand was definitely rubbing up and down my hard shaft. My jeans were still on but I was bulging like I could bust out of them at any moment.

I assessed the situation. Julia was stroking me, so she was interested in not being just friends? This was what I wanted. This was the ideal situation. Certainly I couldn't turn this down.

But then this part of my brain that I absolutely hate started taking over. She was vulnerable right now. This was a big deal for her and maybe she thought I wouldn't stay around if she didn't sleep with me or something. I wasn't exactly sure what was going on. I let my fingers glide through her hair as I enjoyed her hand on me for a minute while I tried to decide what I should do. Surely we could figure this out. Maybe this was going to be a fun thing for us, we could be friends with benefits or something like that.

"Julia, I thought you just wanted to be friends?" I said softly.

She didn't respond.

"I'm open to this if you're interested but we should probably talk about it."

Again, she didn't respond at all. Yet her hand continued to stroke and play with me. I was so confused as to what was going on here. Surely she was awake, wasn't she? I mean a girl didn't just start stroking you while she was sound asleep, or did she?

I leaned over and tried to get a good look at her face, but her head was tucked in so close on my chest that I couldn't get a good look. She was slumped down pretty good as well.

"Are you awake?" I finally asked.

No response.

Slowly I pulled her hand off of me and moved her head so

she was resting on the side of the couch. She was asleep! Julia didn't even know she was stroking me. Quickly I moved to the other side of the couch and tried to take in the whole situation.

We had been asleep for so long that the sun was starting to come up now. I didn't want to leave without waking her up but I couldn't exactly wake her up at the moment since I was throbbing through my jeans.

Instead, I started picking up the mess we had made and went into the kitchen to clean up a little bit. Julia started to stir a little on the couch and I moved even quieter around the kitchen in the hope that I wouldn't wake her up just yet. But sure enough she started to wake up and was looking around to see where I was at.

"Oh, well I should invite you over more often if you're going to clean for me," she said sweetly as she came into the kitchen.

"You can invite me over anytime."

"You know, I was having a delicious dream, and it was about you," Julia said as she moved in closer to me.

"Really, what was it?"

"I don't know if I should say. I mean we are friends and all."

"Yeah, definitely don't tell me then. You wouldn't want to share something like a dream with your friend."

"I dreamt that we were cuddled up in some lounge chairs

on a beach somewhere. It was really romantic."

"Oh, that's nice."

"And well..." she drifted off as she pulled herself up onto the counter next to the sink where I was doing dishes.

"Well, what?" I asked trying not to have any idea what was going on in this dream of hers.

"We were about to have sex. I was teasing you."

"Really?" I said with a fake surprised expression.

"Yep, and I think you were liking it."

"Oh, I'm sure I was liking it. I have no doubt in my mind at all that I would have been loving having your hands on my body."

"I was wondering," Julia said as her hand traced up my arm. "Are you fully committed to being friends?"

"Of course. I want to be involved as much as you're comfortable with. I'm actually excited about this idea."

"I mean, what if I just couldn't resist," she said and then grabbed me and pulled me in for a kiss.

I dropped the plate that I was washing and enjoyed every second of Julia's lips on mine. She was definitely awake. There was no doubt that she knew exactly what she was doing in that moment.

Chapter 11

Julia

I couldn't help myself. Having Mike right there all night long was torture. I might be pregnant with his baby but if I hadn't been doing all of this the two of us could have given a fun relationship a try. Hell, I wasn't sure at all what I was doing at the moment. All I knew was that I wanted to kiss Mike, so I was kissing Mike!

"Julia, we should probably talk about this," Mike said as he pulled his lips away from me but moved his body right in front of me.

"Did you want to talk about it?" I teased him and pulled him close.

"We should."

"It doesn't have to be serious. We are already friends. I might be carrying your baby already. We can just relax and have fun. How about it?"

"Like a friends with benefits thing?"

"I'm sure they never work out like people think, but we will be different. If either one of us meets someone else, then we will just stop this whole thing and move on. No hard feelings. It's just fun."

"So we are going to do this more than once?" Mike asked with a little smirk on his face.

"Probably," I said and wrapped my legs around him and pulled him in closer to me. "Deal?"

"Um, yeah we can see how it goes."

That was all I needed to hear and I quickly pulled him back in close to me. This time I didn't kiss him though. Instead, I just let us stay right there in the close proximity of each other and I waited for him to make the move.

Sure enough he leaned in closer and gently put his lips on mine. This was going to be a hell of a lot of fun. No worries about a relationship, no worries about getting pregnant. None of that. Well, assuming I was already pregnant, then I wouldn't have to worry.

"Do we need a condom?" I asked curiously.

"I guess not. But I'm fine with wearing one if you want me to."

"Yeah, why don't you wear one," I said just to ease my mind.

I'd just spent thousands of dollars for a doctor to squirt Mike's sperm into me. I didn't want to feel like that was all a waste of money. Plus, there was just something about wearing a condom that allowed me a little bit of distance emotionally. I thought it would be good to have a little emotional distance since this relationship was going someplace I wasn't at all ready for.

"Cool," Mike replied and lifted me up and started carrying me into the bedroom.

I laughed at his enthusiasm. He didn't seem to care one way or the other about the condom. He just wanted to know the answer so we could move onto the next step of fun. It was fun too. The last time we were together it was hot and heavy. The romance seemed in high force that evening, but this time we were so much more comfortable with each other that we were actually giggling as we took each other's clothes off.

"Get your butt on that bed," I said playfully and pushed Mike back onto the bed.

"Yes, mistress," he teasingly replied.

"Mmm, I kind of like that. Maybe I'll be in charge tonight. I don't usually get to be the one in charge," I said as I grabbed the condom.

"Yes," he said roughly as his throbbing cock moved with excitement.

"Oh, do you like that? Do you like me being in charge?" I asked.

"Yes," he said again.

"Mmmm maybe if I'm in charge tonight I should take my time with you. Tease you. Play with you." I knelt down next to Mike and let my hand slowly drape up and down his leg. I moved it near his cock and then away again. One time I let my fingers circle the tip of him before I let go and moved to his other leg.

His body was pulsing so hard that he started to drip with excitement. I couldn't help but lick it up. My tongue moved slowly around the tip of him and took in the salty taste of his precum. Soon I had my lips wrapped tight around him though and slid down to the base of him before sliding back up.

Slowly, I moved ever so slowly as I tasted him. Even though his hips thrust slightly against my mouth, Mike stayed fairly still and took in the power I had with my mouth around him. The faster I moved the more Mike appeared to settle back down. He liked the faster motion but I knew that the slower movements would torture him. I wanted to torture him. Not in a bad way, of course. I just wanted to sexually torture him and bring his orgasm to such a peak that he wouldn't forget it ever.

I continued to suck slowly. So slow that at some point even I really wanted to speed things up. He was groaning and moaning like a crazy man. Then it happened, the word I'd been waiting to hear.

"Please," he moaned out. "Please."

"Oh, do you want me to get on top of you?"

"Yes, do it. Get on."

"Mmmm, maybe in a minute," I teased mischievously as I looked up at him.

I was having so much fun playing with him! It was fun to

be in charge like that. Fun to get to do what I wanted and take my time with him. I could see what the fascination was with being a dominatrix. It was exhilarating knowing that someone was at your will and you were the one bringing them pleasure.

After another couple of minutes torturing Mike, I finally decided that it was torture for me to wait any longer. I ripped the condom open and started to climb on top of him when Mike grabbed me and gently flipped me over on the bed.

"Oh no, you're not getting off that easy," he said with determination in his eyes.

"I thought I was in charge tonight," I smiled.

"I lied. Now I'm going to pay you back for that little bought of torture."

I just laughed at his plan. It wasn't really the same level of torture if he was going to lick me like I was licking him. I'd enjoy every second of it, no torture at all.

But then he started to tease me. He spread my legs wide and looked down at my wet body. His hands held onto my ankles and very slowly moved up my thighs, all while staring right at me.

"Mike," I laughed uncomfortably as he looked at me.

"You're so wet."

"Because you make me excited. Put that condom on and come here," I urged.

"Just a second."

He leaned down and let his tongue gently lick some of my wetness. It was true, I was excited by him and our evening so far. I was probably dripping wet at that point, there was no denying it.

His tongue moved softly from the bottom of me up to the tip of my clit. He took his time with each stroke but spent a little extra time around my clit. Each one of his licks were hard and slow, which really built up my arousal in that moment.

As he finished licking me Mike knelt there between my legs. I was ready for him. I was drenched with excitement and absolutely ready for him to be inside me. But then I saw the childlike face of a troublemaker looking down at me.

Mike smiled and put his hands on my inner thighs to open me up as much as possible. Then he looked at me again. His eyes navigating every curve of my body. Taking time to look at each of my nipples, down at my stomach and then harvesting the curve of my wetness.

He wasn't just purposely taking his time, Mike looked like he was loving every minute of looked at me. The first time we were together I was very self conscious of the way he looked at me. But now I saw it. I saw the lust in his eyes, the desire he had, there wasn't a shred of judgment in the way he was looking at me. He did want every inch of me, I could see it in his eyes.

"Okay, Mike, that's enough torture," I said softly. "I want

you inside me."

"Mmmm," he growled. "You look so hot. I'm going to remember every curve of your body."

"Yeah?" I asked.

"Oh, yeah."

Then I thought for sure he was about to slide the condom on and continue our night, but he had other plans. Mike laid on his stomach between my legs. He kept me pressed wide enough that I couldn't move against him as he devoured me.

He even grunted and growled a little as he was licking and eating me. I pulsed against him hard but the position he had me in made it nearly impossible to buck against his tongue like my body wanted to.

The slow pressure of before was gone and this time Mike was eating me as if I was the last meal of his life. He licked and even nibbled my body, taking in my juice like it was going to keep him alive. He spent just enough time on my clit to get me more excited, but then let his tongue go back to exploring other parts of my wetness. Soon I felt it, the torture of wanting to cum, the amazing feeling of being so close to orgasming and yet so far away.

"I need you inside me," I groaned and grabbed at Mike's hair.

He wanted to be inside me. He needed it just as badly as I did, but Mike had the self control to continue torturing and playing with me. He wrapped his mouth around my clit and pulled it softly into him. The gentle pressure was delightful and I pressed against him for more.

"I'll get on top now," I tried to order him. But Mike was no longer interested in having me be in charge. He had taken control of our little rendezvous.

The slow sucking of my clit had me engorged with excitement. I could feel a deep pulsing in my body like I hadn't felt in a very long time. I needed to release. The full level of my excitement was almost too much for me as I held my breath and pushed against him hoping for more and more from his tongue.

Then it happened. My body didn't need to wait anymore. I felt the tingling building up and the blood rushing to my center as I started to cum. It was a different level of orgasm than I was used to though. It was slow, deep and unsteady as it built up longer and longer. My legs were shaking, my hands gripped tightly on the sheets. Finally I was going to get the sweet release my body needed. I couldn't wait to feel that release. Every inch of my body was ready to explode.

Then he released me. Mike let go of my body with his mouth and his hands. He knelt in between my legs, not touching me at all. Just watching me as I looked up at him in terror. He'd stopped! No, no, no, he couldn't stop. I was so close. I was nearly going to explode and he just stopped. What sort of torture was this man putting me through?

Mike smiled down at me, knowing exactly what he had just done. He relished in this high level of torture that he put me through. He was loving every second of my shock. At one point I was pretty sure he even laughed at me as I looked up at him.

"What?" he asked playfully.

"You put that condom on and get inside me right now," I said forcefully.

"Oh, so you're saying that I'm good at sexual torture? Tell me I'm good," Mike said and held the condom in his hand.

"You are good. Now get moving."

He started to open the condom wrapper and then pretended like he couldn't get it open. He hilariously dropped it and then picked it back up. Fumbling with the thing like he was a teenager who hadn't opened one before.

"Oh, man, these things are so hard to open," he said dramatically.

"You are so dead," I laughed.

"I don't know. It's just so hard to figure out," he continued his joke.

Then I did something that I didn't even know I knew how to do. I slid down closer to Mike and wrapped me legs around him. I pushed him to the side and before I knew it, I was on top of him again. I was positive he was going along with my move, because any sort of resistance and it wouldn't have worked at all. But there I was, back in control of the situation, but this time I wasn't interested in wasting any time.

I grabbed the condom from Mike and ripped it open with my teeth. I rolled it onto him as I hovered above waiting to slide down. It was more like one motion than two and I thrust my body hard onto his erect cock.

"Wow," I said as I took him in so deep that I had to adjust for a moment. "Wait, is this okay for the baby?"

"The chemicals released during sex actually help relax you which is very good for the baby," Mike said in an official sounding voice.

I wasn't really sure if he was telling the truth or not about the chemicals and relaxation. But I knew he wouldn't be having sex with me if it would endanger my pregnancy. So I did relax and take him into me as I started rocking softly on top of him.

Even though I'd been so close to orgasm only a few moments before, I wasn't close at all as I started thrusting on top of Mike. The change in sensation at put me back a few steps, but not all the way to the beginning.

His hands held onto my hips as I rocked on top of him. Moving slowly but forcefully I was in control, although I was pretty sure that Mike would have taken over at any moment if I'd stopped moving or tried to tease him again.

We moved together so softly and perfectly, it was as if we'd made love thousands of times before. The pressure of a relationship was gone and I was able to relax and just have fun with our time. I'd never felt so relaxed with a man before. It was rather sad that I'd made it to twenty-five years old and hadn't felt this level of comfort with a man before. Apparently, it just took a guy agreeing to donate his sperm to me, then I finally trusted and was able to relax around him.

I also liked that we weren't worrying about a relationship. We were friends. We'd already decided that I was going to have the baby and I was going to be in charge. There was no co-parenting or anything like that. He donated his sperm so I could make my own dream of motherhood come true. Our friendship was just a bonus with the whole situation and this new plan of a friendship with sexual benefits was the absolute icing on the cake.

I watched Mike, as he watched me on top of him. He continued to delight in looking at me as I moved. It was such a turn on to see that desire in his face. The genuine longing to know my body warmed me and gave me the courage to stay on top of him, exposed to his view.

My hands rested on Mikes chest as I found the perfect position on top of him. My hips moved in a short thrusting motion and I rubbed my clit softly against him with each movement. Slowly, but surely, I felt the buildup of excitement becoming unbearable.

My thrusts slowed as I tried to hold back my orgasm a little. I hated losing control. I hated not feeling like I was in full control of my body. But Mike saw what I was doing. He saw how close I was to losing my control and he held my hips firmly and helped me continue on top of him.

His added control guided me to continue moving and soon I was thrusting hard on top of him. I had lost my control. Harder and harder I moved. I closed my eyes so I could concentrate on the delicious sense of pleasure that was going on.

"Yes," I muttered as I continued to move. "Yes."

"Cum for me, baby," Mike groaned as I felt his thrusts coming harder too.

I'd never been a fan of dirty talk in the bedroom before but Mike's words drove me to cum. His permission wasn't needed, but it was welcomed as I finally let my body release with such an intense orgasm that my fingers latched onto Mike's chest hard.

He didn't yell out from the pain though. Mike thrust deep inside of me and then released his own explosiveness. I was shaking from my release and fell on top of Mike's chest in exhaustion. I literally couldn't move of my own free will at that moment, although my body was still shaking from the pleasure quake that had just happened.

His fingers glided up and down my back softly and then wrapped around me in a bear hug to hold me. The intimacy was welcomed. I relaxed almost instantly and felt myself drifting off to sleep there in his arms with his body still inside of mine.

I fell asleep. Right there on Mike's chest as I straddled his still throbbing body, I fell asleep. There was such a sense of perfection with my life at that moment. Everything was exactly as I had hoped, even better than I could have imagined. Life was so good that I finally slept deeply for the first time since my insemination.

Chapter 12

Mike

I stayed the whole weekend with Julia. We didn't just have one night together, it ended up being both Saturday and Sunday night. Although most of Sunday was spent sleeping after our early morning romp in bed. We did manage to wake up and eat some food late in the day before finding our way back to bed after sunset.

I'd never had a true friend with benefits before. It was one of those relationships that guys talked about but I wasn't sure really existed. What sort of woman actually didn't want a relationship? Up until that weekend with Julia, I honestly didn't think such a woman existed.

But we didn't talk about a relationship at all. In fact, Julia and I talked about her and her baby. She talked about saving money over the last year, so she could buy a condo of her own, paying off her bills, and getting herself financially ready. Julia talked only about a future on her own with this new baby that she wanted so desperately. We never talked about going on dates again, or what I wanted; it was amazing.

It was a release to be able to have sex and not have to

worry about calling for the next date. I didn't have to worry if we would like each other in a few weeks or how I would get out of the relationship when things didn't work out. Julia didn't want those things from me and that gave me the freedom to actually enjoy our time together.

By the time I left early Monday morning, Julia and I had already made plans to go to a celebratory dinner after her pregnancy test. It didn't matter if it was positive or negative, we were going to celebrate our friendship and her journey.

We did set some ground rules, at least for the time being. We were going to continue to use the artificial insemination process if Julia needed to try another round. She just thought it would help her separate things emotionally. And I was going to keep using a condom if we decided to have sex again, although we might not continue that side of our relationship. I didn't get a lot of clarity on that.

Julia wasn't going to call me every day, those were her words and rules not mine. She said she was concentrating on herself and wouldn't be reaching out to me very much. Perfect, I couldn't have thought of a more perfect situation. We were going to actually be friends. Just two people who happened to enjoy hanging out with one another and might be having a baby together as well.

By the time Julia came into the office to see Bruce for her two week check up, our friends with benefits situation was pretty solid. I'd even come over after her home pregnancy test was positive and we had some celebratory sex.

Julia and I were texting every day. Not because either of us were obligated to, but because we both genuinely wanted to see what the other was up to. We were friends and part of that meant that we liked to talk to each other.

On the morning of her appointment with Bruce, we talked on the phone to make plans for that evening. "Where do you want to go celebrate?" I asked as we decided on her celebratory dinner.

"Nothing spicy. Is it a thing to have indigestion so early on?"

"Everybody is different," I offered. It was a pretty standard answer for most questions women had about their bodies so early in pregnancy. Every woman reacted very differently to the rush of additional hormones in her body as the baby began growing rapidly.

"What about a salad place?" Julia asked.

I liked meat. I enjoyed a good steak and I absolutely hated going to salad restaurants. It was like handing over my money and then getting nothing in return. I could eat a giant salad and half the time I still had to go somewhere else to get more food because I didn't feel full at all.

"Sure," I replied. More than willing to adjust my needs for Julia's in that moment.

"Well, maybe pizza?" She asked, totally not worrying about her indigestion at all.

"We can decide after your appointment," I laughed. "I'll

see you later today."

"Yeah, I'm coming in at four. Will you be able to head to dinner after my appointment?"

"I should be able to head out shortly after," I lied. "Have a good day at work, I'll see you later."

As I hung up the phone I realized just how many charts I still had to update from the previous day of seeing patients. I'd been getting behind on my work since Julia and I got together as friends. I was distracted, in a good way. But now I had yesterday's work to finish and still had a full load of patients for that day.

I dove into my charts and was still working hard on them at eight o'clock when Bruce arrived. The nurses were checking in our first patients of the day and Bruce and I took a moment to get organized and catch up.

"You look like a well fed man," Bruce joked.

A few days before I'd made a crack about the possibility of living off of oral sex as my sustenance alone. He thought it was hilarious, but also agreed that he believed he could live off a woman's juices as well. There was something so nurturing about eating a woman out, so deliciously erotic that it made me feel fuller than any salad ever could.

"Yeah," I laughed. "She's coming in today for her official test. We are going to go to dinner after to celebrate."

"So you're dating?"

"No, not really. It's more like a friends with benefits

thing."

"Oh, those never work out," Bruce laughed.

"Well, our situation is a little unique. Isn't it?"

"Yeah, but sooner or later one of you is going to get attached to the other. I'm just saying, they never work out. So keep yourself ready for that."

"I know," I said without really agreeing with Bruce.

Sure, most of the time this sort of thing didn't work out. I hadn't even believed girls were into it at all. But Julia and I were different. She wanted to be independent. She was the one who had suggested the whole situation. It was going to work out for us. At some point I could see us going back to being just friends without benefits. Sooner or later I'd meet some girl and start dating and I wouldn't keep sleeping with Julia if that happened.

"But I think it's cool what you guys have going on," Bruce said giving me his thumbs up of approval. "It will help her relax through the pregnancy and it's good for you too.

"Yeah?"

"Yep, she seems like a nice girl. I think this whole thing could go south pretty quickly, but it's possible she'll help you be less of a jerk with the ladies," Bruce laughed.

"Me? I'm not a jerk."

"I bet your last few exes wouldn't agree with that statement." He laughed and left my office.

"I'm not a jerk," I yelled after him as Sheryl turned up at my office door.

"That's a matter of perspective," she retorted.

"Any possibility of me getting out of here by five o'clock today?"

"Not if you want to get your paperwork done," she showed me the long list of patients we had.

"Okay, I'm going to bring my notebook and take notes and put them into the chart later. Not ideal, but I really need to get out of here by five today."

"Big date?" Sheryl asked with a mischievous smile.

"Not a date like that. I'm just going to dinner with Julia after her pregnancy confirmation appointment."

"Ohhh," Sheryl replied with a knowing look in her eye. "So you have a time picked out and you shaved this morning. You're rearranging your day so you can leave by a certain time, but it's not a date?"

"It's not a date," I said again.

Sheryl wasn't having any of my talk though. She just smiled at me and then went over to her nursing station to get ready for the day. It was only a minute later that she was at my door again, trying to pull me away from my paperwork and get me in the room with my first patient.

"If you're going to make it to your date on time, you'll need to see your patients on time," she winked at me.

"It's not a date," I defended again.

But she was right. I had to stay focused throughout the day to get through my extra long list of patients. Even on the best of days, I never got out of the office by five o'clock. Inevitably there were delays or additional time I had to take with patients to ensure we covered all the bases. Not to mention the fact that any number of my patients could go into labor at any moment.

Bruce and I tried to alternate evenings and weekends that we were on call, but if a patient went into labor during the work day, we each handled our own patients. The whole process of building up our business was exhausting though and some months I swore I only got a few nights of full sleep the entire month.

Luckily, the business analysis had come back saying we could sustain two new doctors and we would be able to move forward with that plan for expansion. Although neither of us seemed to have the time to do in-depth reviews of the resumes for potential candidates. It wasn't that much of a hurry since the tech firm across the hall still had six months on their lease. As much as I didn't wish harm on anyone, I wasn't going to be sad if their company went bust and had to terminate their lease early.

I made my way in to my first patient of the day with a fresh notepad and a determination to get through my day on time. I couldn't wait to take Julia out and celebrate her exciting day. It was exciting to me too.

The Baby Package

My day drudged along with patient after patient. I did my best to stop thinking about Julia while I was in the room with each patient, but the second I walked back to my office I was looking at the clock and waiting for her to arrive. Four o'clock couldn't come fast enough for me.

Julia send a couple of texts in the morning talking about how excited she was for her appointment but other than that I didn't hear from her for the rest of the day. This appointment she had with Bruce was purely an official checking in with her hormone levels and confirming the pregnancy. There wasn't a lot to the appointment and I was relatively certain she'd be disappointment by how fast it was. The fun appointments wouldn't come for a few more weeks when she got to hear the baby on the monitor and see him or her growing.

For me it was different than I'd expected things to be. I was invested in her pregnancy much more than I thought I was going to. I worried if she was sleeping and eating right. I wanted to tell her all the advice I had to give and it took everything I had not to butt in with my opinion.

She was having *HER* baby. This wasn't technically my baby, at least that was how I was looking at things. I found myself trying to think about her separate from the pregnancy and separate from the idea that it was my sperm that helped to make the baby. We signed the legal documents for this. I'd agreed that she would be the parent and I would not have rights to the child, so therefore I didn't have rights to anything while she was pregnant.

I was Julia's friend. We had some delicious side benefits, but we were friends and that was it. Maybe in the future I'd have some sort of optional interaction with her and her child but I had to stop thinking about the baby as if I had any claim on him or her.

By the time four o'clock rolled around I was stuck with a patient for a good half of an hour before I could come out and see how Julia was doing. Sheryl had let Julia wait for me in my office without clearing it with me first, but I didn't mind.

"Hey, I should be done shortly. Just one more patient. How did your appointment go?"

"It was good. It's official. I'm having a baby!" She said loudly and jumped up to give me a hug. "Thank you, Mike."

"Yeah, you know, it was a lot of hard work. I'm sure you'll think of a way to thank me," I joked.

"I am actually going to lay down and take a little nap while you finish working. I didn't sleep well last night and I'm exhausted. Would that be alright?"

"Absolutely. In fact, we have a special sleeping room here for when we are on call and running back and forth to the hospital a lot. How about I get you set up in there?"

"Yes, that sounds nice."

"I wouldn't call it nice, but it's better than sleeping on this hard couch," I laughed.

Together we walked to the room at the back of our office

where I showed her our not so fancy sleeping room. It used to be a closet and we had converted it to the sleeping room with a single bed in there and a small night stand next to it. We had investing in a good quality mattress and some nice linens for the bed purely to ensure we could get a good sleep when we were only able to be in there for short amounts of time.

"Thanks, I probably won't be able to actually sleep, but I'll give it a try."

"I'll come get you when I'm done," I said as she sat down on the bed looking utterly exhausted.

After seeing my patient I went back to the sleep room to check on Julia and I was pretty sure what I was going to find when I got there. Sure enough she was fast asleep and I wasn't about to wake her up. I wrote a note telling her I'd be in my office and for her to come over when she woke up. If she hadn't slept at all the night before she needed her sleep more than we needed to hurry off to a date, or dinner, whatever we were calling it.

"I thought you and Julia were going out?" Bruce asked as he walked past my office when he was leaving around six o'clock.

"She fell asleep in the back room and I didn't want to wake her up."

"Oh, you're good," he shook his head as if he knew what secret plan I was up to.

"I'm just letting her sleep for a little bit. She was tired."

"Yeah, you're being the good guy. Let her sleep, be there for her, slip in as the friend she can't live without. I see the long game here."

"I don't know what you're talking about. I'm just trying to be helpful."

"And get laid," he grinned. "I'll see you tomorrow. Enjoy your night," he laughed a little as he headed out for the evening.

Bruce made me sound like some calculating individual that was plotting every detail of the interactions between Julia and I. That wasn't how I was at all. I didn't think and plan things through between us. If at any moment Julia decided to pull away or asked me not to be as involved, I'd comply in a moment. But she seemed to really need someone around. She seemed to like having me around and I liked being there for her.

While I waited for Julia to wake up I worked on my paperwork. By seven o'clock I went to check on her and she was still sound asleep, so I continued with my notes and finished them up for the day of work. I finished around 8:30pm and I didn't want to wake her up but it was getting rather late and I decided I should get her up.

"Julia," I said softly as I sat on the side of the bed.

"Oh, yeah. Sorry. What time is it?"

"It's almost nine," I smiled back at her.

"What? Oh, why did you let me sleep that long? I'm sorry. I bet you're starving," she said up quickly and then looked like she was dizzy and quickly laid back down.

"Stay there, I'm going to check your blood pressure," I hurried and grabbed what I needed and took her pressure. "Have you been eating and drinking okay?"

"I wasn't really hungry today, or thirsty. It was probably the nerves."

"Julia, you're hypotensive. We need to get some fluids in you. If I get you a Gatorade do you think you could drink it?"

"Yes."

She was able to sip on the Gatorade drink for a little bit but I was still worried about her. We certainly weren't going to go out for dinner and I wasn't even sure I felt comfortable having her go back to her house.

"Is Kendra at your apartment tonight?"

"No, I think she's out."

"How about you come home with me then?" I suggested and then quickly added the qualifiers to my question. "Just because I'm really close to here. I have a spare bedroom you can stay in and I have plenty of food and drinks to keep you nourished."

"Okay," she responded without much contemplation.

"Perfect, let's get you some rest."

It was a relief that she had willingly agreed to come with

me. Otherwise I would have had to take her home and stay with her to make sure she was taking care of herself.

We took an Uber to my place. Normally I would have walked but I didn't want Julia exerting any more of her energy than she had to. We pulled up to the building and I noticed her looked at it in awe.

"It's a little big, but the condos are really nice."

"I thought this was an office building. There are all condos?"

"Yep. I think there are forty five or fifty floors. I'm not sure, I guess I don't pay much attention. My condo is on the thirty-fourth floor."

"Wow this place is beautiful," Julia said as we entered the lobby.

"It really is a nice place. Best door staff in the city," I said loud enough so they could hear me. "Oh, and 47 floors," I said as we got in the elevator and looked at the buttons.

"Is there a pool?"

"Oh yeah, there is actually a full gym, pool and business lounge here. They have an outdoor patio area too off the fifth floor. It's a great place."

"Yeah, it looks really expensive too," she laughed.

There was no denying that. It was an expensive place to live, but I had plenty of money and just wanted an easy place to live and get around town. I'd actually bought a two bedroom condo just to make sure I had room for a home office if I ever decided to do that, but I never did. Instead, I used my second bedroom as a spare room for when people came to stay over, like my parents and other friends who wanted to come to town to visit. Although, it really hadn't gotten much use in the last few months at all.

"This is me," I said dramatically as I opened the door to my condo.

"What? Oh, my God, this view. You can see the whole city. Mike, this is so pretty."

"I'm sure all the condos on this side of the building have similar views," I joked. "It is nice though. Especially at night."

Julia stood in front of the floor to ceiling windows for a few minutes while I went to the spare bedroom to make sure it was in order. I hadn't been back there in a while and hoped I didn't have a big mess of things to deal with.

"How about some left over Chinese food?" I asked when I returned to the living room.

"Yep, sounds great," she replied without taking her eyes off of the view.

"Okay, well sit down then. I don't want you passing out. I'll definitely make you go to the hospital if you do that."

"That's silly, you're a doctor."

"Then do as the doctor ordered and sit down so you don't end up at the hospital."

"Wow, you're a mean doctor," Julia laughed as she moved over to the table and sat down facing the view.

"I'm the worst. Good thing you got Doctor Simon instead of me. You would have hated me."

"Probably," she laughed.

"Okay, how are you feeling about sweet and sour chicken vs broccoli and chicken?"

"Sweet and sour."

"And I don't have Gatorade but I do have some flavored sparkling water, will that work?"

"Yep."

"Perfect," I brought over her food and drink and then grabbed mine before joining her at the table.

Julia was distracted by the view and it dawned on me that I really hadn't just sat and enjoyed the view in a long time. It was nice to sit there with her and eat dinner while taking in the magnificent sights of the city.

"I can't believe I actually went through with this," Julia said while still looking out at the city.

"You seemed pretty determined."

"I know, but I often give up on things that take a lot of work. I'm pretty proud that I continued on with this. I'm so excited. This is going to be the start of the rest of my life."

"I bet you're going to be an amazing mother."

"Thank you," she said with a small tear in her eye. "I am going to do the best I can."

Chapter 13

Julia

I slept better than I probably should have over at Mike's. The guest bed was more comfortable than my own bed and once I fell asleep I didn't toss or turn at all. When the sun started to peak in the next morning, I couldn't believe just how great a night of sleep I had gotten.

"Hungry?" Mike asked when I came out of the bedroom after freshening up in the bathroom.

"Starving."

"Then let's get you some food, little lady."

Mike started piling on a bunch of food for me. He had made some sausages, eggs, and pancakes. He poured me a big glass of orange juice and then sat down to eat with me. It was nice being there with him. I felt so safe around Mike, not just physically, but emotionally. I didn't have to worry about chaos at all with him and that was a relief. Plus, it was amazing to know that he could answer any of my pregnancy questions, that took a lot of worry off my plate.

"You're going to get me fat," I laughed as he poured some syrup onto my food.

"You should gain twenty to thirty pounds. And don't worry about what you gain. It's important to eat and take care of yourself. That's all you should worry about. You can always lose the weight after the baby is born."

"Yes, doctor," I said as I ate the food in front of me. I hadplanned to try and be a little picky with my food. Ideally I wanted to eat healthy foods and stay away from sugars and unhealthy carbohydrates, but for this meal I was just going with the flow.

"So what do you have planned today? Your color looks better. Are you feeling dizzy when you stand at all?"

"Nope, no dizziness. I'm feeling pretty good. I was thinking of going shopping for some comfortable clothes. I know I'm not going to be showing anytime soon, but I'd like at least one outfit I can wear when my pants start getting too tight. And if I keep letting you feed me, I suspect that will happen sooner rather than later."

"No way I'm going to stop feeding you, so I guess you better get those pants."

"Yeah, I'll buy a couple pairs just in case."

"Are there shops like that around here? I'll go with you if you'd like. I'm not afraid of a little shopping."

"It's New York, Mike. There are shops for everything all over the place. I'd love some company shopping. I think Kendra is busy this afternoon and I haven't really confirmed the news with anyone else yet."

"Deal. I'm at your service," Mike said as he dramatically bent over.

Shopping with Mike turned out to be really enjoyable. He had a decent sense of style and was able to quickly adapt to the trends in the maternity world. We went into a couple boutique stores and I quickly ruled them out as anything I was willing to pay for. Many of them were charging a couple hundred dollars for their jeans; it was outrageous. I certainly wasn't going to pay that much money for pants that I'd only be wearing for a couple of months.

Finally we found a shop that was in one of the malls. It was a national chain store but they had reasonable prices and a variety of options that I really liked. Not to mention the prices weren't crazy.

"You should get them all," Mike said after I finished trying on a few outfits.

"What? No way, I'm not even showing yet. How do I know what they will look like when I get big and fat? I'll just get this outfit."

"I think you'll look amazing with your baby tummy."

"Really? Amazing?" I asked a little skeptical.

"Yep. You're so darn beautiful now, you'll only get more beautiful as the pregnancy progresses."

"You're such a suck up," I laughed.

"I'm serious, Julia. Do you really not see how beautiful you are?"

"No, not at all."

"I just don't get that. I mean you're a smart, intelligent woman. You have to know you're stunning. Like ten out of ten level of beautiful."

Mike was laying it on thick as he complimented me. There was no way I thought I was a ten out of ten. Maybe an eight on the relative scale for female beauty but sometimes I thought even that was pushing it.

"I'll admit that I'm not hideous," I said.

"Oh, that's all you're going to admit to?"

"Yep, I'm not hideous. Maybe a little above average," I laughed.

"Oh, wow, I can see we have a lot of work to do with you before you're a mother. You don't want your daughter to worry about how she looks, right? You have to see how beautiful you are. It's not like you need to lead with it, but you need to understand it. I bet guys are throwing themselves at you every time you're at the bar."

"No, that does not happen," I laughed.

"I practically threw myself at you."

"No way, I was totally the one flirting with you more. You were all cool and collected."

"I'm good at pretending," Mike said.

I ended up buying one outfit and then we called it a day for shopping. It was fun hanging out with Mike. I'd definitely enjoyed it and as we were saying our goodbyes I decided to see if Mike wanted to visit some more later that evening.

"I'm going to be watching a few more episodes of our series if you want to come over tonight. Kendra will be home and I think she might watch as well. She saw the series already but says she'd like to watch it again."

"Yes, I'd love to," Mike responded freakishly fast.

"Okay then, come on over whenever you'd like."

"Five o'clock sound good?" he asked.

"Yep. I'm probably going to go sleep until then," I laughed. "I'm so tired. I just can't shake this feeling that I need more and more sleep."

"Julia, you are literally making a new human inside you. Sleeping is good. Eating is good. Drinking water is good. You have to do those things to keep your body working."

"Thanks for that reassurance, Mike, I appreciate it."

"Okay, go sleep. I'll see you later," he said as he opened the cab door for me and sent me on my way.

When I got home Kendra was there waiting for me. I could have sworn she said she was going to be gone all day but she looked really worried. Then I pulled my phone out to see what if I had missed any messages from her. Sure enough she'd been texting me all morning and I hadn't responded to any of them.

"So, you're not dead. That's good," she said and rolled her eyes.

"Nope, I'm alive. I'm so sorry I didn't see your messages. I totally got wrapped up with Mike and shopping and I didn't check my phone at all this morning."

"Girl, I thought you were dead on the sidewalk somewhere. Geesh. You text me and tell me you're up and heading out from his house and then don't text me back at all. What are you doing to me, woman?"

"I'm sorry. But Mike is coming over here to watch television and visit tonight, if you'd like to yell some more."

"He's coming here?" She asked and started messing with her hair. "When? How long do I have to get ready?"

She looked like someone who was excited for a boy that they had a crush on to come over. It was a little confusing since Kendra didn't date white guys at all. She exclusively dated men of color and hadn't ventured away from those preferences since I'd known her.

"Why? Are you trying to steal my baby daddy," I laughed.

"No! I don't want him, but I bet he knows some damn fine doctors in this town and I'd really like to meet those friends of his."

"Oh, I see what you're plan is. Make a good impression so he can fix you up. I got you, girl. I'll help you out," I laughed.

She rushed out of the living room and back to her room where she remained for the rest of the evening. By the time

Mike showed up she was done up like she was going out on the town, except she had her sweats on to stay in and watch television.

Kendra was a pretty girl without all the hair and makeup, but she was drop dead gorgeous when she did herself up. A little piece of me thought I should have done my own hair and makeup, but then I remembered that Mike and I were just friends and it didn't matter if I had my hair done when we were hanging out.

"Well, don't you ladies look pretty?" Mike said as we let him into the apartment.

I could tell he was good with people. New people, friends, pretty much anyone felt comfortable around him. There was no denying the charisma he had. It was one of the things that had thrown me off so much when I first met him, but I was started to get used to it now that we had hung out a bit.

Our night of Netflix watching went fantastic. We got through five episodes and it was really fun having Kendra there too. She took the pressure off of the romantic stuff that had been going on between Mike and me so we were all able to just hang out and have fun.

Mike even told her about a few friends of his that he thought she would like, both of them doctors, and when he pulled up his softball league photo, it was clear that Kendra would have taken either one of them. Nearly all the guys on Mike's team looked like they could have posed for GQ magazine. It was a little intimidating knowing that he had so many good looking friends.

"So let's make a plan to go out sometime and we will invite Kendra and I'll invite one of my friends," Mike said when he finally headed home for the night.

"Yes, let's do that," Kendra interrupted and gave Mike a hug. "I swear if you get me one of those men I will owe you for the rest of my life."

Mike just laughed and shook his head. I was pretty sure women tried to get him to hook them up with his friends a lot. But they were probably more interested in hooking up with him if they knew him.

"He is so perfect. I can't believe you're having his baby," Kendra squealed before the door of our apartment was even closed all the way.

"Kendra, he can hear you."

"I don't care," she yelled. "Mike is so handsome," she said teasingly.

"Okay, okay, he is handsome. But he is also a really smart guy and very kind too," I added.

"And you're not going to date him? Tell me you've changed your mind on this. He's perfect Julia. He's the guy for you. This is meant to be, I feel it in my bones."

"Okay, I'll admit that the thought of being more than just friends with Mike has crossed my mind. But I'm planning on just seeing how things go between us. There is no telling how he's going to react as the pregnancy progresses. There is no telling how I'll react. But yes, I'm going to keep the option open of having something more than just friends," I said as Kendra started smiling and jumping up and down. "But only if you stop jumping around like a teenager," I laughed.

***

A few weeks later Sarah and Kendra had put together a list of condos for us to go look at. I had my preapproval from my bank and I was ready to make an offer if something came up that I couldn't live without.

The housing market in New York moved fast. Placed were often sold before they were even put on the market at all. Sarah had come around quickly to the idea of me having a baby. At work she was constantly talking about the best preschools and how I needed to get my unborn baby onto the wait list.

Preschools were not even on my radar yet. I hadn't looked at daycare either. All of that was a little overwhelming for me considering I hadn't even made it to my first ultrasound appointment yet or bought my new condo.

One thing at a time was about all I could do. On this particular weekend I had my eyes focused on the condo search and nothing else. I gave Sarah and Kendra my ideal requirements and they were excited to put together the list of places to see. We invited Mike to come too, but he was on call for the weekend and apparently tons of ladies were going into labor. My realtor arranged a vehicle to take all of us around and we started our search early Saturday morning.

"This first place is a little run down inside, but the building has been updated in the common areas. The price is well below what you were looking for so you'd have plenty of wiggle room for remodeling," my realtor Beth said.

"I'd prefer not to have a remodel job, but I'm open to looking at it since it does have some good square footage."

"That's the big selling point of this place. It's bigger than any of the other places we will look at today."

"Great, let's take a look," Sarah said enthusiastically.

I walked into that first condo with an upbeat opinion and totally open to liking it. But it was a pit. The building was really old, even though they had remodeled, it still didn't look all that great at all. I knew it wasn't the right fit for me.

We continued down the list of places and one after another I was disappointed. Sometimes there was a glaring issue like super small windows, or tiny bedrooms, and other times I just didn't get a good vibe from the building or the location. I was exhausted when we pulled up to the final building for the day.

"Maybe I'll have to do some research on my own," I said.

"I could narrow some places down online."

"Sure, let's just look at this place though. It was over your preapproval budget but they just lowered the price. The owners moved overseas and would really like to unload it."

As I looked up I realized we were at Mike's building. I loved his building. It sounded like an amazing place to live but I really didn't think I could afford a place there. Not a two bedroom like I wanted.

"It's a two bedroom?" I asked.

"No, it's a one bedroom with a den. But I believe the owners added double doors to the den so it's pretty much a two bedroom. It's small, but very nice inside," Beth said.

She went on to list all the amenities of the building and I was hooked. I knew I liked the place when I had visited Mike, but the idea of living there was just amazing. I could see raising my child there. I could see living there for a very long time. It felt right. The building felt right.

When we got into the apartment I knew it was mine. I felt at home from the moment I walked in there. The place was empty and as the sun was starting to set I walked up to the windows and looked out at the view. It was a little different than Mike's view, but still unbelievably gorgeous.

"It's eight hundred square feet, but that's big for this area of town. Plus, it's a newer building and you shouldn't have many issues for several years."

I walked into the bedroom, explored the bathrooms, but

when I stepped into the den I knew I was going to make an offer. It was the perfect size for a baby room and had some beautiful built-in book shelves.

"Let's make an offer," I said to Beth.

"What are you thinking? Maybe go in about ten percent below their asking?"

"Sure, but I'll pay their list price if I have to."

"They just lowered the price today, so they might want that list price. But your preapproval will go far with them. A guaranteed sale at a little lower price might just go through. Sign these and I'll get the offer over to them. It's late and they are overseas so we probably won't hear back until tomorrow though."

We did all the things that needed to be signed right there in the apartment and Kendra, Sarah and I went out for drinks to celebrate afterwards. Of course, my drink was just a fruit juice, but it was still nice to have a night out with my friends.

"Do you think I should have asked Mike before buying a place in his building?" I asked the girls.

"Oh, Mike lives in that building?" Sarah said looking really worried.

"Yeah, is that bad? I stayed there the other night. Loved the building but didn't think it was in my budget."

"So he doesn't know you were considering a place in his building?" Kendra chimed in.

"No, but now you guys have me worried. Is this bad? I mean he likes the building. I would think he'd be okay with me being in a nice place."

"I don't think it's about you being in a nice place," Sarah added. "I'm just worried he might think you're trying to get him to co-parent or be more involved than he wants to be."

"He's pretty involved right now," I laughed.

"I know, but there's no actual baby right now. I'm just worried that he will not take it well," Sarah added.

"I'm sure he will be fine," Kendra said reassuringly. "He's not going to care. But you should text him or tell him before you end up running into him in the elevator."

"Of course. I mean, we are talking all the time. I'll tell him right now," I said as I pulled my phone out.

"Oh, no, this is not a text messaging sort of thing. He needs to see your face and you need to see his. Tell him in person. Where is he right now?"

"I think he's at the hospital," I said.

"Then go there. Offer to bring him dinner or something and talk to him," Sarah added. "The last thing you need is him freaking out and thinking you're some sort of stalker."

"Stalker?" I laughed. "He wouldn't think that!"

"Did you forget how he reacted when you showed up at his office?" Kendra added. "You need to nip this in the bud early so you don't have to worry about it. I'm sure it's going to be fine, but you need to tell him tonight."

"Fine," I said as I sent Mike a text and offered to drop off dinner and tell him about my condo shopping. "I'm texting him now."

Within five minutes he responded and I made plans to meet up with him in an hour. The girls decided to stay at the bar and keep drinking their real drinks, while I grabbed a cab and made my way to the hospital.

I stopped and grabbed some delicious burgers for us to eat and only ended up being a few minutes late. Unfortunately, Mike had just been called into deliver a baby and I ended up sitting in the lounge for two hours before he was finally able to get a moment free.

"Well it's cold, but mine was delicious," I said when he finally came in.

"Thank you so much. You didn't have to wait though. It's getting so late."

"I know, but I had to tell you about the condo I put an offer in on. It's in your building," I said going straight for my news.

I'd decided that showing any sort of trepidation would only make it seem worse that I hadn't talked to him first. Instead, I was going full force with the excitement and I was putting on a good show too. I smiled big and tried my best to look really excited, which I was, but I was also really nervous to see how Mike was going to react to my news.

"That's good. It is a nice building. But I thought you said you couldn't afford it?" He asked as he ate his burger.

"I didn't think I could. But there was a one bedroom with a den that was just reduced. It will work nicely for a baby room. It's on the fifteenth floor. Looks over the water more than the city but it has a nice view."

"Julia, that's great. You're really going to like that building and it will be a great place to raise your baby," he said and then went right back to eating.

Mike continued to eat his food without talking at all. We sat there in silence and I realized there was definitely an issue with me buying this condo and not giving him a little warning about it first. He wasn't rude about it at all, he was kind and said all the right things, but Mike was pulling away from me for sure.

"So we will see if I end up getting it or not. The offer is in, so I should know by tomorrow."

"That's good news, I better get going. It's a busy night," and just like that Mike was gone.

He didn't give me our usual hug goodbye. There were no sweet reminders for me to eat more or drink more water. He was just gone. My heart sank at the possibility that I had upset him by buying a condo in his building, but I was trying to give him some time. He didn't say he was upset. He didn't act upset. Perhaps he was just busy.

The next morning when the condo sale was approved, I

sent a text message to Mike to let him know it had gone through. I didn't get a response back that morning at all. That's when I knew something was really wrong. He didn't text me back later that night either. In fact, it wasn't until Monday afternoon that he finally replied with a thumbs-up emoji. That was it, two days later and all I got was an emoji. This was not good at all. This was bad.

Mike probably thought I was trying to force him into a co-parenting thing or make our friends with benefits relationship something more. And although I definitely wouldn't turn him down for either of those options, I honestly didn't buy the condo intending for him to be anything more than a friend.

Nothing had changed. I was still perfectly fine with being a single mother. I was just going to do it from a kick ass condo that happened to be a few floors down from where he lived. Where I lived didn't have to matter. The building was huge and it was likely I wasn't going to see him at all even if we lived there together. There were thousands of people that lived there. But I couldn't shake the sinking feeling in my stomach and the idea that Mike and I might have just broken off our friendship because of my condo purchase.

Chapter 14

Mike

A month went by with Julia and I only barely talking over text messaging. I definitely didn't want to be that jerky guy who blew her off, but I also didn't like how fast she had moved into my building without giving me any sort of heads up. I didn't care that she bought a condo in my building, but I also wasn't sure I wanted to be locked into this thing we had going on. A nice, fun, friends with benefits relationship seemed ideal, but if she was living right next to me I honestly didn't know how to handle that.

I threw myself into my work that month. Taking on more patients and working on our business plan for expansion. It took every bit of my energy, mostly because I didn't like the guilt that was eating away at me because I had been blowing Julia off.

When Taylor called and wanted to head out for drinks at the local sports bar, I agreed. A night on the town might be just what I was looking for.

"I can call up some girls to keep us company if you want?" Taylor offered.

"Not tonight, man. I just want to drink and watch the

game."

"I hear ya. Ladies are just trouble."

"Very true. Trouble and a headache," I added.

When we got to the bar there wasn't a table left in the place. It was packed with people there to enjoy their weekend. Taylor and I found a spot at the bar after a few minutes of rummaging around and finally settled in with a couple of drinks.

"So what's new with you?" He asked.

"Not much. Well, I'm expanding the practice soon, that's exciting."

"Really? I'm surprised."

"Why? We are doing great. I'm surprised you still work under the big umbrella of the hospital. You know you'd make a ton more money out on your own."

"I don't know, it seems like a lot more trouble than it's worth. The way things are now I can show up, clock my hours and go home. I don't work weekends. I'm never on call. I get a flat salary and don't have to worry about billing; it's a pretty sweet gig. I actually thought that you would end up coming over to my side sooner or later."

"But what are you getting paid, like two hundred thousand?"

"Try four," Taylor said with a flashy smile.

"You're just a family doc and they are paying you four?

That's outrageous," I was in shock. I'd always assumed the pay through the hospital was much lower.

"I mean, it doesn't hurt that I made New York's most eligible bachelor list. You know I've got a full practice and no one is cancelling their appointments."

"Ahh, so you have all the hot mom's coming to see you. I get it."

"Yeah, but I think it's mainly about productivity. Still, I know you're making well into the seven figures at your practice. But you're working all those nights and weekends. You are going to burn yourself out sooner or later."

"That's why we are..." I trailed off as I looked toward the doorway and saw Julia coming into the bar with Kendra and two of my friends. One of them was the guy who I shared Kendra's number with and the other was a mutual friend of both of ours.

"What?" Taylor asked as he noticed my attention had clearly been diverted. "Oh, damn those girls are hot. Devon and Patrick have some good taste in ladies."

"That brunette is the one having my baby," I said and then realized I hadn't exactly filled Taylor in on the whole back story to that comment.

"You're having a baby? Why is she out with him then? She's a knock out. Is she crazy? Did you have to dump her because she was crazy?" Taylor had known a few crazy women of his own over the years, so that was of course the first thing that popped into his mind.

"It's a long story. She's an old friend and asked me to be her sperm donor."

"That wasn't very long."

"I can't believe she's dating," I said almost to myself as I watched the bar manager open up a table just for their group in the corner.

Patrick was a high powered real estate agent in town. He knew everyone and everyone knew him. If you were buying a large business property or a multimillion dollar condo, you went through Patrick.

I could barely contain myself as I watch Julia flirting with Patrick and him returning the affection. They clearly liked one another. They looked more comfortable than a first date. I couldn't take it any longer and looked back toward Taylor.

"Why can't you believe she's dating? She's a beautiful girl."

"She's pregnant. She wanted to have a baby so bad that she asked me to be a donor. I would have thought she was going to concentrate on motherhood."

"She doesn't look pregnant in that dress. She looks like she's trying to get pregnant," Taylor laughed at his own joke.

"Well, she is pregnant. About two months along so she's not showing yet. I really hope she told Patrick about the baby. It would be a pretty shitty thing to be going out with him and letting him like her if she wasn't planning on continuing to date him."

"Wow, okay, so did you sleep with this girl to get her pregnant? Is that what's going on here?" Taylor looked a little confused by all my emotion over Julia being out on a date. Hell, I was even a little confused about it.

"We slept together but she used a donation for the insemination. It's part of the long story I was talking about before."

Just then Patrick and Devin happened to notice us and motioned for Taylor and me to come and sit with them. We all played softball together and hung out a lot. It wasn't unusual for any of us to invite the others over, but I absolutely didn't want to sit next to Patrick while he was flirting with Julia.

"Let's go over," Taylor said as he hopped up.

"I'm not going."

"Now that would look weird. You have to go. And if you don't want her dating other people then maybe you should consider dating her yourself. Just an idea," he walked over to the table and left me there at the bar. I had no other choice but to go join them.

The walk over was torture. I did my best not to look Julia in the eyes, but eventually we made eye contact. She smiled at me and that just made me feel worse for not keeping in touch with her the last few weeks.

"Hey guys, what are you doing out without some pretty ladies on your arms?" Patrick asked.

"Just grabbing a drink and having a chat," Taylor said.

"How are you?" I mouthed toward Julia as the guys were talking.

"Good," she smiled back at me.

She looked good. Her hair was pulled back in a tight ponytail and she had a skin tight black dress on. It showed off all her curves which I absolutely thought were becoming more defined. She was rocking a pair of black heels and had her makeup done. She was dressed to impress Patrick and that made my stomach swirl.

Why was she dating? I mean really. Wasn't the whole purpose of going on a date to see if you could find someone for a relationship? There was no way Patrick was going to want to date her if she was pregnant and no way Julia was going to get herself in some sort of relationship mess while she was preparing for her baby. I didn't understand at all what was going on.

When the waiter came to the table to drop off the drinks that Kendra, Julia, and the guys had ordered, Julia was drinking plain ice water. If that wasn't a tell-tell sign that she was pregnant I wasn't sure what was. No girl went on a date with a guy like Patrick and just ordered water, they usually wanted to drink for free all night long with him.

"Julia's pregnant," Patrick announced to the table as if

the child was his or something. "Don't worry, it's not mine. We haven't been on that many dates yet," he laughed. "But isn't that exciting? I think it's really brave of you to do this on your own."

I'm pretty sure my mouth was actually open as I watched Patrick lean in and give Julia a kiss on the lips. What sort of weird parallel world was I in? I had no idea what was going on. And then I felt sick. My stomach had been rumbling since I saw Julia and I finally couldn't take it any longer. I excused myself and made a bee-line for the restroom.

I barely made it into the stall before everything in my stomach was emptied into the toilet. My hands were shaking, I was sweating, I felt like I could hardly breath and yet I'd felt fine only a few minutes earlier.

"Everything okay in here?" I heard Taylor ask from the doorway.

When I came out of the stall it was clear that I was not okay. My breathing was rapid, I was having a full-blown panic attack. I'd had them before, not many over my life, but I knew what it was. Normally I was only panicked about things like the ten year lease I signed for my business or the tests I took in college. This was a whole new level of panic and over a woman, which I'd never had before.

"A panic attack, eh?" Taylor said as he got a paper towel wet and handed it to me. "On your neck. You know the drill."

"Dude, I don't know why I'm freaking out. She's not my

girlfriend or anything. She can date whoever she wants to."

"Maybe you should figure that out sooner rather than later."

"So Patrick is just dating her and doesn't care that she's pregnant?"

"Well, I don't think he knows it's your baby. He wouldn't have been acting like that. But nowadays you have to hold onto a stable woman when you find one. I've dated women with kids before; it's not a big deal."

"But she's still cooking her kid. Like she literally just got pregnant. You don't think that's weird that he's dating her?"

"I think pregnant women are sexy as fuck. I can't wait to be married and bone my wife all throughout her pregnancy." Taylor wasn't even the person I thought he was. I had no idea what was going on. My hard line friends were now pro-pregnancy and talking about their sexual fetishes with pregnant women.

"Go talk to her. Or talk to her tomorrow when she's done with her date. Just clear whatever is going on between you. I've never seen you this crazy over a girl."

"I know." I didn't actually know until that moment though.

"You need to ask her out. You can figure the rest out on the way. Don't let her run to Patrick."

"She might not say yes. Patrick didn't dick her over like I did," I shrugged.

"Trust me, I saw how she looked at you as you walked over. She would rather have you."

I hoped Taylor was right about that. I really did. There was no possible way I could sit back and watch Patrick become the father to my baby. Was it my baby? No, not in the legal sense, but I felt responsible and I wanted to be in Julia's life.

There was no way I knew what to do next. Nothing was certain. Nothing was planned. All I knew was that I had to let Julia know that I wanted to date her. Not like a casual thing where we were messing around and just being friends. I wanted to give it a go. A real try.

Taylor left me in the bathroom while I calmed down a little more. It was nearly fifteen minutes before I finally felt put together enough to head back out into the bar. When I finally came out and walked down the hallway, there was Julia waiting to talk to me.

She had her arms crossed and looked like she had been standing there for a long time. It was a little embarrassing how long I'd been in the bathroom; certainly she was thinking I was doing something on the toilet and not throwing up.

"Hey," I managed to say as I leaned next to her on the wall. "So Patrick, he's a nice guy."

"He really is a nice guy."

"How long have you two been going out?"

"This is our second date with Kendra and Devin. Sort of a double date thing we have going on. It's nice. Takes the pressure off of the need for conversation and stuff like that. There is always someone who's willing to talk if I don't want to."

She laughed nervously and that made me feel much better. But things between us were weird, off, or different from how they had been a few weeks before. It was all my fault and I knew it.

"I'm sorry I've been quiet lately," I said trying not to totally admit to purposely not responding to her messages.

"Oh, is that what you call it? I just call you a jerk when I talk about you to Kendra," she teased and elbowed me a little. "I know you're just trying to figure things out. That's what I'm doing to."

"And dating Patrick," I threw in there.

"Well I wouldn't exactly call it dating. We have been on a couple of dates. But nothing serious," she said sweetly as she leaned toward me.

Instantly relief washed over my body as I saw the expression on Julia's face while she was looking at me. She clearly had feelings for me, or at the very least she liked me. I was such an idiot for pushing her away.

"Would you be interested in going on a date with me?" I asked, unsure of what her response would be and feeling less confident than I normally did when I asked a woman out.

"A real date?"

"Yeah, like one where I come pick you up. You wear a sexy dress like this. I buy you dinner, you know the kind," I said and motioned with my head over to the table where Patrick was still sitting.

"Hmmm, I think I've vaguely heard of such things."

"But yes, it would be a real date. I think we should give it a try. I mean we can always go back to ignoring each other if it doesn't work out," I laughed.

"Or you could go back to ignoring me?" She raised her eyebrows. "Because I wasn't ignoring you at all."

"Yes, or you could join in this time if you need to."

"Yes, Mike, I would like to go on a real date with you. I would like to dress up and do my hair and have you pick me up and take me out. That sounds like a great idea."

For a minute I thought Julia was going to lean in and kiss me. Her mouth was pouty as she licked her lips and leaned in closer to me. Patrick was only a few feet away. I couldn't believe she would even consider kissing me like that. But she didn't, instead she gave me a hug and motioned for the two of us to rejoin our group at the table.

As we slid back into the booth I immediately noticed that Julia was not flirting with Patrick nearly as much as she had been doing earlier. It dawned on me that she could have been flirting with him on purpose to make me a little jealous. Although, she had gone on two dates with the guy with no intention of making me jealous at all; she just was having a good time.

My heart skipped a little at the notion of Julia 'having a good time' with Patrick. Normally I wouldn't have thought a girl like Julia would sleep with a guy on the first date. She seemed like the sort of girl who tested the waters a little before she ever considered sleeping with the guy. Maybe a couple of dates first or even a half dozen dates. But I knew she made exceptions to that rule because she had made one for me.

The entire rest of the evening I stared at the television screens in the bar and avoiding conversations among our group. I could hear them talking and I tried to keep up with what they were saying, but I couldn't stand the thought of seeing Julia sitting there with Patrick. I kept wondering if they'd kissed yet. Or if they had gone to bed together. My mind was a horrible place to be when I was thinking about Julia, but then other times it was the best possible place in the world.

When the night wrapped up Patrick loaded Julia and Kendra into a car and went with them back to their place. Apparently Devin was going in an entirely different direction home and Patrick was going to have the Uber drop the girls off first and then go to his house. He was a good guy.

That was probably one of the reasons I worried so much

about Julia being out with Patrick. Not because he was a terrible guy for her to go on a date with, but instead I worried because he wasn't a terrible guy. I couldn't help but think that Julia might actually like him and that just killed me to think of.

Chapter 15

Julia

"I'm so tired of packing boxes," I groaned as Kendra and I were putting together another box in the kitchen. "Are you sure you don't want to just keep all this stuff?"

"No, you can't afford to buy all new kitchen stuff and I'm looking forward to restyling this place after you leave."

"What? You don't like my style?"

"I like it just fine, I just want to try something new. Plus, it will be nice to move over to your bedroom. I've always wanted the big bedroom here."

Kendra and I were the best roommates. Even the arguments we had weren't actual arguments. I couldn't have imagined sharing an apartment for as long as I had with anyone else.

I was a home owner now. If something went wrong, it was my responsibility to pay for it. That was huge for me. All the changes in my life were good though. I sort of liked the idea that everything was happening at the same time. That meant that when everything was done, then I'd have this whole new life that was super cool.

"Have you gone on that date with Mike yet?" Kendra asked as she lifted a box of cups and brought it to the pile by the door.

"Not yet. We have both been so busy that it's crazy. I'm actually going later tonight. Well, if no one goes into labor before five o'clock. After that Bruce is going to take call for the rest of the evening."

"Oh, you call your doctor Bruce now?"

"Just because that's what Mike always calls him. When I go to the office I still call him Doctor Simon. I'm actually going in for an ultrasound soon. Should get to know the sex of the baby, if I want to. But I haven't really decided yet. Do you think I should find out?"

Kendra was laughing as I talked, but not because of me, she was looking at a text message on her phone. She had been seeing Devin for a few weeks now and the two of them were really hitting it off. He was an ear, nose, and throat doctor. Not exactly the sort of doctor that I would think of as a sexy profession, but he made good money, had a stable career, and Devin was really into Kendra.

"Sorry, what were you saying?" She said as she looked up and realized I was standing there waiting for her.

"How is Devin?" I laughed.

"He's so good. I mean really, really good. I like him at dangerous levels."

"What are dangerous levels?"

"I'm not even looking at dating anyone else. I haven't responded to other people's text messages flirting with me at all. I agreed to go out with him both Friday and Saturday nights. Something is wrong, it's dangerous. I don't think I'm ready for this level of relationship yet."

"Kendra, you have to go with the flow. Just see how things turn out. It's okay to just date one guy at a time. You should have some fun and stop worrying about what things are supposed to look like. Just have fun."

I was talking to her like I had some expert experience in serious dating, which I absolutely did not. I could be the worst dater in the whole city, or pretty damn close. Now I was pregnant and trying to date; that was silly and I knew it.

The only way I could mentally wrap my brain around going on the double date with Patrick and Devin was to come out and tell Patrick what I was doing. I did my best to push him away and make the whole thing a friendship date that we were going on just to support Kendra and Devin, but Patrick didn't care at all that I was pregnant.

In fact, a lot of guys had been flirting with me lately, more than usual. Not the normal type of guys like at a bar, I'd been getting hit on at the gym, the coffee shop and even by potential clients from the hotel. I chalked it up to the pregnancy glow and told most of them no, but Patrick ended up being a fun date. Well the first one was, the second one I saw Mike and how pitiful he looked when he saw me out with another guy.

When Mike finally called to schedule a real date with me I was well beyond the stage of needing to keep him as a friend. I clearly had some feelings for him and he had some for me so going on a real date was a good idea. However things turned out from there was up to us. If dating wasn't our thing we would just have to figure out how to go back to being friends. The truth was, I didn't have the energy to worry about my relationship with Mike any longer. I had too many other things going on in my life to worry about now.

"I like this new Julia. The super chill, laid back girl who is telling me to relax," Kendra smiled back at me.

"Yeah, I'm liking the new me too. I can't believe I was so worried about everything all the time. Clearly I just needed to get knocked up and I'd be able to calm down."

"Ha, I'd be crazy if I was pregnant. I couldn't handle that level of responsibility."

"Yeah, sometimes I'm worried about being a mom. But most of the time I think about how amazing it's going to be. I'm lucky that I have a good job and good friends like you though. That makes it easier for me to think that I can make it through all of this in one piece."

"Girl, you are going to make it through this just fine. You are one of the most put together people I know."

"Thank you, Kendra," I said as I hugged her and started crying.

"Oh, no, this again?"

"I know, I just can't help it. I'm going along fine and then suddenly my emotions overwhelm me and I'm sobbing. I guess pregnancy hormones are to blame, right?"

"Probably. So do you know what you're going to wear on your date tonight? It doesn't look like you are showing much, are you?"

"Not really. I mean my tight jeans need to be unbuttoned, but other than that I could wear just about anything. I don't like the tight dresses though, my boobs feel like they have doubled in size and are going to explode out of them."

"Your girls have gotten bigger. A nice side effect of pregnancy I guess."

My breasts were busting out of everything I owned. I found myself wearing a sports bra to work just to keep them in check and fit into my shirts that I own. It was one of the after effects of pregnancy that I hadn't really considered. I didn't own many shirts for work that fit, even if I wasn't showing very much, purely because of the level of boobs I had going on.

Kendra and I talked about going shopping for some more clothes but instead I made adjustments where I could for my work outfits. All my casual stuff fit just fine because it was t-shirts and other stretchy materials.

"I don't know how nice it is, but I suspect Mike won't mind."

"How about that sun dress I got when we were in

Cancun? I bet it would fit you now with those new jugs of yours."

"Sure, I'll give it a try. But it is November; not sure a sun dress is the most appropriate thing to wear," I said as I looked out at the blustering day.

"We will pair it with some tights and a cardigan. It will be fantastic."

Kendra went right to work putting together a perfect date outfit for me. I couldn't have been more grateful. Planning what to wear was so low on my priority list I honestly might have just gone out in the sweatpants and t-shirt that I'd been packing in all day.

After an hour of sorting through both of our closets for the perfect pair of tights to go with the perfect cardigan, we had the outfit. The dress did fit me well, but there was no doubt my breasts were bigger. They could barely be contained by the dress. I sort of liked the new look though.

Even when I was younger I'd imagined getting breast augmentation or hoped that my boobs would get bigger, and now they were. The flowery dress fit me nicely and wasn't too tight around my belly. Even though I wasn't really showing yet, I did have a fuller stomach than normal and was really self conscious of it. People would just think I was fat, instead of pregnant at this stage of the game.

"He should be here soon," I said as I looked at the text from Mike.

"What? No!" Kendra hurried into my bathroom and then motioned for me to get in there too. "Your hair, your make up. Come on, girl. We need to finish you up."

"He's seen me without my hair and makeup done plenty of times," I laughed as she plugged the curling iron in and started working on my face.

"This is your first official date, Julia. Don't be lazy." Kendra handed me my makeup pallet so I could do my face while she started working on my hair.

I really had no choice in the matter and did as Kendra ordered. I kept my makeup light but did put on an extra coat of mascara to highlight my eyes. When all was said and done I didn't look half bad for a woman who was three months pregnant.

"He's here," I said and hurried out to the speaker to wait to buzz him in.

"Okay, keep your cool tonight. This is just a date. It's no big deal. Don't worry about the happily ever after stuff. Just have fun and be yourself," Kendra said acting more nervous than I was.

"I'm fine, Kendra. But you look a little nervous."

"Awww, I want you two to work out so badly. You're the cutest couple. But I know it might end up with you guys just being friends and I totally get that too. Okay, I'm going to stop talking now," she pretended to zip her lip as the buzzer sounded and I let Mike into the building.

"I'm just going on a date like any other date between the two of us. I'm relaxed. I don't know why you're so worried."

Kendra just shook her head back and forth and pretended to zip her lip again. She was funny and a great friend too. I knew what she was talking about. The idea of ending up with Mike was obviously crossing my mind too, but I wasn't focusing on it at all. My expectation was that we were going to go on a date or two and then end up deciding to just be friends.

Having a baby was a huge deal and dating someone who was having a baby was a big deal too. Plus, Mike had some emotions going on about being the donor to my baby and as much as I tried to separate my mind from the Mike in front of me and the Mike who was growing inside me, I couldn't. I suspected that Mike had a hard time with it as well.

I pulled the door open on the first knock. Expecting to see him standing there in a something casual, instead I was surprise to see he had on a button-up shirt with nice slacks and fancy shoes.

"For you," he said sweetly and handed me a bouquet of flowers. "I picked them myself... from the flower shop," he joked. His smile lit up my apartment. It was contagious. The flowers were amazingly beautiful, a perfect combination of yellow, pinks and reds. Not just roses, but a mix of several different flowers that all worked together very nicely.

"Thank you. I'll put them in some water," I said as I went toward the kitchen and realized we had packed up most of everything that was in there.

"Give me those. I'll figure it out. You two go have fun," Kendra said as she smiled like the Cheshire cat at the two of us.

"You are moving into your new place soon?" Mike asked looking at all the boxes.

"Yep."

"I could get some of the guys to help you move if you need help."

"That's so nice of you," Kendra said as she stepped in between the two of us. "Isn't that such a nice thing to offer? I mean moving in New York, wow, that's a tough thing. You're a really nice guy, Mike. Don't you think he's a nice guy, Julia?"

"Thank you for the offer, but I've hired a company to do it for me. You're more than welcome to help me unpack once I get there though. I am not looking forward to that. And I think we should get going," I said as I looked wide eyed at Kendra and hoped she wasn't going to keep pushing with her agenda.

"Have a great night, guys. You look adorable together..." she said as I shut the door on her and hurried Mike down the hallway.

"She likes you," I said.

Mike held the elevator door open for me and then came in and stood right next to me. His hand grazed against mine and the soft touch of his skin was welcomed so much by my body that I tingled all over.

"I like Kendra. She's a good friend to you. Seems like a very nice woman. You look amazing tonight. Did I tell you that yet? I was thinking it, but I might not have said it out loud."

"Thank you. It's getting a little harder to find things that fit well," I adjusted the top of my dress and pulled it up to cover my breasts a little more.

"That dress fits you perfectly," he mischievously smiled as he watched me adjust it.

"I know. They are huge, aren't they?" I said looking at my own breasts. "It's like they have a mind of their own."

"Hello, ladies," Mike said leaning down and talking to my breasts. "I'm excited to take you girls out tonight."

"Stop," I laughed and pushed him playfully away as the elevator opened on the main floor. "They are getting so big and they hurt too."

"They are just doing their job. Part of the amazing job a woman's body is capable of," Mike said as if it was no big deal.

Sometimes I forgot that Mike was so familiar with the pregnancy stuff. He obviously knew more about pregnancy than I did and I really should have been using him more for questions.

It had been nearly a month since we saw each other at

the sports club and a month before that since we had argued about the new condo. As Mike held the door open for me and we loaded into the hired car he had waiting, I realized that I definitely missed having him around as a friend.

Once inside the fancy black SUV, Mike moved over so he was sitting next to me in the long bench seat. He gently grabbed my hand and pulled it up to his lips, taking an extra long time kissing the back of it before placing both of our hands in his lap.

"I missed you," he said softly. "I'm glad we finally got this date scheduled."

"Yeah, I missed talking to you for sure."

We sat in silence for a little bit, but it wasn't that weird sort of silence that happened when people were arguing. Instead, I was wrapped up in how comfortable I felt there with Mike. Even after two months of barely seeing each other, I felt safe and calm sitting with him in that car. My leg was bouncing up and down with a little bit of nerves though and I was doing my best to control it.

Going out with Mike was a big deal. It was a bigger deal than I had let myself understand until I was there in the back of that car with him. This was the real deal. This was our first true effort at seeing if what was between us was more than just friends.

"How do you feel about steak?" Mike asked.

"Oh, my God are we going for steak? I've been craving

meat so bad lately that I made myself a steak at home the other night."

"I know," he smiled back at me. "This is the stage where your body is lacking iron and other nutrients. Are you taking your vitamins?"

"Yeah, of course."

"Make sure to eat lots of dark green vegetables too," he added and then quickly flipped back into date mode. "This restaurant is supposed to be really good. I read some reviews online and everyone loves it."

"Did you have to murder anyone to get a table?"

"Nope, actually Patrick got the table for us," Mike said only showing a small crack of a smile.

"You told Patrick that we were going on a date and he helped you get a reservation?" I asked, a little surprised that Patrick would put that sort of effort in after I told him I couldn't see him anymore because my life was too complicated.

"Yep, he likes me," Mike joked.

"You know I only went on a date with him because Kendra needed a double," I added.

"And because he's an awesome dude."

"Well, there was that," I laughed. "But I saw you and right away all I wanted to do was be with you that night. I'm glad we figured things out and are going out tonight."

"Me too," Mike pulled my hand in even closer to him. "I've missed you," he said again.

There was a true sincerity in Mike's words that hit me hard. I felt my eyes welling up and the tears forming faster than I could stop them. I looked up and tried to count in an effort to distract myself, but then I felt a soft piece of fabric being placed in my hand.

"What's this?"

"For the tears," he said softly as I put the handkerchief up to my eyes.

"You carry a handkerchief around?" I had to laugh a little. "I'm just a little surprised by that."

"I carry it around when I'm going on a date with a highly hormonal woman who is at the end of her first trimester of pregnancy."

"Wow, I can see that your level of knowledge about my medical state could get really annoying," I laughed.

"I'm not trying to be annoying about it. Just sensitive to what you are going through."

"Yeah, yeah, yeah," I teased as I finished wiping my tears.

"Thank you for agreeing to go on a date with me. I'm excited to show you a good time tonight," Mike said thoughtfully.

He held my door open for me and set his hand at the base of my back as he guided me into the restaurant. Mike held my seat out for me and made sure he was sitting next to me instead of across from me for our meal. When the steak came I could hardly hold myself back from eating it up so quickly that I could have choked on it. A little conversation in between bites was about all I could manage as I did my best to feed the growing beast inside of me.

"Did you have an ultrasound with Bruce yet? I don't think I saw you come in."

"Just a quick check of the heartbeat with a Doppler thing so far. I'm having the ultra sound in a couple of weeks. Would you like to come?"

"I would."

"Sure, I'll let you know when I get back to my calendar. I think it was on a Wednesday, but not sure. I'd love to have you there."

"Are you going to find out the gender?" Mike asked trying to look casual about the question.

"I'm not sure. I mean I really want to know, but I also like the idea of it being a surprise. The problem is that I want to buy nursery items and I don't want everything to be yellow. I don't really like yellow at all."

"I'm sure you'll come to a decision that is right for you," Mike said and then shoved a piece of meat in his mouth as if he was trying not to say anything more.

"Do you think I should find out?" I asked as I ate my steak too.

"It's your pregnancy. I don't want to intrude with my ideas. This is your thing. You do whatever you feel is going to work for you."

"That's a very politically correct answer," I put my fork down and leaned in. "What would you do if you and I were together? If this baby had come naturally and you felt like you were an actual partner in this decision. What would you say then?"

"I'd say that this is one of the last true surprises out there and you could always decorate the nursery after the baby is born. The baby won't be in there at first anyways. You'll have them in your room in a bassinet next to your bed. But that's just my opinion and I know that doesn't matter in this situation."

"Shit! I have to get a bassinet too?" I said and put my fork down as I rolled my eyes. "I swear I'm going to be the most unprepared mother in the world."

"No," he laughed. "You would have figured it out after the first night of having your baby in the other room and realizing you didn't want to be that far away from them. Trust me, mother nature has a way of helping moms figure out what they need."

"I do like the idea of not finding out the gender. I'm a bit of a planner though so it's hard to imagine waiting until after the baby is born to do all the nursery stuff."

We sat and ate quietly for a few moments and then Mike glanced at his watch and looked a little panicked. He motioned for the waiter to bring the check and then downed the rest of his glass of wine as he nervously waited for me to finish eating.

I was waiting for him to tell me where we were going or why it was so urgent that we hurry up, but he never rushed me. He sat there quietly watching me finish my meal. When I finally managed to wrangle the last bite of my steak into my mouth Mike threw his napkin on the table and came around to pull my chair out.

"Where are we going in such a hurry?" I laughed.

"The show is starting in twenty minutes. I guess I timed the date a little poorly."

"We are going to a show?" I said as I started to tear up again. "I haven't been to a show in ages."

He handed me his handkerchief again and we rushed out to the waiting black SUV. After helping me into the vehicle, this time Mike just slid in next to me and moved me into the middle seat.

"Need to get to the Booth Theatre as soon as possible," Mike told the driver.

"Yes, sir," the driver responded.

"Man I hope we aren't late. They won't let us in. The Booth Theatre is a stickler on showing up on time. We'd have to wait until intermission and then we would have missed the whole first half of the show."

"It's okay," I replied and grabbed Mike's hand. "We will

make it."

Sure enough we did make it. We were probably one of the last people to get through the doors before they shut them, but we quickly shuffled into our seats just as the lights went down and the show started.

Seeing a Broadway show seems like something we New Yorkers would do all the time. Before moving to the city I imagined that I'd spend every weekend at the theater. But life didn't turn out like that. I often had a full day of plans on Saturdays and Sundays and never put aside the time to go to the theater. That was why going with Mike was even more special.

We sat holding hands throughout the first act and both were mesmerized by the performers. One was a highly known movie actor who was doing a short stint on Broadway. I always assumed those actors just did theater as a way of boosting their name a little, but this guy truly was good. He was fantastic on stage. So good that I forgot all about the last action flick that I'd seen him in and only saw him as portraying the character he was in the play.

"This was a great idea," I whispered to Mike at intermission. "I'm so glad we came."

"I thought you might enjoy it. It doesn't hurt that the actor is shirtless the whole show either," he teased.

"I hardly noticed because his acting is so fantastic."

Mike just laughed as he guided me up to the lobby and

we grabbed something to drink while we talked for a few minutes. I absolutely loved being at the theater and being around other people who enjoyed going to the shows.

"I wish I came to the theater more often. I feel like a bad New Yorker," Mike said.

"Me too! I was just thinking that. It is always what people ask me to do when they come visit and I think that is the only time I go. It is a waste to not come more often."

"I'll take you anytime you'd like," he said and pulled me in close to him.

I liked being there in his arms. We leaned against the wall and he kept one arm around me as we sipped our drinks and enjoyed a few moments together. I was so calm there with him. It wasn't at all like a first date. I didn't feel the need to constantly be flirting with him or pretending he was funny; I was just myself and that was relaxing.

Mike smelled like a combination of cologne and bacon. I thought I'd smelled it before when he picked me up but I dismissed my senses as being disrupted because of my pregnancy, but as we stood there I could definitely smell bacon.

"Did you cook bacon today?" I said as I leaned in and took a big whiff of his shirt.

"Are you smelling me?" he laughed.

"You smell like bacon. I'm pretty sure it's bacon. Did you could bacon?"

Mike was laughing at me as he sipped his drink and didn't answer me. I was much more sensitive to smells now and I was sure that he smelled like bacon. That was just weird. Not that I minded. I'd been eating way too much bacon lately and been a little addicted to it. I ended up eating two pieces before bed almost every night. It wasn't the healthiest, but I just couldn't stop.

"I did cook some bacon recently," Mike said as he dramatically pulled out a baggie with two pieces of bacon in it.

"Why do you have bacon?" I said and grabbed it from him.

Something had come over me. I didn't care how old that bacon was. I'd smelled a scent of it all night long and couldn't wait to have a taste of it. But it was still really weird that Mike was carrying around bacon.

"I thought you might like a fun snack during the show."

"How did you know?" I said as I hurried and ate the two pieces he had for me.

"I asked Kendra what you were snacking on lately," he said with a boyish grin.

"You made bacon, carried it around all night, just to give it to me at intermission?" I asked as I looked at him in total awe. "You are the best friend a woman could ever ask for," I said dramatically.

"Could we cool it with the best friend talk?" Mike teased.

"Sure," I had to laugh a little at his expression. I knew he was trying to get out of that dreaded friend zone.

After the show, Mike walked me up to my apartment and used my keys to open the door for me. It had been the best date I'd had in a very long time. And although it wasn't technically our first date, it felt more like our first real date.

"Did you want to come in?" I offered as I wrapped my arms around his neck. "I've missed you."

My hormones were going crazy as I practically threw myself at Mike. But to my surprise he didn't agree to my offer.

"I had an amazing night, Julia," he leaned in and softly kissed my lips. The sweet taste of his tongue jetting into my mouth only briefly before retreating again. "I can't wait to take you out again very soon."

He pulled my hand up to his lips and kissed the back of it like he had done earlier. I couldn't help but jump back into his arms for one last kiss before heading in for the night. I made it a quick one and then opened my door and stood in the doorway.

"Thank you for a great night, Mike. I can't wait to see you again," I said as I closed the door.

"Goodnight, Julia," he said from the other side.

I bounced up and down with excitement as I turned and watched him leave through the peep hole in my door. Things were changing between us, a glorious change that I was so excited for.

Chapter 16

Mike

Things were much better between Julia and I after our date although we still couldn't manage to get time together. The more I tried to schedule out time to see Julia, the more my schedule was getting booked up.

We were in full force now trying to get the details for our expansion up and going. The tech guys across the hall didn't go out of business like we had hoped and were going to ride out their lease, but Bruce did talk with them about moving to a different location. Patrick helped the tech firm find the perfect new place and we were set up to take over their lease in just a few months.

Bruce and I were going over dozens of potential hires and trying to figure out how we wanted to organize the company with this new addition. Bruce wanted me to be the head of everything and he planned to take a step back to concentrate on himself a little, in a good way. He had really been working on his own issues lately and was turning out to be a really good guy after all. Of course, I knew he was a good guy when we partnered up, but somewhere along the way he had gotten a little lost.

Julia and I were relegated to text message flirting for the last several weeks, but I didn't mind it at all. It was nice to see her name pop up on my phone and she always put a smile on my face.

JULIA: Today is the big day! Ultrasound at 3!

MIKE: Do you want me there?

JULIA: If you want to be, but I can just tell you afterwards too.

MIKE: Okay.

JULIA: Kendra and Sarah are coming. ☺

I wasn't sure if she really wanted me there or not. If she had her whole crew of girlfriends, she probably didn't need me. It was hard for me to separate myself from the baby she was carrying, and it seemed like Julia was doing a better job of it than I was.

I figured I'd let her have the moment with her girl friends and then maybe I'd pop in at the very end of her ultrasound. I certainly didn't want to push my way into the moment and she and I were doing so good at this level of our relationship that I didn't want to mess that up. We were going slow, but still had a very strong connection.

"You're smiling like you are texting your high school crush," Sheryl said as she saw me in my office that morning.

"I do have a crush on her."

"Julia? How is she doing? Are you two still dating or are

you friend zoned?"

"We are in the beginning stages of dating. She has a lot going on in her life right now and I messed up early on. I'm just trying to be cool about it and not push things too fast."

"How do you feel about dating a woman who is going to be a mother?"

"You know, I don't know. I like Julia and I know this is part of her life so I just think about her. I haven't thought too much about what is going to happen when the baby comes."

"You should think about that. Breaking up with a new mom is a jerk thing to do," Sheryl said and left my office.

I didn't know why she assumed I'd be breaking up with Julia after the baby came. I might keep dating her. If we were getting along there was no reason to stop dating. Sure, we would take it slow and she would be busy with the baby, but I liked talking to her better than any other woman around so there was no need to break things off.

I'd read through the last chart at least three times and still didn't know what I was going to put for my note. It was as if I couldn't focus at all. The more I tried not to think about Julia, the more I was actually thinking about her.

Julia was really an impressive woman. So were a lot of the women who came through my clinic. To live on your own in New York was a big deal. It wasn't like smaller cities that you could afford to live in an apartment by yourself, but then to live on your own and also have a child, wow, I was in awe of the women I worked with for sure.

But Julia was an independent woman. Even in the last few weeks after our date, she hadn't been texting and calling me all the time. She returned my messages at her own pace and always seemed to be plenty busy. She was working her butt off at work since she was feeling good and trying to drive in as many sales as possible before it was time for her to go out on maternity leave.

Although I hadn't been able to arrange a convention to book with her hotel, I did manage to point a few other high powered friends of mine in her direction who booked events with her. It was the least I could do to try and help her meet her sales goals before the baby came.

It was getting frigid outside and snow was on the ground now. Julia said that it became harder to book people in the winter because they didn't want to come take a look at the large group spaces and only wanted photos. Everyone waited until early spring and then tried to rush with their bookings, but Julia was worried that she'd be too far along in her pregnancy and not be able to handle the influx of customers.

The last time she talked about her work she said she was making over forty calls a day with clients and potential clients. It seemed to me she was pushing herself too hard, but I didn't see it as my place to bring that up. Obviously she had goals for work and I didn't want to be the person who was trying to hamper those.

Instead, I made an effort to help in the ways I could. I had deliciously healthy lunches delivered to her work each day. Although I paid for them anonymously, Julia knew it was me who had sent them. I'd tried desperately to get away for a long lunch or early dinner over the last few weeks, but just couldn't manage it. Business was terribly busy and with just Bruce and I as the doctors, we both were working our butts off to maintain the patient load until we got some new people hired in the spring.

"Today's the big day, Daddy," Bruce joked as he plopped down on my couch in my office.

"I know. She's coming with some friends though. I'll just wait and talk to her afterwards."

"She's doing great. I saw her a few weeks ago. The baby's heartbeat was perfect and she's eating well and gaining some weight. I hate when these ladies try not to gain weight during their pregnancies."

"Me too. They worry way too much about it. I love the added cushion," I winked at Bruce.

"Oh, so you and Julia are spending some time in the bedroom?"

"I wish. No, we are taking things slow for now," I said and rolled my eyes. "But man I'd be happy to get my hands on her any day of the week. She was looking fantastic the last time I saw her. Delicious even," I said as my body reacted to just the thought of Julia from out date night.

"You will, I'm sure."

I wasn't exactly sure what Bruce was implying. It might have just been a joke, but I didn't take it well at all. Was he assuming that I'd keep moving things along until I got my way with Julia? Because I wasn't going to push her into a sexual relationship again. If she just wanted to date and not do anything else that was fine with me. Although she had offered to invite me in on our last date, it didn't seem right. If we had been on a real first date she wouldn't have invited me in and I knew it.

I wasn't as nervous about the upcoming ultrasound as I was sure Julia was. Throughout our text messaging I always heard about the baby flutters and it sounded like she was feeling very well. Soon she was going to feel the first real kicks and I couldn't wait to hear her excitement when that happened.

Being a doctor I had talked to women about the kicks several times, but I'd never had such a close personal relationship with a woman who was going through pregnancy. It was fun for me to hear all about it from her end of things.

By the time three o'clock rolled around I was deep into my day of seeing patients and decided to keep working unless Julia asked me to come in. I heard her and her friends after they called Julia's name and even when they got into the ultra sound room I still heard the uproar of the group of them together.

It was hard for me not to burst in there and just sit and watch the whole thing. But Julia hadn't text me back and asked for me to come and I didn't feel like she really wanted me there. I kept my eye on the room as Bruce went in with the ultra sound tech.

"She'll be okay," Sheryl reassured me.

"Oh, yeah, I know. I'm just excited to see if she if finding out the gender."

"You should go in."

"No, I'll let her have the moment," I said as I grabbed my next patients chart and went in to visit with her and her husband.

I'd become pretty good at zoning out the outside world when I was in with a patient. There were always things to worry about. Always something going on with the business or some commotion in the waiting area. But when I was in the room with a patient I did my absolute best to devote myself to that person and only them.

About halfway through meeting with the new couple I was with, I heard a scream. It was not something we heard very often around our office. Except in bad situations, like when a baby didn't have a heart beat or some other dramatic issue had arisen during the test.

"I better go make sure everyone is okay," I said as I excused myself from the patient room and hurried down to the ultra sound.

I should have just gone in with her. Why was I such an ass?

"It's okay. Everything is okay," Bruce said as he stood right by the door when I burst in there.

"What's going on?" I asked.

Julia was staring at the ultra sound and hadn't even noticed I was in the room. Sarah and Kendra were jumping up and down and screaming like wild women. The ultra sound tech was casually going about her job and getting measurements. Then I saw what the commotion was all about. There were two babies!

I went over to Julia and squeezed my way in next to her. Her hands were resting on her chest and I grabbed one of them as I stared at the picture on the screen with her. We could hear the loud beating of two heart beats and I was overcome with emotions as I looked and saw Julia looking up at me.

"I'm having twins," she said with tears rolling down her face.

"You sure like to do things big, don't you?" I said and gave her a sweet peck on the forehead.

"Congratulations, you two," Bruce said as he stood at the end of the bed Julia was on.

We continued staring at the ultra sound picture as the tech moved the device around and did all the things she needed to for her report. Julia looked really pale though and she wasn't talking at all.

"Are you okay?" I asked.

"Girl, I can't believe this. This is amazing. Twins is like the jackpot. Do you know what gender they are? Do you want to have one of those cool gender reveal parties? I could totally help throw you one of those."

"No, I don't think she wants to know," I said when I realized Julia wasn't even listening to any of us. "Write it down and put it in an envelope for her for later though." I asked the tech.

Kendra and Sarah were still bouncing off the walls with excitement but I could tell something was wrong with Julia. She wasn't happy or sad at the moment. Instead, she was blankly staring at the ultrasound screen even though the procedure was over.

"Girls, I think she might need a minute. Maybe I could bring her home later?"

"Sure, she's at the new place now anyways. They just brought her boxes over the day before yesterday," Kendra said.

"Perfect. I'll take care of her. Thanks, ladies."

"It's going to be amazing," Kendra said as she leaned down and hugged Julia.

"We will help you whenever you need us to," Sarah added. "It's going to be fantastic. Think of all the adorable

The Baby Package

sweet pictures you'll have and all the fun times at the park. It's going to be so awesome," Sarah added in an effort to get some sort of reaction from Julia, but there was nothing.

Julia barely managed to hug her friends and after helping her sit up I was really worried about her. She was still staring off into space a little, very pale, and I thought for sure she was going to pass out at any moment.

"Julia, I need to know if you're feeling okay," I said as I stood right in front of her.

She shook her head yes, but I didn't believe her at all. I had seen this reaction to multiples before. It was often what happened when a single woman decided to have a baby on her own and didn't consider the natural ability of the body to make more than one baby. When couples were in my office for fertility issues and such, they were excited about multiples. Well except my favorite couple, Nathan and Mary. They had been trying to have a baby for ten years and used all their money for the process. So when they found out they were having triplets and were still living in a tiny one bedroom walk-up in Queens, it wasn't the best news.

"Sheryl, will you come stay with Julia for a second?" I hollered from the room.

She was there in a second and stood in my spot as I hustled around the office to get what I needed for Julia. I made up a comfortable spot on the couch in my office. Grabbed some snacks from the fridge and some Gatorade for her to drink. I pulled a pamphlet that we had on multiples and being a single parent, since we had this happen every now and again with our fertility practices. Then I hurried back to Julia's room and Sheryl helped me get her into my office.

"Rest here. Eat some food. I have a few patients I need to see. Sheryl and I will be right out there if you need anything," I said as I sat her down.

Julia leaned back on the couch but still wasn't exactly reacting to me. She was still staring off at the wall when I closed the door, leaving it open a crack so we could check on her.

"She doesn't look good," Sheryl whispered.

"Yeah, I don't think she paid attention during the part of the insemination process where we talk about the possibility of multiples.

"Did she do hormones?"

"I think she was on a low level one from her primary before the insemination. But it looked like identical twins from what I saw of the ultra sound. Same amniotic sac."

"Boys or girls?" Sheryl asked.

"I didn't get a good look. But I think the surprise will be nice," I said before hurrying back into the patients room that I had left earlier.

I apologized profusely before getting back on track with the new couple. Luckily they were very understanding of the interruption and we were able to finish our appointment rather quickly. I had four other patients I saw throughout the rest of the afternoon and made sure to look through the crack in my door whenever I had a break to check on Julia.

She had moved to lying down on the couch and at some point had eaten a few of the snacks I brought in there and sipped the drink. She looked like she was sleeping when I finally wrapped up my day and opened the door to come in. But when I sat next to her on the couch I realized she wasn't sleeping at all. She was crying softly into the pillow that she was hugging tightly. Julia looked so sad, so utterly devastated.

Chapter 17

Julia

I couldn't believe it. I didn't know anyone in my family that had twins. It wasn't even on my radar during the initial appointments. I had only taken a couple doses of the hormones my other doctor had prescribed and he said it wasn't a strong one at all. He said the hormones would just ensure a viable egg was released each month.

Being a single mom sounded so exciting when it was just one baby. I had wrapped my brain around all of that responsibility. I hadn't considered the possibility that there would be more than one baby.

I had gotten myself into this situation and I had no way of getting out of it. Somehow I had to find the courage to figure this out and it was overwhelming me. The problem was that I could hardly breathe. The whole thing was going to be an absolute disaster and instead of having a wonderful time being a young mother I was going to hate it, I just knew it. I wasn't going to sleep at all because I'd be up all night feeding them. How was I ever going to keep my career on track with twins at home? Somewhere down the line I would start gaining a ton of weight because I wasn't taking good care of myself.

I sobbed quietly in Mike's office until he finished his work and came in to sit with me. I couldn't stop crying when he got there and when he sat next to me and rubbed my leg, it just made me cry more.

"Why are you crying? This is exciting. You're going to have two beautiful babies," he said delicately.

"I know I should be happy. I know, but how am I going to take care of two babies? I was already going to be pretty bad at taking care of one of them," I said through my tears.

"It's just the same as one baby, you just do everything twice." Mike tried to be upbeat, but that just made me even more overwhelmed.

"It's not my plan," I managed to get out.

"Was it your plan to meet me?" Mike asked as he leaned

down and put his face in front of me. "Sometimes plans don't go the way you want them but they still turn out pretty damn good. I mean, I think it turned out good. And those babies of yours are going to be so adorable since they have my genes," he continued on until he finally got me to crack a smile.

"It's not funny, Mike. How am I going to take care of two babies?"

"You will figure it out. You're one of the smartest women I know. I don't think having two babies is going to bring you down. You'll rise to the occasion. You'll make the absolutely best out of it. And I have a feeling once you meet those two bundles, that you'll be perfectly happy with having twins."

"Thanks," I said and started to wipe my tears as I sat up on the couch. "It's just hard to see past all the stress right now." It was nearly impossible to see past the stress, actually. But having Mike there trying to cheer me up was really helpful. He stayed there with me and we ate more of the snacks and talked for hours about my stress and worries over bringing two babies into this world.

Some of the things I was worried about were logical. Like the logistics of paying for a nanny or getting two cribs into the small den of my new condo. Then there were other things that were less logical, like how big my boobs were going to get if I wanted to breast feed. Or what combination of foods I'd always have to keep in the house when they were teenagers and didn't like the same things. My mind was all over the place with the idea of having two babies, which would turn into two kids and two teenagers and then two adults.

"How about we concentrate on the here and now before we start worrying about the feeding habits of teenagers," Mike said with a small smile. "One day at a time here. For right now, you should concentrate on relaxing. All this stress isn't good for the babies or for you."

"Relaxing, I don't even know what that is anymore. I just got over to the new condo and I can't find anything in my boxes. I don't even have my bed set up. I slept on the mattress on the floor last night," I laughed.

"Well, that's something I can help you with. How about I stop by the fifteenth floor and help you get set up a little bit so you can get a good night sleep?"

It was the sweetest thing Mike could have offered to do. I didn't want to lift all the heavy wood pieces to my bed and hadn't gotten around to having Kendra and Sarah over to help me yet.

"Perfect. And let's get some food on the way home, I'm starving," I said as I looked at the pile of snacks we had just devoured.

"Of course," Mike agreed without making mention of the plethora of food I'd already devoured. "I'm starving too."

I didn't think he was telling the truth about still being hungry, but it was really sweet that he was trying to make me not feel bad about it. Mike arranged a car for us and we swung past my favorite Indian joint to grab some take out before heading back to our condo building.

The building didn't feel like home to me yet, but it was so inviting to arrive in the front doors and have the smiling doorman greeting us. I was going to like it there; I knew it the moment I'd decided to buy my condo.

The elevator had glass mirrors throughout the inside and as Mike and I got in I noticed my stomach was showing more than I thought it was. I turned and admired the growing bump in the mirror and Mike stood behind me and did the same.

"You'll start getting big faster now. Those two little ones are going to be growing a lot the next few weeks."

"I can't believe I didn't realize I was having twins. Should I be bigger than this by now? Am I not eating enough?"

"It's your first pregnancy so a lot of times women don't start showing until around now. I think you are right on track."

I lifted my shirt a little and looked at how round my stomach was from that angle. It was amazing how I was growing two human beings inside of me at that moment. I suddenly felt more at peace about everything. Of course, I was still really overwhelmed about how I would manage with two children. But nature was a powerful thing and I knew that I would be more excited after I got to meet my two little ones.

"Did they say what the gender was?" I asked as I realized I hadn't been fully paying attention during the ultra sound after I found out it was twins.

"She wrote it down and I had her put it in this sealed envelope. Did you want to open it and see?"

"Oh wow," I grabbed the envelope from him and just held onto it. Now I really wanted to know what gender the babies were. "There's going to be twice as much planning and decorating as before. Maybe I should look so I can get started on everything."

"Maybe," he said going along with what I wanted.

"But wouldn't it be exciting to find out when they are born? I mean you are right, that would be the best surprise ever. I do like that idea as well."

"You've got plenty of time to think about it. How about we put it in one of your kitchen drawers for now and you can decide another time. Tonight we should eat, get your bed up, and get you some relaxing sleep."

"Or other things to relax me," I said playfully as we got off the elevator.

Mike just smiled back at my flirting with him. The idea of having his hands on me did seem really relaxing though. I wasn't going to say no if things heated up between us. In fact, I was hoping there would be a little heat when we got to working on my bed.

Having all these hormones running through my body just

had me wanting to have sex all the time. It didn't seem like a logical thing for a woman's body to still want to have so much sex after she was already pregnant, but maybe nature meant it that way since couples wouldn't have to worry about contraception if the woman was already pregnant. But then again, contraception was more of a modern thing and nature just wanted women to have babies, so I had no idea.

"Let's eat," I nearly growled as we entered my condo and went up to the counter where I had a couple cushioned chairs.

"No table?" Mike asked as he looked around the mess I had there.

"I don't think I have room. Where would I put one?"

"By the windows, of course," he stood over by the window and looked out at my view. "I think you'd like waking up and eating your breakfast over here. But you also don't have a couch or a television either. What is in all these boxes?"

"I don't have much of my own furniture. Kendra owned the living room set. I just have my bedroom stuff. All these boxes are the rest of random stuff I had around the apartment and in the kitchen. I should have tossed some of it away, but I didn't know how much I wanted to worry about purchasing new things just yet."

The truth was that I hated most of the stuff I had but I thought my feelings might change once I got my stuff over to the new condo. I wasn't a very sentimental type of person, but I didn't want to throw items away that I might wish that

I'd kept later down the road and I thought I should wait and go through my boxes slowly and plan out the condo better.

I was hoping to buy some modern furniture for the living room and a trendy baby bed for the den. But now I'd be buying two baby beds and that was going to change everything. Surely I was going to have to save my money for baby stuff now and wasn't going to want to spend it on furniture for the living room.

"Your place looks really big for a one bedroom. I think you made a great choice," Mike said as we sat at the counter eating our dinner.

"I know. I was a steal," I said between shoveling food into my mouth.

Knowing that I was having twins, made my constant need to eat feel much more reasonable. I had been worrying that I was eating way too much over the last few weeks. The problem was that I was always hungry. I was constantly wanting food and sex. And now I had my food, next I wanted Mike in my bed.

As much as I liked thinking about having Mike in my bed, I wasn't going to push that plan too much. Things were really good between the two of us and there was too much room for error if I started pushing a relationship with him. I was going to take a back seat and just see how things turned out.

Mike got a text message on his phone that seemed to distract him a lot. I just sat there waiting for him to tell me what was going on but he was so engrossed in a back and forth texting session that I didn't want to interrupt him.

Something was wrong. Whomever had texted him didn't have anything good to tell him at all. I continued eating my dinner while he finished his conversation.

"Sorry, just some work stuff. Some legal issues came up with the new expansion. That thing has been so stressful. And one of the people we interviewed ended up turning something into the medical board like a tattletale. Our lawyer has it handled because everything we do is legal; it's just got me a little worried now."

"What did they turn in?"

"Oh, Bruce made a crack about being a sperm donor on the side for cash. And the uppity guy we were interviewing didn't think it was legal or ethical or something. I didn't really think anything of it but our attorney just texted to tell me the board is doing an official review of both Bruce and I."

"It wasn't legal what we did?"

"It was legal. I'm one hundred percent sure of that. I think the questionable part is having a doctor from a fertility and obstetric clinic, donating to their patient. Bruce is probably in more trouble than I am ethically. He's remained the doctor after donating. But you stayed with Bruce for your doctor so I don't think I would be in trouble."

"But this could affect your whole practice, couldn't it?" I said, a little worried for Mike and the new expansion he was planning.

"I'm not sure the extent of the consequences just yet and I don't think talking about it will help you relax at all. I'll let you know if I hear of any news as this whole thing develops."

I was stressed out for Mike just thinking about having some sort of investigation like that going on. He looked like he had already forgotten about it though as he slipped his phone back into his pocket and finished eating his meal.

Oh, how nice it would be to have the type of personality that could just let things roll off your back like that. One minute he looked extremely anxious and the very next he had totally forgotten about it and was enjoying his meal.

We moved into the bedroom when he finished. I had boxes all over the room but I did have the bed pieces set up in the general area where it was supposed to be put together. I was also organized enough to have all the bolts and screws in a bag sitting next to the bed and the tools I needed to get it all put together.

"This shouldn't take long. I might need you to hold the headboard steady while I put the pieces on."

"I can handle that," I said as I found a spot by the headboard and held onto it for him.

Mike used a box to balance the long side boards for the bed and made quick work of putting the frame together. He had the slats for the bottom of the bed attached quickly after that and was loading up my mattress all within thirty minutes.

I was positive that the girls and I would have spent hours trying to get that thing put together. Even though it was relatively easy, the three of us managed to make a mess of things rather quickly when we were all together.

"Do you have sheets? I can help you put them on," he offered.

"Yep," I grabbed my set of nice hotel quality sheets and threw one side of them over toward Mike. "I love these. They are so soft. Like staying at a hotel."

"Are these hotel sheets? Did you steal these Miss Rivas?" He asked with a stern look on his face.

"I wouldn't exactly call it stealing. I mentioned that I really liked the sheets that our hotel used and a set of them turned up in my office one morning. I didn't question it," I laughed. "Sometimes you just have to go with the flow."

"They are really soft," he rubbed his hands on them after we finished making the bed. "I bet you'll sleep great tonight."

I walked around the bed and stood next to Mike. We were close to each other. Closer than we should have been if we were planning to keep our relationship platonic.

"How are you feeling?" I asked him.

He laughed. "I think I'm supposed to ask you that."

"Oh, I feel fantastic."

"Yeah?" he asked as he pulled me in closer. "You sure you're feeling okay?"

"Yep."

His eyes gazed into mine as we stood there with our bodies pressed against one another. Being with Mike was calming to me. It was like home to me. Just having him there in my apartment made me more comfortable about all the unknown things coming ahead for me.

His hands rubbed up and down my arms and then we leaned in and kissed softly. He moved slowly and sensually as we kissed and touched each other, both of us climbing onto the bed and lying down as we continued to make out for a little bit.

Mike's hands were soft and gently as he rubbed one of them on my stomach while we kissed. It was exciting having him there and I wanted all of him. I needed to have him.

He pulled my shirt up and over my head and then started kissing every inch of my stomach. He was gentle, yet firm with his kisses and even stopped to rest his ear on me and see if he could hear anything going on inside.

"Any grumbling in there?" I laughed.

"Nope, all quiet."

Mike rolled me over and unhooked my bra before diving full face into my booming breasts. They had to be twice the size they had been before. I was so swollen and big that it made me more sensitive than I'd been before too, so as Mike pulled my nipple into his mouth I moaned out in pure pleasure at the sensation.

"Mmmm yes," I said and arched my back to press my body into him even more.

"You're so sexy," he groaned and then took in the other breast.

Mike played with and sucked on my breasts for a while before finally turning his attention to licking me. And I was swollen down there too. My whole body had extra blood flow and I felt the pleasure right away when his tongue hit my naked center.

Quickly I felt the pleasure building like I'd never felt it before. Within minutes of his tongue touching me I was screaming and moaning and trying to catch my breath as a huge orgasm was building up.

"Come here," I said as I pulled on his hair.

"Now?" he asked pausing for just a minute. "Right now? Where's the condoms."

"Yes, I want you inside me right now, fuck the condoms," I urged and literally started pulling his head up toward me.

Mike hurried and pulled his pants off and then held himself over me. His body pressed slowly into mine and I closed my eyes and let the full feeling engulf me with excitement. Soon I found myself thrusting hard against his body wanting more and more from him. I couldn't get enough. I couldn't get the feeling that I was searching for and then Mike shifted his hips a little.

"There, how about that?" he asked as he moved slowly and rubbed his body against mine as he thrust inside of me.

"Yes," I groaned.

It was perfection. His body was hitting my clit as he moved and I vibrated from inside with utter excitement. My hands held onto Mike and I used my legs to help me move against him as we made glorious love. We kissed sweet and softly as I finally released an intense orgasm which was followed shortly after by Mike having his own release.

Our night was perfection and I was more relaxed than I'd been in months as I cuddled up in his arms. He pulled the blankets up over us and kissed my forehead before the two of us drifted off to sleep.

***

For the next several weeks Mike and I were pretty inseparable. We both stayed at each other's apartments from time to time but sometimes we did stay on our own. We went shopping together and texted all the time.

He was crazy busy with work and so was I but we both made an effort to see each other throughout the week. It certainly didn't hurt that we lived in the same building. Sometimes Mike wouldn't get done with work until nearly midnight, but he'd send a text and see if I needed him to do anything before he went to bed.

We hadn't officially defined our relationship, but it was going good, whatever it was. For two and a half months we basically had a normal dating life, except most of our conversations were around my growing stomach and the babies that would soon be joining us.

Us. That was a word we had been using a lot lately. Not in the sense that Mike would be responsible for the babies at all. I was always careful not to expect anything like that. But he did talk about us all going on walks and exploring the city from their point of view. He wanted to be more involved than I had expected, but I knew we still had to have a real conversation about how things were going to look once the babies were here.

The last thing I wanted was more miscommunication between the two of us. But talking about the situation was really anxiety provoking and not something I wanted to bring up when things between the two of us were going so well.

The other thing that was happening a lot was our sex life. We were exploring all sorts of fun positions and having a blast in the bedroom. I was more sexually free with my large stomach than I'd ever felt with flat abs.

Mostly it was because of the way Mike looked at me. He lusted after me just like he did when we first met. My growing size only enhanced his desire for me and that was a huge turn on. He was instantly hard any time the suggestion of us making love came up. It didn't take but the smallest of hints and he was all over me. I'd never had so many orgasms in my life. We were good together. The chemistry between us was off the charts and the more time I spent with Mike the more time I wanted to spend with him.

He was making this whole pregnancy less stressful for me. He made me feel excited about having twins and about the future that was ahead for me. Mike was careful not to suggest that he'd be the father to the babies though. Of course, he was the genetic father, but he was careful not to make statements about taking care of them or being there every day.

By the time March hit I was as big as a house, or at least I thought I was. We were making plans to meet up with his friends Nathan and Mary, the couple who had triplets. I was getting so excited to meet the babies someday soon. Fourteen more weeks would bring me to the ideal of 40-weeks pregnant, but Doctor Simon said if I made it to 36-weeks that would be fantastic. Many times women with twins just weren't able to keep them in there for the whole 40-weeks.

I was utterly determined to take the best care of my unborn babies as possible. If that meant resting more, I was resting more. If that meant eating more green food, I was doing that. I was doing everything I could to make sure this pregnancy progressed as long as possible and my two sweet little ones came to me healthy.

Chapter 18

Mike

"Double date time," I hollered as I used my key to get into Julia's apartment. I knocked slightly as I entered, but she knew I was coming. We had finally managed to arrange a date with Nathan and Mary to talk about the joys of parenting multiples. They were such a great couple so I couldn't wait to hear what they had to say to help Julia with some tips for what was to come.

"I'm not going," Julia said from her bedroom in a muffled voice.

"What are you talking about? You have been looking forward..." I stopped when I saw her hiding under the covers and did my best not to laugh. "Julia, what are you doing?"

"I'm not going. I'm hideous," she said peeking her head out from the covers for just a second.

"I happen to know that isn't true. You look amazing. You still have six weeks to go, babe. You can't hide in here for a month and a half."

"I can and I will."

"Julia, we have been trying to schedule something that

worked for all of us for months. Come on, let's get you dressed and get to the restaurant. I'm sure it was very hard for them to find a babysitter for triplets."

"Don't play that guilt game with me, mister," she said finally coming out from under the covers. "Nothing I have fits me. Or if it does fit me I look like a house wearing it."

"How about this dress? It's nice and flowing, I'm sure it will fit beautifully."

"House."

"Okay, these leggings with this shirt?" I tried again.

"House."

"Maybe you'll just have to go as a house then," I said frustrated at her stubbornness. "We really do need to get going. I don't want them to be waiting for too long."

"Fine," she grumbled at me as I left the room and she finally got up to get dressed.

Julia threw on the first dress I had offered and pulled her hair up in a messy bun. When she opened her door she looked absolutely adorable, except for the grumpy expression on her face of course.

"There," she said. "Let's go."

"You look beautiful." I stopped to pull her in for a kiss and she pulled away from me. "Stop it, you look beautiful and I'm going to kiss you."

She finally smiled a little bit and let me kiss her. Then she liked the kissing so much that she wrapped her arms around me and we were full on making out. Her hormones were large and in charge and in any other situation I would have happily put her to bed and taken care of all her needs, but we were late and I really wanted to get moving.

I pulled her off of me as softly as I could and held her hand hoping that she wasn't going to get emotional about it. Emotions and hormones were a tricky combination for us guys to navigate around women during this time of the pregnancy.

Sometimes I wondered how she and I were going to get along for the rest of the process. It was getting dicey at times with our little arguments and trying to be there for Julia without stepping on her independence.

"I know. I know. We need to get going," she said reluctantly.

It was a relief when we arrived at the restaurant to find Nathan and Mary still waiting for our table. I hated being late for things, especially when I was the one who had planned them. Luckily, Julia perked up once she met Mary and the two of them hit it off instantly.

They were off in their own little corner talking about pregnancy and babies while Nathan and I caught up a little over a beer at the bar. It was nice to be around a guy who knew a little bit about what I was going through at the moment.

"So, hormones. Wow, they are a trip," I said taking a long

swig.

"Yeah, and get ready for them to get worse after the babies. Then you'll have crying and happy and crying all over the place."

"Thanks for meeting us. I know Julia has been really nervous about the babies and I thought Mary might be able to help her get used to the idea."

"Of course."

When our buzzer finally sounded Nathan and I waved for the girls to join us and we all made our way through the crowded restaurant to our table. Once we managed to get past the crowd at the front of the restaurant, it was actually rather quiet in the back.

"So this is exciting for you guys. I never thought of you as a family man," Nathan said when we first sat down.

"Oh, I guess I should clarify. Julia is my friend. She's having these babies on her own, I just thought it would be nice for her to talk with Mary a little," I said. Instantly, I regretted my comment. Julia went from looking happy as could be to scooting her chair out quickly and rushing off to the bathroom. Mary followed closely behind and I sat there with Nathan feeling like a total ass.

"I thought they were your kids?" Nathan asked.

"Technically they are. She used me as her donor. But she was always talking about how this was her chance to be a mother and she was going to be independent."

"When was the last time she said something like that? Because from the look on her face I think she was expecting more from you in the involvement area."

"It's been a few months, I shouldn't have said it. Damn, now I feel terrible. I do want to be involved. I just don't know where I fit in. She has her own apartment. She has her own plans for the babies. She doesn't include me in this stuff. How am I supposed to know what to do?"

"I'm sure she will be fine. Mary will calm her down and they will come back and we will all have a great evening. Nothing to worry about just yet."

"Yet?"

"No, not until there is yelling involved," Nathan said without cracking a smile at all. "That's when you need to worry."

I appreciated the tip. And when Mary returned with Julia I jumped up and told her I was sorry as I pulled her chair out. She shook her head in agreement and we continued on with the evening as if the comment hadn't happened at all. Well, sort of.

The conversation stuck to what it would be like for Julia to take care of two babies at a time. Mary was delicate when she talked about breast feeding and having a helper around when possible. She did look over at me but never specifically said that I should be there to help her.

"The hardest part is the night time. You'll be tired and it

would be helpful to have someone there to occupy one baby and change them while you breast feed the other. And then you could rotate. But you can do it on your own too."

"I'm not sure I can breast feed twins. I know it's healthy and I'll give it a try, but it is really overwhelming to me."

"You can do it for a few weeks and then supplement with bottles. That's what I had to do. Nathan went back to work after two weeks and I had my sister come stay with us. She was a lot of help."

"I've only got brothers," Julia said and rolled her eyes. "But I have a couple girl friends who are really excited to help out. I'm sure I could get them to come over a few nights at first."

I just stayed quiet. I didn't want to say anything that would make her feel bad again. We could talk about it all a little more in the next few weeks. I would be happy to help out where she wanted me to be. Hell, I liked the idea of having us be together and raising the babies together. The only reason I had brought up the statement that they were hers was because of how the pregnancy had started. She didn't want a baby daddy. Julia didn't want anyone telling her what to do or how to raise her babies and I was just trying to follow along with that and be supportive.

Of course, I did see how that might have changed for her over the past few weeks since we had been spending so much time together. It was more like a relationship than our situation had ever been. We should have talked about it before dinner. I should have asked her how we were going to explain things. It was all my fault. I took full responsibility, well I would after dinner was done and the two of us were able to have a good conversation.

"Have you decided on your birth plan?" Mary asked Julia.

"I'm just going to the hospital and letting Doctor Simon do his thing. My biggest fear is that I'll have to have a c-section. I just don't want to go through that recovery and have the babies at home. That sounds really hard."

"Maybe your mom could come stay with you?"

"That wouldn't be helpful," Julia laughed.

"I know what you mean, that's why I had my sister. But start working on lining up your help for those first couple of months. You'll need to get some sleep so you have to have a few extra sets of hands. Even with Nathan, we still had two or three people at our house helping us out at times. These little ones require a lot of time and attention."

"I'm a shit," I whispered to Nathan as the women talked.

"You're in shit, that's for sure," Nathan laughed.

"Maybe I could help out?" I said to the ladies as they talked.

"No, I wouldn't want to force you to help care for *MY* children," Julia said with a stare that looked like she could have killed me.

"Yeah, you're in trouble," Nathan leaned over and whispered.

For the rest of the dinner I did the best I could to lay low. I laughed at the jokes Mary told and tried to appear sympathetic to the plight of the pregnant woman, but the whole time all I could think about was that I needed to talk to Julia in private, so we could straighten this whole thing out. Certainly, I wanted to help with the babies. I wanted to keep seeing Julia. And I wanted to be part of her life and their lives; we just had to figure out how that was all going to work.

When dinner was over, and we finished saying our goodbye's, I helped Julia into our Uber and tried to hold her hand while we pulled away. She yanked it away from me though. She was upset and I had done this to her.

"I'm sorry. I thought you wanted to do this alone. Tell me what you want."

"You're right. I do want to do this alone. It's okay. I'm just emotional," she said suddenly softening up a little. "We can figure it all out later. I was just caught off guard and a little embarrassed."

"I'm sorry."

"If you want to be involved in their life and my life you can. If you don't want to be you don't have to be. I did this for myself and I was the one who wanted to have the babies. I understand if you want to move on with your life and not be a co-parent."

"I didn't mean..." she interrupted me by grabbing my cock and rubbing it hard right there in the back of our Uber.

"Did you mean it when you asked me what I want?" she asked.

Julia looked like a woman who had been possessed by hormones as she eyed me like a piece of meat. We definitely needed to talk more about everything that was going on but at this point I was pretty sure I needed to give her a few orgasms to calm this lust that had taken over her body.

If I wasn't a physician the rapid change in her emotions would have worried me much more than it did. But I knew she was using sex as a coping mechanism for all the emotions that were going on inside of her. I also knew that trying to talk about it at that moment would be a very bad idea. She had primal needs that needed met before we would ever be able to flesh out how much parenting involvement I was going to have.

When we got back to her apartment she practically threw me on the bed as we walked into the bedroom. She had her own clothes stripped off long before I was able to get mine off. And she was climbing on top of me before I even managed to get my pants all the way off.

She slid onto my throbbing cock and rode me so hard I thought for sure she was going to break me in half. She was a beast as she pressed into my chest and thrust her hips against me and I fucking loved every minute of it. Watching her beautifully round body on top of me was a sexual turn on that I wouldn't forget any time soon. Making love to Julia throughout her pregnancy was much more erotic than I'd imagined.

My patients often talked about how turned on they were all the time or how they couldn't get enough of their man during the pregnancy. Seeing it first hand with Julia was a treat for me. I was lucky to be there with her and wished I wouldn't have made her feel so bad at dinner.

"Grab my nipples," Julia suddenly ordered of me. "Hard."

I did as I was told and squeezed both of her nipples as she moved faster and faster against me. She yelled out with pleasure and I throbbed with lust. It took everything I could muster not to cum right then and there, but I didn't want to have the wrath of my primal woman turn on me.

Her fingers dug in and I thought for sure she was about to release when she jumped up off of me. She moved to the side of the bed and bent over. She motioned for me to get behind her and I dutifully did as she asked.

My hand rested on her soft ass as I slid into her. Slowly, gently, I moved as I enjoyed every moment of being inside of Julia. Her head was on the bed and she moaned with pleasure with each of my thrusts. It was a huge turn on to see her so engrossed in the pleasure of the moment. I grabbed her hips as my thrusts got deeper and she pressed hard back against me. There was no way I could hold back any longer. I had to feel the sweet release of letting go as I thrust hard a few more times and then finally couldn't handle it another second.

I came hard inside Julia and she pressed back against me with delight at the explosion. We both crawled back up onto the bed and I knew right away that Julia wasn't finished with her own primal explosion.

Her hands played with my exhausted body. She teased me and was already working to see if she could get me excited again. Oh no, that wasn't about to happen so fast; I knew my body well enough to know that.

I also knew that she wasn't going to stop until I had utterly satisfied her needs. So I pressed her back onto the bed and let my fingers touch her softly.

"Yes," she groaned as I played with her.

Julia pulled me down to kiss her while I played. It was exciting to have her in my mouth while my fingers played with her wetness. I titillated her clit and rubbed on her in every direction as I worked up her excitement.

When I finally slipped inside her Julia grabbed my lip and bit down on it as she thrust her hips toward me. I was pretty sure she'd drawn blood with that lustful move but I didn't care.

I stroked in small circles, feeling her body react to my fingers. Feeling the excitement growing more and more for her. She was getting close and I knew what I needed to do to help bring her over the edge.

Slipping away from the delicious taste of her lips. I kissed down her body taking my time to suck on each of her nipples for a just a moment. I then moved over her sweet belly and touched the right and left sides with my kisses for the babies growing inside of her.

When I made it to her center, she was dripping with pleasure and I took her in clit and held onto it. My fingers stroked hard and deep as Julia grabbed the sheets and propelled her clit farther into my mouth.

Then it happened, the sweet release that Julia had been dying for. Her whole body tensed up and her back arched. I didn't stop doing what I was doing but continued on in an effort to prolong her pleasure as much as possible.

"Yes, she moaned, "fuck, yes," she finally fell back to the bed in total exhaustion.

I moved up beside Julia and put her head on my chest as we wrapped up in each other's arms. For weeks we had been making love and hanging out together. It had been the best time I'd had in a very long time. I was so happy to have her there. So excited to see what the future might have in store for the two of us.

"Are you thirsty? Do you want me to grab you a drink?" I offered.

"Sure," she said as she rolled off of me and curled up on her side of the bed.

I hurried into the kitchen and grabbed a bottle of water

from the fridge and placed it on Julia's side of the bed. I was just about to get back into my side when she sat up and looked at me with tears in her eyes.

"I think you should sleep at your place tonight," she said looking so utterly sad that I didn't know what to say or do.

We'd just made love for an hour. She'd been so into it. We were both into it. What had happened? What had gone wrong? Was this just a burst of hormones? I didn't want to leave her there like that. I couldn't leave her in that state.

"Honey, what's the matter? We should talk. You don't want to go to bed upset."

"I'm tired. We can talk another time."

"Julia, is it about that crack I made at dinner? I'm sorry. I didn't mean it. We should talk about it. I want to be here for you if you want me here."

"But you don't want to be here, so let's not worry about it. I will abide by the contract. I'll make sure you get your yearly cards and a visit if you want to."

"Julia, I know you're hurt, but we have time to talk this through. I'm going to go because I don't want to make this more of a thing than it needs to be. But I'm open to being a part of this if that's what you want."

"Again with what *I* want? When are you going to step up and tell me what *you* want? What about saying that you want to be part of my life, of the babies lives? Just go," she said as the tears rolled down her face. "Just go."

As much as I wanted to explain my position, it just wasn't the right time. Julia was clearly very emotional and she had to be exhausted after all that we had just done in bed. I decided to leave and give her some space. We had weeks to work through this before the babies arrived and I was certain we would come to a solution once we were both able to have time to think about it.

"I'm going to go, but I want to talk more about this later."

I leaned down and tried to give her a kiss but she turned away and I was only able to kiss her cheek. For a moment I stood in the doorway of her apartment contemplating not leaving at all. I thought about sitting in the living room and just waiting for the morning so we could talk, but I decided to do as she asked and I left.

All the way up to my apartment I felt sick to my stomach. Julia meant a lot to me. She was important to me. I didn't want to lose her. I wanted to be in her life. This was all just a big miscommunication and I was sure we could straighten it out.

I didn't sleep much at all that evening and had to go to work the next day. I tried stopping by to see Julia before I left but decided not to wake her up. Instead, I send a text message, hoping that it would calm her nerves a little.

MIKE: Julia, I care about you a lot and I would like us to sit down and talk soon.

At work I went about the day as normal seeing patients and dealing with our business troubles. Both Bruce and

Sheryl noticed I wasn't myself that day but I wasn't in the mood to talk with them about what was going on either. It was more of a self reflection sort of day as I figured out what I wanted in this relationship and how that was going to look for me.

"Hey, hospital just called. We have an emergency patient in there," Bruce said.

"Who?"

"No name yet. I'm waiting for a call back. Is it your turn or mine?"

"Let's see who the patient is," I said as we waited for the call back.

I had a few patients that were getting close to full term and I knew Bruce had a couple that were past their due date. Either one of us could be the lucky doctor who was going to be up all night long delivering a baby.

The phone rang and the look on Bruce's face told me that something was wrong. He was not longer smiling or light hearted at all. Instead, he was serious and took some notes as the person on the other end talked.

"Yes, get her stabilized and I'll be right there," he said and then hung up. "It's Julia."

My heart sank. She was still very early along. She had two months before her due date. There were so many things that could go wrong at this point. So many things that could go wrong with her and with the babies.

"I'll take care of things here," Sheryl said as she motioned for the two of us to get out of there.

It was the middle of the day and we would have to cancel all the patients for the rest of the day. But at this point I didn't care and I could tell Bruce didn't either. He knew how important Julia was to me. She wasn't just his patient. She was a friend now and we rushed to the hospital as quickly as we could.

Chapter 19

Julia

At first I wasn't sure what was going on. I was having some major cramps but thought my night with Mike had brought them on. I'd orgasmed pretty hard with him and certainly believed my body was just reacting to that.

But as the contractions continued and got worse, I knew something else was going on. I'd read all about Braxton Hicks contractions and how a lot of women had them when they were as far along as I was. I called the doctor's office and made an appointment to go see Doctor Simon later that afternoon. The problem was, I definitely wasn't going to make it to that appointment.

I tried walking around to relief the pain from the contractions but soon I realized I was in full labor. I was pacing around my condo and the contractions were hitting exactly five minutes apart. That was when the panic set in. What was I supposed to do? Just go to the hospital on my own? I could barely walk, there was no way I could get myself there.

"Kendra," I said as I put her on speaker phone. "I'm in labor. I need you to help me get to the hospital."

"I can't. I just landed in Vegas with Sarah, remember?"

"No!" I had totally forgot they were going away for that trip. "What do I do?"

"Call Mike," Sarah said as I was put on speaker.

"No, he doesn't want to be involved. I need to do this on my own. What do I do? I'm so scared, guys."

"Just call him, Julia. He will make sure you are safe," Kendra said.

"Okay," I said in order to deal with the contraction that was building up. "I'll let you guys know how it goes."

"Wait, aren't you too early?" Sarah asked. "You better get to the hospital right now. This is way too early. You go right now. Just go downstairs and the staff will get you there."

"Okay," I grunted through my contraction and hung up on my friends.

This was it. I had to be the independent woman that I kept saying I was. I didn't have a hospital bag or anything like that ready yet so I just grabbed my purse and slipped my sandals on my feet.

I waited for a contraction to end and then hurried to the elevator and down to the lobby. But by the time I reached the lobby I was already having another contraction. They were coming much quickly than every five minutes and I was terrified that I was going to lose the babies.

"I think I need an ambulance," I grunted from the elevator as I leaned against the doors and breathed through the contraction.

"Shit, yes ma'am," the young man at the front desk said as he dialed his phone.

"Can you help me to the chair?" I asked.

"He had the phone on his ear and hurried over to me to help me while he was giving the 911 operator directions to our building and which entrance to use. Luckily, the building was really easy to find and the ambulance was there in less than five minutes.

"How far along are you?" the paramedic asked.

"Thirty-one weeks," I said through another contractions. "I'm having twins though."

"Okay, let's get you to the hospital. Is there a doctor we can call?"

"Yes, Doctor Simon at Reproductive Medicine Associates."

The paramedics got me onto the gurney and began taking my vitals before we even left the lobby of the condo building. I couldn't figure out why they weren't just rushing me into their vehicle and to the hospital.

One of them was attending to my vitals while the other strapped me in and then started listening to hear if the babies were okay. He seemed pleased with what he heard but the woman who was working on me wasn't as happy with what she saw.

"It's elevated," she said looking at her partner. "We need to get her OB on the line."

They hurried me out to the ambulance and to my hospital. The driver was on the line with dispatch who was communicating all the details that the paramedics were giving them about my condition.

From what I could gather my blood pressure was elevated enough that it was a concern for them. But I was in the middle of labor so they had to assume there would be a little spike in my blood pressure during such a physical event.

"Approval on the injection," the driver said to one of the paramedics.

By this time I already had an IV line in me and the paramedic had medication waiting to shoot into it. Normally I would have had tons of questions about a medication that was being shot into my veins but in that moment I was in so much pain that I didn't care what they were doing. All I wanted was to get to the hospital and make sure the babies were okay.

When we pulled into the emergency room a handful of people came out to help take care of me. There was a doctor there in a set of scrubs, but it wasn't Doctor Simon. Although I was worried about having my doctor there I also knew that at this point I was going to be delivering these babies with whatever doctor happened to be on hand.

The doctor and nurses moved me over to a hospital bed and started working on me so quickly I didn't know what was going on. One of the nurses helped me get out of my clothes while everyone else was working on things around the room. This was when I knew the situation was more urgent than I had though, when they wouldn't even spare the time to give me privacy to change into a hospital gown.

"Are you allergic to any medications?" A nurse asked.

"No."

"You are thirty weeks along?"

"Yes."

"You are having twins?"

"Yes."

"Is there someone we can call for you? Do you have a partner that you'd like to have here for the delivery?"

I paused and contemplated having them call Mike. He would have wanted to be there; I knew he would, but at that point I was still upset with him and didn't feel like reaching out. I figured he'd probably hear I was in labor when the hospital called looking for Doctor Simon and decided not to take any extra measures to notify him of what was going on.

"No."

"Okay, well I need you to sign this and we do need to have someone to contact in case of an emergency."

I filled out her paperwork and put my brother Rob down as my emergency contact person. I could have had them call him and bring him down to the delivery, but I didn't feel like listening to him tell me how gross it all was. I also didn't want to have him looking at me naked while I went through the labor and delivery.

The nurses went back to hooking me up to monitors and wrapped some straps around my stomach to listen to the babies. I had a blood pressure cuff working and squeezing my arm and electronic things on my chest listening to my heart. I felt like some sort of experiment as the nurses whipped around me hardly stopping to look at me at all.

Finally a young nurse came and sat down next to me. She grabbed my hand and held it while I labored through another contraction. They were coming nearly constantly at this point and I could hardly take it any longer.

"When this one is done the doctor is going to check you to see if we have enough time to bring you up to the labor and delivery floor. It would be better to deliver up there since we have all our equipment there."

"Okay," I said through my pain.

"Nice and slow. Remember that breathing is your friend. Take in a deep breath and then blow it out," she said as if she knew exactly what I needed to hear.

As soon as I started listening to her I was able to calm down and focus a little better. I had taken the weekend class to learn all of this stuff, the problem was that I hadn't remembered any of it when the panic of my contractions hit me.

"Okay, it's almost done," I said feeling the tension in my

stomach letting up.

The doctor was watching the contraction on a monitor next to the bed and waited until it had finished before checking me. He looked happy when he was done and nodded to the nurses that they could bring me up stairs.

"She's going to go soon, but the sac is intact and I think you have enough time."

"Perfect," the young nurse said as she unhooked me from all the monitors but kept the wires and chords connected to me. "We have all this stuff upstairs. It's a quick ride in the elevator and we will have you in the delivery room."

"Okay," I said and closed my eyes as we zoomed down the hallway. "There is someone I should call," I finally said.

"When we get to your room we will get that information and call them."

I should have just given Mike's information to the first nurse who had asked. This wasn't the time to be holding a grudge against him.

"Okay, let's get you into this bed. It will be much more comfortable," the nurse said as she put down one side of the bed that I was on.

I slid myself slowly over to the big bed in the room. She was right, it was much more comfortable. Plus it looked like the bottom of the bed could be taken away so you could deliver right there without moving. That was fantastic.

Another contraction hit and it hurt so bad that I felt like I couldn't catch my breath. The nurses hurried to hook up the machines and I heard a commotion at the door as Doctor Simon and Mike came busting in.

There was no time for modesty. The nurses had the whole top half of my gown off while they were making sure all the electronics were connected correctly and Doctor Simon quickly got right up there to see how far dilated I was.

"Do you want Mike here?" Doctor Simon asked.

"If he wants to be."

"It's a yes or a no," Bruce said looking a little annoyed at me.

"Yes," I finally said.

Mike had stayed over by the doorway and when Bruce motioned for him only then did Mike make his way over beside me. He looked nervous but I grabbed his hand as another contraction hit.

"I think we are going soon, people. Let's get ready," Bruce yelled to the nurses in the room. "I need two incubators in here too. Let's get the teams ready. Come on, people," he barked as a swirl of nurses and other staff started to fill the room with equipment.

"How are you doing?" Mike asked as he kissed my forehead.

"Just perfect," I grunted through my contraction. "I think I need to push."

"Not yet, Julia," Mike told me as he anxiously watched everyone getting set up.

I did my best not to push as the contraction tightened down on my body. I could feel so much pressure and pain that I knew the babies were coming soon.

"I'm going to break your water," Bruce said as he and a nurse set up the bottom of my bed and put something below me to catch the liquid. "You will deliver quickly after this."

He was right! The next contraction after he broke my water I started pushing. It didn't take long before the first baby was out. I heard him scream and they brought him quickly over to be evaluated.

"They have to take care of him first before you can hold him, just because he's so early," Mike said as he held my hand.

"Thank you," I cried as I looked over at all the people working on baby number one. "Is he okay?"

"He's crying. That's good," Mike said. "Now let's concentrate on the next one."

"Breach," Bruce said looking up at Mike.

"No, give it a minute. The baby just needs some time to move," Mike urged.

"No, man. His butt is coming out. I'm going to try and rotate. Take care of her," Bruce said as he looked at me only briefly and then started pushing on my stomach.

"He's maneuvering the second baby trying to change the position so the delivery will go more smoothly. It might hurt a little. Take some deep breaths."

Honestly, Bruce pushing around on my stomach and trying to change the position of the baby didn't hurt any more than the contractions I was already going through hurt. Whatever he was doing seemed to have worked because Bruce went back to his chair and shook his head positively as he and Mike looked at each other.

"Did it work?" I asked.

"Yep, so the next contraction you have I need you to push," Mike said.

"Okay," I screamed as I felt the next contraction coming.

It was only a few minutes later when baby boy number two was born. He started crying almost immediately after he was out but he also had to be rushed over to the team waiting for him to assess how he was doing.

"You did such a great job," Mike leaned down and held onto me.

"I can't believe I did that."

"I can. You're amazing."

"Are they both boys? I think he said boys, right?"

"Yep, two boys. You're the mother of two perfect baby boys."

"Go check on them please. Make sure they are okay.

When can I hold them?"

Mike went over to the teams that were working on the babies and watched what they were doing for a moment. He talked with the baby doctor that was there and motioned to me at one point during the conversation. I wasn't sure what the two of them were talking about but Mike looked like he was trying to convince the man to do something.

When he finally came back over to me Mike was smiling big. His expression put me at ease instantly.

"They are doing fine but they will need to go to the intensive care unit since they were born so early. It's necessary for them to be on oxygen but everything else is looking nice at this point. I did talk the doctor into bringing the boys over to see you before they have to go to the NICU."

"I can't go with them?"

"No, but as soon as you're feeling up to it I will take you down there in a wheel chair and you can stay by their side as long as you'd like."

"Okay," I said as I started to cry.

"Do you have names picked out yet?" One of the nurses asked.

"No," I said through my tears.

"Okay so for right now we will name them Baby Boy A Rivas and B Rivas, is that okay?" she asked and looked at me and then at Mike.

"Yes," I said feeling absolutely terrible that I didn't even have names for my babies yet.

"It's fine. A lot of people don't have a name picked out yet. You'll come up with something after you spend some time with them. Rest for a couple of hours first though," the nurse said. "They will be busy with their doctors for a little bit."

The first bassinet was brought over to me and I got my first glimpse of Baby A. He was in a covered incubator type bassinet and had a breathing tube on his tiny face. It broke my heart to see him in there but he did look like he was breathing well on his own and was a beautiful shade of pink.

"You can put your hand in through here and touch him," Mike said as he moved the incubator as close to me as possible.

I reached in and touched my sweet baby for just a moment before they had to take him away. It was heart breaking and I was sobbing as the second incubator was brought to me. Again I reached inside and briefly got to feel the soft skin of Baby Boy B before he too was taken away to the NICU.

As the room emptied out I couldn't stop crying. They were here. This was all so real and yet it didn't feel real yet at all.

"Can I get you anything?" Mike asked as he sat on the side of my bed.

"I don't know," I said through my tears.

"The nurses are going to come in and look after you for a minute. They have a bunch of girlie stuff to do with you and then if you're hungry they will bring you some food. Make sure and drink plenty of water and we will see if the babies are doing well enough to suckle in a little bit."

"Oh yeah. If I don't breast feed soon won't they have problems latching on?"

"No, the nurses will bring you a pump and show you how to use it. Then you can feed them breast milk through a special dropper or they will even put it directly into their stomachs through a small tube if needed. Then when the babies are ready you can breast feed. It will be just fine."

"Thank you, Mike. I'm glad you are here."

"There is no place else I would be. I'm so happy for you, Julia. This is so exciting. They are actually here."

"I know, this is crazy. I'm not ready at all," I laughed.

"Sorry to interrupt, but we do need to get you cleaned up. Do you want your guest to stay?" The nurse asked as she looked over at Mike.

The nurses obviously knew who Mike was. He was in there delivering babies for patients all the time. On this particular day he wasn't the doctor though and the nurse was treating him just like she would any other guest that was there to see a patient.

"I'm going to step out. I actually have a few phone calls to make. You ladies take care of business," Mike said before leaning down and giving me one more kiss on my forehead.

The nurses helped to give me a sponge bath and washed my hair for me. They changed the sheets and even brought me a new gown to wear. It took a good hour and a half before we were all done and they left to get me a food tray.

"Could you see if Mike is around?" I asked one of the nurses. "Doctor Cooper."

"Oh, yes, he said he had to leave really quickly but he would check back with you tomorrow and hoped you had a good night."

"He left?"

"Yes, he was going to come in and say goodbye but looked like he was in a hurry to leave."

"Oh," I said as my heart started to beat faster and faster.

I was trying the best I could not to jump to conclusions about why Mike left so quickly. Unfortunately, after just giving birth to twins who I couldn't even see yet, I was not in a good emotional state to contemplate why Mike had left me like that.

He had promised to take me to see the babies and then just left the first chance he had. If that was how he was going to be around me and my boys, then I didn't want to push him to be part of our lives. It was better for me to know that I had to do it all on my own than to think that I could count on someone else and not have them there. Although I was devastated that Mike had left me without even saying goodbye, there was no time for me to dwell on him and his issues. Instead, I ate my dinner and took a nap until the nurse came back later in the evening and told me I could go see the boys in the NICU.

The nurse helped me into the wheelchair and brought me to the other end of the hospital where the boys were being held. There were dozens of babies in a variety of different bassinets and incubators. Lots of noises from beeping monitors and other machines throughout the room. I felt my anxiety increasing the longer I was in there but the second we pulled up to my boys, I was calm as could be.

They were both breathing easily with just some tubes in their noses. They did have some monitors on their chests and IV's in them, but overall, they were looking really good.

"You did good, momma," the baby nurse said to me as she brought me closer. "Both of them are very healthy. I think a couple of weeks in here to make sure they are eating well and you'll be able to bring them home."

"Thank you," I said through my tears. "Can I hold them yet?"

"Not yet, but really soon. You can touch them though and talk to them. They will like that."

For the next two hours I stayed in the NICU talking to my boys and reassuring them that I was ready to take care of the two of them. It didn't matter to me that they were early. It didn't matter if Mike stuck around or not, because now it was me and the boys and I was going to do everything I could to make sure their lives were perfect.

"I have names for them," I told the nurse as I was wrapping up my visit. "Brody and Ben," I said to the nurse as she wrote them down. "I've got middle names too."

"Here, write down how you want them spelled and I'll make up their name tags for them," she said softly.

"Brody Philip Rivas and Benjamin Parker Rivas," I said as I wrote their names down for the nurse.

"Beautiful names," the nurse said as she took the paper from me.

I felt so much better after seeing them and giving them their names. When I finally crawled back into bed all I could think about was what a wonderful life the three of us were going to have.

***

The next few weeks I spent at or near the hospital. When I was released I was able to rent a special hotel room near the hospital from the company I worked with. They gave me a special rate of five dollars a day because they couldn't technically give it to me for free.

My work was absolutely amazing and supportive when I had to go out on my maternity leave two months early.

Sarah and Teddy took over my clients and they even gave me the commission from the people that I had already started to work with.

I was at the hospital nearly all day long caring for the boys, pumping my milk and just being there for them as they grew and got strong enough to come home soon. I did go home for a few brief trips to I grab some clothes and I managed to order the boy decorations I wanted for the nursery.

Mike had been trying to call and text me but I didn't have time for him at that point. He tried to explain that the legal stuff with his work had gotten out of control and I wasn't mean to him but I also didn't really care at that point. My priority was my children and Mike would have to deal with his own priorities however he saw fit.

"Can we take you to dinner?" Kendra asked when her and Sarah showed up at my hotel room across from the hospital.

It was nearly ten o'clock at night and I tried to let the babies sleep at night so I could get some sleep too. I was actually about to crawl into bed when the girls showed up at my door but I couldn't remember the last time I had actually eaten anything.

"Sure, there is a place across the street. I don't want to go far," I said.

"Of course."

Both Kendra and Sarah had been to see me a few times

but they weren't able to see the babies just yet. As soon as they were off of oxygen the boys would be moved to the lower level of care and in there I could bring guests to see the babies.

"What's going on? How are the boys?" Sarah asked as we ordered our food at the diner across the street.

"They are doing good. I think only another two weeks and they can come home. Both of them are over four pounds now so that's nice."

"Very good. And what's going on with you and Mike?" Sarah asked.

"What do you mean?"

"I mean he's calling me and Kendra all the time checking on you because you won't call him back or answer his text messages. He wants to talk to you. Are you really still mad at him?"

"I'm not mad. I just don't have any extra energy right now. He doesn't want to be involved with me and the babies. I don't want to deal with him. That's all there is to it."

"Hmm, he seemed really worried about you guys," Kendra said.

"He said the babies were mine and I could take care of them," I blurted out as I tried not to cry, but was unsuccessful.

"He said that?" Sarah looked appalled. "What a total jerk!"

"Yeah, well I thought so too. I mean we needed to talk some more things through but if he was willing to say something like that I just don't want to even deal with him. I have more important things. I've got the boys now."

"We are here for you. Whatever you need," Kendra said.

"Yep, anything. Do you want me to go kick his ass? I'll do it. You know I could take him out if I wanted to. One quick kick to the knees and he'd go down hard."

I couldn't help but laugh at Sarah and her willingness to go to battle for me. It was a good quality to have in a friend.

"I'm so lucky to have you guys. Thank you both for being here for me. I really appreciate having you two. Oh, and I'd like to see if you guys want to come stay at my house a little after the babies come home?" I said with a little trepidation. "I'm going to need some help. My mom is coming next week and the babies will still be in the hospital. She can't come back for a little bit after that."

"I'm there," Kendra said with so much excitement the people at the table next to us turned around. "I can't wait to change some diapers."

"I'll come over and help too. Plus I know Teddy wants to help if you'd let him. He's really looking forward to being Uncle Teddy."

"Sure, and thanks again, guys."

We finished our dinner and the girls decided to come stay with me at the hotel to keep me company for the night.

The nurses had talked about moving the boys down to the next level of care soon and it was possible that would happen the very next day. If it did, I couldn't wait to bring Kendra and Sarah in to see them. The girls were going to go absolutely crazy over my sweet baby boys. I was exhausted and not much of a host though as I fell asleep less than five minutes after we got into the room.

Chapter 20

Mike

"So we are okay? No sanctions or whatever the heck the board likes to do to people?" I said to the attorney as I sat in his office.

"Yes, but from now on I'd just say no if I were you guys. In this particular case the woman that Bruce had donated to was well known and went to bat for him. It might not turn out as well if they got wind of a second case."

"Deal. We will close up our sperm donations," I said trying to keep things a little light.

"Mike, this was a close call. If they would have taken your license or Bruce's you two wouldn't have a way to make a living. If we are moving ahead with this expansion I think you should look at taking on a business manager at the site.

Someone who I can work with and we can make sure you are protected."

"I agree. We need some additional staff as we grow. I also think it might be time for me to take a little step back and manage more than I'm seeing patients."

"Whatever you need to do."

"Thanks, I've got some new life changes going on and I think I'll need some time to get acclimated to everything."

With Julia having her babies I knew I was going to want to help her out as much as possible. There was no way I could keep a full load of patients at work. The legal scare that we had only helped me to realize that there were some major changes I had to make in my life.

It wasn't until the next day when I realized Julia hadn't returned any of my text messages that I really started to worry. I had hurried out of the hospital so fast that I didn't get a chance to tell her what was going on with our legal stuff and I was really worried she was still angry with me.

As the next couple weeks went on it became glaringly clear that Julia was still angry. Or she just had decided that she didn't want anything to do with me. I tried texting and calling her. I even tried reaching out to her friends to see if they could put in a good word.

When I was at the hospital I swung by the NICU and a few times I'd seen Julia in with the boys, but I didn't want to interrupt them. If she needed some time I was going to give it to her. But by the time I heard the boys were getting ready to go home I was beside myself with worry that Julia and I were never going to work stuff out.

It wasn't like me to push myself on a woman. If she was pushing me away then I stayed away. If Julia wanted to talk to me she knew how to reach me. I also knew that we would probably be running into one another in our condo complex and we should try and settle on how we were going to interact.

As I walked down the hall of the hospital after visiting a patient, I was engrossed in planning some way that I could reach out to Julia without being overbearing. It was harder than it seemed. I had obviously tried calling her over and over again. I'd sent text messages just asked if there was a time we could talk and none of it was working.

"Hey, asshole," a woman's voice said as I walked around the corner near the cafeteria.

"Oh, hey Sarah. How are you?"

"Seriously, Mike. You are the lowest of the low. I can't believe you."

"What?"

"You know what. You deserve to burn in hell for how you treated my friend. What sort of total asshole just disappears like that? And saying she could take care of her own babies, I mean, wow. That was rude."

"Sarah, I don't think you have the full story."

"I'm sure you have a lot of excuses. But save them, I don't want to hear it. You stole my girls heart and then crushed it in a million pieces. I know she won't admit that her heart is crushed but it is. She was devastated by you."

"I've been trying to talk to Julia since the babies were born. She won't return my calls and I didn't want to stress her out while the boys were still here. I want to be involved with her. I love her," I said and paused when I realized the words had just come out of my mouth.

"You love her?" Sarah asked skeptically.

"Yeah," I reassured myself. "I do love her. I've had a lot going on with legal stuff at work and I fully admit to being a total jerk when we went out to dinner. But I didn't want to say I was going to be an involved father if that wasn't what she wanted. She said she wanted to do this all on her own. I didn't want to take that away from her or make her feel like I had to be involved."

"Have you two talked about any of this? I mean it seems like a pretty big deal and something the two of you should have talked about at some point over the last few months."

"No. We haven't had a chance and I've been trying to reach her."

"You guys have been hanging out for months. How have you not talked about what was going to happen after the babies came?" Sarah looked at me as if I was an idiot.

The way she asked the question did make me feel pretty

stupid. Julia and I had been spending tons of time together. We were enjoying one another and having fun. We both were avoiding the topic. It wasn't just me. Julia didn't bring it up either.

Sometimes I would say something like I couldn't wait to have all of us go for walks to the park. Instead of speaking up and saying that it sounded like a good plan, Julia simply shook her head in agreement.

Other times when Julia talked about how hard things were going to be for her taking care of the babies all by herself, I wanted to speak up. I wanted to say something about what it would be like if I helped out more. One time I even wanted to tell her that I could stay the night and help with the babies. But the nerve to say something passed and we went back to both being quiet and avoiding the topic.

"Well, we need to make this happen. You two just need to be in a room together and hash this out."

"That's what I've been trying to do. I've been trying to talk to her but she won't talk to me. This whole thing is just her being stubborn. Okay, not just her. But she is being really stubborn. I can't believe she hasn't returned any of my phone calls. I mean, at some point I just needed to take the hint and stop calling."

"And you being unwilling to communicate what you want," Sarah added. "You should have told her a long time ago that you wanted to be involved."

She was right. If I had come out and told Julia that I

loved her a long time ago then I wouldn't have had to worry so much about figuring all of this out now. I'd been keeping my feelings close to my chest and waiting for Julia to tell me her feelings. I shouldn't have waited. I should have just gone for it and told her. But now everything was a mess. She was angry with me in the midst of trying to care for her newborn babies. The last thing she needed was for me to get her all worked up with my feelings.

Everything was out of control now. Julia was busy with the boys and it had been weeks since we had talked. It wasn't going to be easy for me to get close to her without the help of her friends. I didn't even know if her friends could help at all at this point. Julia might already have her mind set; she might have decided to move on.

"I've been visiting the boys at night after Julia leaves. I love them so much. I want to be involved. I need to be involved. Not out of obligation or anything like that. I just need Julia and the boys in my life."

"Then we need to figure out a way for you to tell her that. Let me get Kendra and Teddy, so we can all talk this through and figure out a plan."

Sure enough Sarah found Kendra and Teddy and the four of us ended up in one of the hospital conference rooms trying to figure out what to do next. Julia clearly wasn't going to call me back just yet and if she didn't want to talk to me I wasn't going to just show up somewhere.

The three of them were like super heroes coming to my

rescue. They believed in my feelings for Julia and somehow believed that me being involved in her life was a good thing. There was no way to know what Julia was going to say about the whole thing, but having her friends support me in my quest was a really good thing.

"Maybe we could have you surprise her in the nursery holding the babies?" Kendra said. "You could do that whole kangaroo care where the babies are resting on your naked chest. Oh, yeah that would be awesome."

"No, absolutely not," I replied. "I'm not going to hold the boys without her permission."

"What about if you just waited for her outside the nursery?" Teddy suggested.

"I don't think it should be done at the hospital. I can wait a little bit. I'll just come visit her once she returned to her apartment." As much as I wanted to straighten things out with Julia right away, I didn't want to push myself on her in the middle of getting ready to come home. She had enough to worry about without worrying about me too.

We sat in that conference room for over an hour throwing around ideas before we finally settled on one. I wasn't one hundred percent sure I loved the idea, but it was exciting to have a plan and something I could look forward to.

"Okay, well I'm going to work with Julia so I know when the babies are coming home and I'll keep in touch with everyone else," Kendra said.

"Yes, I can't wait," Teddy added.

"This is going to be fantastic. I'll help you with your part, Mike so you don't have to worry about any of that. Within the week the two of you love birds should be on your way to a happy future."

"Thanks for your help everyone. I really hope this works."

After some reassuring hugs, everyone took off and left me in the conference room to contemplate our big plan. That was when I started to get really nervous. This was going to expose me more than I'd ever been exposed. I was going to have my raw emotions laid out there for Julia to see and she could decide to stomp all over my heart.

Of course, I hoped she had the same feelings for me as I had for her but there was no way to know for sure. I was already nervous about the whole thing. My hands were sweating at the thought of this surprise. Not just because of what it might mean for Julia and me but for what it could mean for our future.

Chapter 21

Julia

"It looks like the doctor is going to release the babies tomorrow," the nurse said as I was wrapping up my visit for the night.

"Really?"

"Yep, they are doing fantastic. Neither of them need breathing assistance and they have been gaining weight steadily. You'll need to set up an appointment with your pediatrician for one week from today."

"Oh wow, I don't even have a pediatrician yet," I said realizing that there was one more thing that I hadn't prepared for.

"No problem. If you'd like I can set you up with one that we recommend?"

"Perfect, that would be wonderful."

As I left the nursery to head back to my apartment for the night I couldn't stop worrying about all the things I still didn't have situated. I hadn't even been staying at my condo; the times I was there I had very little energy to get things situated.

I'd ordered some baby stuff for the nursery but I hadn't even made the beds up yet. I also had two bassinets for my bedroom for the boys to sleep in the first couple of nights but neither of them were assembled at all. There was a changing table, rocking chair and swing that had to be assembled to. Basically I felt totally unprepared to be bringing the boys home already.

I should have had more ready by now. They had been in the hospital for weeks and even though I stayed at the hotel most of the time I had come home several times over the past weeks. I was just exhausted.

The truth of parenting twins hadn't even started to set in yet and I was already barely able to walk straight I was so tired. I was visiting the boys and taking care of them during the day. I was able to breast feed them when I was there but then I pumped in the night time and they received bottles from the nurses.

My level of exhaustion felt like it couldn't possibly get any worse and yet I knew when the boys came home it was going to get worse. I wasn't going to get enough sleep unless someone was at the house to help me. There was no way I could manage alone. All my confidence about being a single mother was gone. As I stepped into my condo and saw the mess of things everywhere around the living room I just collapsed onto the ground and started sobbing. It was so overwhelming, everything was so overwhelming.

I planned to stay up late that night getting as much ready

as I could possibly manage. I would start with the small bassinets that were in my room and then work down my list by what I felt was most important for when the babies came home the next day. Well, at least my plan had been to stay up late and get things done, unfortunately I fell asleep right there on the floor of my entryway.

When I woke up to my phone ringing I was so disoriented that I couldn't even figure out how to answer the darn thing. It was morning, I could tell that by the light shining in through the window, but I had no idea how long I'd been sleeping.

"Hello," I said as I finally clicked the right button to answer the call.

"Hello, Miss Rivas. I just wanted to let you know that the doctor has written discharge orders for the boys. When do you think you'll be in this morning?"

"I'm on my way," I said without skipping a beat.

I was still in my clothes from the day before and I probably smelled horrible, but I grabbed a sip of orange juice and headed back to the hospital. On the ride over I sent a text message to Sarah, Kendra and Teddy to let them know what was going on. The last few days they were all harping on me to keep them in the loop.

When I arrived back at the hospital it looked different to me. Before I'd been engulfed with sadness as I came to visit the boys each day and that sadness made the hospital look dreary. As I walked through the halls on this morning everything was brighter and full of life. I was bringing my boys home and I couldn't wait.

"Good morning, Julia," the nurse for my boys greeted me as I finished washing up and made it back to their corner of the room. "The boys are both hungry if you haven't pumped recently."

It was then that I realized I'd slept all night long and hadn't pumped at all. My breasts were so full that they were starting to leak through my nursing bra. I quickly grabbed a spot in a rocking chair and the nurse handed me Brody to feed first.

The nursery they were in now was the regular nursery. They had moved there a day before in preparation to go home. Neither of them had any special needs at that point; just the basic baby care like all the other infants in that room.

I was the only mother in the nursery with her babies though. Most of the women just had the babies in the rooms with them. A few of the babies would stay in the main nursery if their mother needed some sleep or if the baby was going to have to see the doctor soon.

After feeding Brody the nurse handed me Benjamin. I had been worried that I wasn't going to be able to tell the boys apart, but I was able to tell them apart from the first day I saw them. They were identical twins, but I could still see a different in them. It was hard to describe but I saw it.

My phone was buzzing in my purse as I fed Benjamin and

I didn't reach for it. Whoever it was would leave a message if it was important. Somehow I'd gotten on some new mother calling list and I'd been getting a lot of sales calls for baby stuff.

"Do you have someone coming to pick you and the boys up?" The nurse asked.

"I was just going to take an Uber," I laughed.

"That's fine."

"Well, maybe I'll get my friend Teddy to ride home with me," I said as I reconsidered how much stuff the boys had and how hard it would be to get them loaded into an Uber.

"The car seats you have will carry really nicely and should be easy to strap into a cab or Uber. But it would be nice to have a second set of hands, especially for your first couple of trips. Is the father not in the picture?"

It was the first time a nurse had flat out asked me about the father of the babies. Most of the nurses skirted around the issue. Sometimes they would ask about my partner or other random questions to see if I would spill the beans, but this was the first time the father of my babies was brought up.

I did need to figure out what my answer was going to be when people asked me such things. I was certainly going to get asked it a lot. A young woman with two new babies and no man by her side; people would be gossiping about that every time I showed up at a mommy and me event.

"He's not in the picture," I said without giving any further details.

"Well, maybe one of your friends could help," she said in a freshly upbeat voice.

"Yes, I'll give my friend a call."

When I finished feeding Benjamin I tried dialing Teddy, but he didn't answer right away. I then saw that I'd missed a call from Sarah so I tried calling her to see if she knew where Teddy was.

"Hey," Sarah answered her phone. "I'm going to drop some stuff off at your place. Is it cool if I let myself into your apartment?"

"Of course, that's why I gave you and Kendra a key. You two are always welcome there. By the way, do you know where Teddy is? I think I'm going to need someone to ride with me and the boys home from the hospital."

"Teddy, can you go to the hospital and ride home with Julia and the boys?" Sarah asked him. "Yep, he's right here helping me out. He is on his way. He says he can't wait to help."

"Now you're just making things up," I laughed. "Teddy is never excited to help."

"You're right, he normally isn't, but I think he's making an exception for those boys. I have a feeling he would do anything for them," Sarah said before she was distracted by a loud noise in the background.

"What's going on there?" I asked.

"Nothing, but I better get going. Will you be home soon? I could wait for you there."

"Yeah, maybe after we get everything sorted out and loaded into the Uber."

"See you then," she said and quickly hung up on me.

Sarah seemed off. I wasn't sure what was going on but she seemed like she was up to something. Hopefully the loud crash I'd heard wasn't her breaking something at my condo. She was notorious for breaking things and then getting rid of the evidence. Then I'd spend weeks wondering where I put something only to find the broken pieces stuffed in a bag somewhere in the back of my closet. The last time she had broken a picture frame right after I moved into the condo and I looked through all my boxes thinking I'd lost it.

When Teddy showed up at the hospital we spent a whole hour getting the boys ready to leave. I fed them both again and we put them into a couple of cute outfits I had waiting for them. Teddy was a huge help to have around and he was much better with the babies than he gave himself credit for.

"I think I'm doing this wrong," he squealed as he tried to change Ben's diaper after a big blowout. "Help, I need help."

"You're doing great," the nurse said as she stood next to him and encouraged him.

I was busy finishing up with Brody and had just finished getting him latched into his baby carrier when he blew out his diaper too. I had a feeling all my money was going to go to diapers in the near future.

When we finally managed to get both the boys fed, cleaned and loaded into the carriers it was time to head out. The nurses filled a cart full of the miscellaneous items that the boys had at the hospital. They gave me the rest of the formula that was in their drawers, diapers, little blood pressure cuffs. Pretty much everything that the boys had used during their stay was put into some bags and loaded onto the cart for me to take home.

"We have the car seat guy waiting downstairs. He will help you load them into the vehicle and show you how to make sure each seat is in right."

"Wow, thank you so much," I said a little shocked that they were going so above board for me.

"Yeah, Doctor Cooper requested it the other night when he stopped by," the nurse said just as we got out to the Uber.

"Doctor Cooper?" I asked a little confused.

"Yeah, he's been checking on the babies most evenings. He must be working all sorts of crazy hours because he usually stops by after regular visiting hours."

"Oh, okay," I said, not knowing what to say to the information I had just heard.

"Let's get these babies loaded," Teddy cut in and lifted Brody up to the big SUV he had waiting for us."

The car seat guy went over all the little details that we

needed to know and helped me connect both of the car seats. He showed me where a lot of the new cars had the extra safety clips for car seats and we talked a little about safety in the city in particular.

When I finally had the boys loaded in, Teddy and the nurse finished loading everything else into the back of the vehicle. Teddy sat up front with the driver while I climbed into the middle seat between the boys. I could already tell that traveling with these two was not going to be easy at all. I couldn't even imagine what it would be like if I needed to take them to a doctor's visit if they were sick.

"Teddy, did you hear what that nurse said about Mike visiting the babies?"

"Um, yeah."

"What do you think about that?"

"I don't know. It seems like a nice thing to do. What do you think about it?"

"I thought he didn't want anything to do with us. It's just weird that he would be stopping by to visit the boys and he didn't ask me first."

"From what I've heard, you haven't been returning his calls," Teddy said as he looked back at me knowingly.

It was true. I hadn't been returning Mike's calls or his text messages. I didn't have the energy to fight with him and I just didn't want to deal with all that emotion at the moment. I had planned on calling him back eventually but then he just stopped trying to reach me.

"So what have you heard?" I asked.

"Not much, that's about it," he said and turned back to the front of the vehicle.

"Teddy, you know something and you're not telling me. I can tell when you're lying, don't even try it."

"I don't know a thing," he replied without turning around. Just confirming that he was lying to me.

I was too tired to push him for more information. I leaned my head back on the seat and closed my eyes for a few minutes on the ride home. Both of the boys had fallen to sleep almost instantly after being put into the carriers. I did like how that worked so quickly to get them to sleep and I wasn't opposed to using it sometime in the future.

When we stopped in front of my condo I sat up and started unbuckling the boys from the car. Each of the carriers were strapped in with a regular seatbelt and another latch that ensured the seats didn't fly out of the car.

Teddy and the doorman loaded up a cart with all my stuff and Teddy was standing next to the door waiting to take one of the boys as soon as I was ready for him. There was no way I would be able to take the boys out alone unless I had a stroller that the baby carriers could lock into. Then I could just take them out of the car and move them to the stroller. I mentally put that on my list of things that I needed to buy in order to survive my new life.

"Which one do I have?" Teddy asked as he looked at the baby carrier.

"That's Ben."

"I still don't know how you can tell them apart. I think it must be a nature thing since you are their mother."

"Probably. Even the nurses who cared for them for weeks sometimes had a hard time telling them apart."

The doorman came up in the elevator with us to push the cart full of hospital items and gifts that people had sent the babies. All of my brothers had sent flowers and gifts throughout the time the boys were in the hospital. Rob had managed a short visit one afternoon, but then promised he would come to the condo and visit more often once we were home.

None of my family really understood what I had done or why I decided to have these babies on my own. Even my mother didn't seem to care much anymore because she was so in love with the boys.

"Here let me hold him," Teddy said as he grabbed Brody's carrier from me so I could unlock the door.

"I thought Sarah was staying here until we got back?" I asked as it took me forever to get the door unlock.

When I finally managed to get the door opened I looked into my condo and it didn't look like my place at all. The living room was organized and beautiful. The boxes had all been put away and even the pile of items I'd ordered online weren't sitting in the room anymore.

"Surprise," Sarah and Kendra yelled from the nursery.

"Guys, you put all this stuff on the beds and organized the living room. Oh, my God you are the best," I said as I hugged them.

Everything was done. They had opened up all the bedding and put it onto the beds. The rocking chair and changing table were put together. Everything looked absolutely perfect and I felt like a huge weight was off my shoulders.

"We had some help," Kendra said as she turned me around and pushed me to walk toward the bedroom.

As I got closer I could see that both of the basinets were set up in there too. My whole place was cleaned and organized and I had the fresh start I'd been hoping to have when I brought the boys home.

Then I saw him.

My heart skipped when I saw Mike standing next to the baby swing in the corner of my room. He was holding two white roses and one red one. He looked so handsome with his blue t-shirt on and sweat literally covering half of it.

"You helped them?" I asked as the girls pushed me into the room with Mike and shut the door behind us.

"Julia, I love you. I'm not going to wait another second to tell you that. I love you and I want to be with you. I have wanted to tell you for a long time and only held back from saying it because I didn't want to push you. But now I can't hold it back anymore."

"Mike..." I started to say before he stopped me.

"You can tell me to go to hell in a second. I just have to get this out so you know exactly where I'm coming form. I'm sorry I had to leave the hospital the night the boys were born. I thought I was going to lose my medical license and was trying desperately to save it. It's not an excuse but I did want you to know."

"Mike..." I tried to interrupt him again.

"I promise to make it up to you if you let us all be a family. I have taken six weeks off from work and I'm ready to be here with you every night and every day as we get to know the boys. I will get up and change them for you and feed them if I need to or do anything else for them because I love them. I know we signed this contract and if you want to keep it we can, but if it was up to me I'd tear it up so we could be a family."

"Mike..." I tried one more time to stop him.

"No, no, I have to finish. Julia, I knew that first night that you were someone special. I knew that I was going to be different after meeting you and it was true. I am different. I am a better man for having you in my life and even if you don't want me to be involved in raising the boys I will always cherish that we made this decision. And..."

"Mike," I put my finger up to his mouth and held it there

so he would stop talking for a moment. "I love you too."

Instantly all the stress and worry that I had disappeared when I saw his smile. It took us a long time to get to this spot but we were in love and I knew that deep down long before Mike confessed his love for me.

There were no more words to be said. Instead, Mike wrapped his arms around me and pressed his lips into mine. Softly we stayed intertwined as we kissed and held onto one another until Kendra opened the door a little to see what was going on.

"Do you want to meet your boys?" Kendra asked as she brought one of the carriers into the room.

"Oh, I've met them," Mike said as he leaned down and started to take Brody out of his seat. "Me and Brody have had some long man to man conversations over the last few weeks."

"You know that is Brody?"

"Yeah, I could tell them apart from the first time I saw them in their incubators."

And in that moment I knew that Mike and I were going to work out just fine. He was their father and not just biologically. I could tell by the way he held Brody that Mike had done that before too.

"So you didn't think you should talk to me before hanging out with the boys?" I asked a little playfully.

"Oh, I tried to wait for you to say it was okay, but I just

couldn't stay away from these guys. I had to see them every night. I just had to come visit them so they knew who I was and that they were loved very much."

"I'm glad you did," I said as I picked up Ben from his seat.

The four of us stood there together rocking back and forth and cuddling like the family that we were. I'd dreamt about having a perfect family. I'd tried to make my own perfect family and fate took over and twisted everything around to make things even better than I could have imagined.

"And they lived happily ever after," Kendra said as she stood in the doorway with Sarah and Teddy and took our first family picture.

Epilogue

"You absolutely have to stay in bed Julia, no more excuses. This is doctor's orders," I said to Julia after she tried to get up and help get the boys off to kindergarten for the day.

"Oh, come on. I'm allowed to get up to use the restroom so I should be allowed to help Brody get his coat on for school."

"Nope. You are using up all your standing time by using the bathroom. That leaves no standing time for helping the boys. That's the rules. I'll bring them to you though and you can help them in the bed."

"I've already made it to thirty-two weeks. I have a feeling this time I'm going to make it full term. There's only one baby. It's a piece of cake to cook this one up the full length of time," she joked.

"Babe, you have to listen to me for the baby's sake. Okay?" I asked a little more determined to get her to listen.

As much as I knew that bed rest sucked, I also knew that Julia needed it. She was seeing the new female doctor in our practice and we had consulted on what to do after Julia had severe spotting a week earlier. If she was my patient I would have put her on bed rest too.

The practice was going so well that we now had five full-time doctors and I was only working a couple days of the week. I did most of the behind the scenes work with our business manager and the legal team. I also worked with our new marketing team to keep new patients coming in.

Bruce had found the love of his life and married her, she happened to also be the new doctor that we had hired, so that was another mess we had to figure out. I was more worried about it when they were dating than I was now though because he was clearly devoted to her and happier than I'd seen him in years.

"Don't cancel the dinner party," Julia yelled from the bedroom as I finished packing both the boys their lunches. "I can still eat dinner. Everyone has already cleared the day and we don't want to cancel just because I'm on bed rest."

"Babe, what are we going to do, bring the table in here and all eat in bed with you? We can schedule something for after the baby."

"No, I am fine to eat. I won't get up and pee that day," she tried to argue with me.

"Julia, come on honey."

"Mike, this is important. I want to see everyone. We have been so busy and everyone else has been so busy. I just don't want to let this date slip by."

"Fine, but only dinner. You can't get up and help prepare it at all but for the actual dinner you can come out and eat.

Then you promise to go straight back to bed."

"Or maybe sit on the couch?" I asked.

"Girl, you drive me crazy," I said as I crawled into the bed to kiss her growing tummy. "Baby, your mother is one of the strongest women I have ever met. Just you wait until you get to meet her out here. You'll see what I'm talking about."

"Dad, Dad, Dad," Brody said as he pulled on my leg. "I'm hungry."

"I just fed them. I swear I just fed them," I said as I slid out of bed. "They must be growing. I can't believe how they are always hungry."

"Wait until their teenagers," Julia laughed.

I couldn't even imagine what our life would be like with the boys all grown up into teenagers and our new one just a few years behind them. I finally managed to give each of the boys one last snack and brought them to say goodbye to Julia before we headed off to school for the day.

Managing school drop-off with my work schedule wasn't hard since I was the boss, but I could imagine it would be difficult for regular families to balance. I definitely saw how families could benefit from the use of a nanny.

When the boys were younger we had a nanny come stay with them during the day after Julia went back to work. It was a hard decision for her but eventually she had to work just to keep herself feeling good. She was a driven woman and sitting at home with the boys was fabulous and she loved it, but she really did like working too.

By the time Saturday rolled around, the night of our dinner party, Julia was going stir crazy from her two weeks of bed rest. I wasn't sure she was going to make it for another month of rest so it was nice that we were having the dinner party to boost her spirits a little.

The bell to the condo rang and I hurried over to answer it. Everyone had arrived at the same time. There was Kendra and Devin, Patrick and his girlfriend, Teddy and his boyfriend, and Sarah came alone.

"Oh, I'm going to die you all look so good," Julia said as she came out to hug everyone.

"You look so good," Sarah said as she rubbing Julia's growing tummy.

We all visited and I managed to get Julia to sit on the couch while I finished preparing dinner. She was alive and vibrant when she was around her friends and I really did love seeing her so happy.

"So when are you due?" Kendra asked.

"It would be nice to go another month but I'm not so sure I'll make it that long."

"She's supposed to be on bed rest," I shouted from the kitchen.

"Yeah, yeah, I'm resting right here," Julia said and then went back to talking to her friends.

The boys were in their room sleeping and weren't phased at all by the commotion going on in the living room. We did have a babysitter who was staying in the spare room and ready to help if the boys needed anything throughout the evening, but I suspected we would be paying her for sitting there texting her boyfriend.

"Uh-oh," I heard Julia say and the room went quiet.

"Mike, you better come here," Teddy said and everyone got up from the couch, except Julia.

"My water just broke," Julia said as calm as could be. "I'm not feeling any contractions though. That's a good thing, right?"

"No," I said without stopped to explain.

I grabbed our emergency bag and gave some quick instructions to Kendra who was going to stay at the house with the boys. Going into labor without her water breaking would have been better than having her water break. Under this circumstance we had to deliver. We couldn't just stop the contractions and continue with the pregnancy. If the amniotic fluid was all gone, then the baby needed to be delivered.

"Mike, you're scaring me," Julia said as I helped her into the Uber that was waiting for us when we got downstairs. "What's going on?"

"I need to get you to the hospital and see if there is any fluid left in there. If not, we have to deliver."

"But I'm not having contractions."

"Then you'll have to have a c-section. Or maybe we could induce you if both you and the baby are doing okay. It's going to be alright though. Don't worry, baby."

"Who is on call tonight?" She asked trying to hide her fear.

"Bruce."

"Oh, that's good. I don't like that new guy you have."

"He's just a little nerdy. He's a very good doctor though," I reassured her.

We bypassed the Emergency Room and went straight up to the labor and delivery floor. I'd already sent a text to Bruce to let him know we were on the say and he was waiting with the team of nurses at the entrance when we got off the elevator.

"No contractions and at least a partial rupture of the amniotic sac," I told the crew.

"Let's see if we have anything to work with," Bruce said as he and I grabbed the ultra sound machine and wheeled it into the room where Julia was getting hooked up to all the monitors.

"Let's take a quick look," Bruce said calmly.

I knew as soon as he put the scope up to her stomach that there was a problem and it wasn't going to be a smooth delivery. The baby had no fluid around her and her heart beat was much slower than it should be.

"Is that the chord?" I asked as he glided the scope near the baby's head.

"Yep," Bruce said and lipped the monitor off. "Prep the OR," he yelled out.

"Surgery, what? Why do I have to have surgery? I can push. It's okay. And did you say her? Are we having a girl?" Julia looked so excited for the news.

"Yes, it's a beautiful little girl but we need to get her out quickly. I need you to stay calm and we are going back to surgery. There is no time for an epidural and I know you really want to be awake but trust me, we need to move fast."

"Okay," Julia said with a calmness I hadn't expected. "You save our little girl."

She had tears in her eyes and kissed me as we pushed her out of her room and toward the operating room. The operating team was there and ready and we lifted the sheet that Julia was on and moved her to the operating table.

The anesthesiologist was waiting and as soon as the IV was in her he started assessing so he could behind putting Julia to sleep. Everyone was rushing around the room and getting things ready to take care of the baby once she was born. They had all the crash cart supplies for the baby there and I desperately hoped that they wouldn't need to use any of it.

"I love you. I'll see you soon," I said to Julia as they put her mask on and started to put her to sleep.

"I love you too," she said through the mask.

I was going to lose it. The tears were welling up and it took everything I could to hold back and not hurry Bruce along as he prepped for surgery. He was still scrubbing his hands in the other room as the nurses prepared Julia's stomach for the procedure.

Everything was moving really fast but it helped that I knew the process and knew what to expect. It was only a few minutes later that Bruce was cutting into Julia and pulling our sweet baby girl out.

She was blue and had the cord wrapped around her next so tight that Bruce had to cut both ends as a nurse unwrapped it. The baby wasn't breathing at all as they took her to the table and started working on her.

"We good here?" I asked Bruce as he was working on Julia.

"Yes, go ahead," he motioned for me to go watch them working on my daughter.

I'm not sure there is anything that makes a person feel more helpless than watching people trying to save your child's life. My hands shook and I felt dizzy but there was no way I was leaving her side. Julia wouldn't have wanted our sweet baby girl to have to fight all by herself.

The doctor was giving chest compressions while a nurse put a mask over the baby's face. I closed my eyes and said a little prayer that my sweet baby could fight hard enough to come back to us.

"We got her," I heard the doctor say and a moment later there was the sweet sound of a baby crying that echoed through the delivery room. "She's breathing," he said to all of us who had obviously already heard her crying.

I was so relieved that I almost fell over. Luckily, a nurse brought me a stool and helped me to sit down. I sat there a little bit out of the way while the neonatal doctor finished assessing our newborn baby girl.

"She looks really good, Mike. We will need to watch her over the next few days, but she is looking really good. Come over here and say hi."

The nurse walked with me just to make sure I wasn't a fainter. But obviously I was alright now that I knew my daughter was going to be okay. I stood next to her and held onto her little fingers as tears rolled down my face.

"You scared us, sweet pea, let's not do that again," I whispered and kissed her sweet little forehead. "Your mom is going to be so excited to meet you."

The doctor had to take her away shortly after that and I had to wait in the recovery area with Julia as she woke up from the anesthesia. She was scared and disoriented at first, but I just held her hand up to my lips and continued to kiss it and try and reassure her as she woke up enough for me to talk to her.

"Is she okay?" Julia finally asked. "Where is she? I want to see her."

"She's okay. She's so beautiful, oh my gosh, you won't even believe it," I said softly and stroked Julia's hair as she finally set her head back down on the pillow.

"But she's okay?" She asked again and started to cry. "I was so scared, Mike. I was so scared we were going to lose her."

"She okay, honey. They are going to keep an eye on her for a few days. You'll have to be here for a few days too so I'm sure they will let you have her in the room with you when she gets cleared."

"I love you so much, Mike. You have made me the happiest women in the world."

"I love you too, Julia. I'm so happy we ran into each other that night at the club and that you wanted this dream of a life and allowed me to be part of it."

"This life wouldn't be a dream without you," she said as I held onto my beautiful wife.

THE END

Made in United States
Orlando, FL
08 October 2023